"Don't you ever shut up?"

He stared down into her eyes for a moment, just long enough for her to draw a quick, startled breath. Then he put his hand to her cheek, slipped his fingers behind her neck, drew her to him and clamped his lips firmly on hers.

An electric shock raced through Hannah's body. Nerve endings tingled which had lain dormant for months. Responses activated which she had forgotten existed. Feelings were aroused she didn't know she had. His mouth was delicious, his hand on her skin sent shivers of delight rippling down her spine.

Her hands flapped ineffectively against his arms for support as her knees turned to spaghetti. His other arm clasped her round the waist, solidly holding her body against the flat angular planes of his. Surprisingly comfortable, a still functioning part of her stunned brain managed to register. Surprisingly. The rest of her brain fired into action.

This was Jack the rotter! She'd only just met him and they'd done nothing but argue. What was his game? Seduction, after all? She'd been forewarned, thought she was forearmed, but he'd slipped through her guard as easily as could be. He must be gloating...

She pulled away, hot and confused. Embarrassed. He let his hand slide slowly from her neck and his fingers left a burning trail on her skin. So easily, he did it so easily. He laughed a soft little laugh, holding her eyes with his, then turned and walked towards the house. He stopped, looked back.

"Hannah? Come on," he said, mimicking her.

Praise for Elisabeth Rose

Strings Attached

by

Elisabeth Rose

Strings Attached

Contact Information: info@thewildrosepress.com

Cover Art by *Angela Anderson*

The Wild Rose Press
PO Box 706
Adams Basin, NY 14410-0706
Visit us at www.thewildrosepress.com

Publishing History
First Champagne Rose Edition, 2008
Print ISBN 1-60154-329-8

Published in the United States of America

Dedication

To Colin, Carla and Nick

Chapter One

Hannah glanced at the kitchen clock. Cripes! Bernard would be here any minute and she was only half packed. And whose fault was it?

"Yours," she growled at the black and white cat squirming in her grasp. "Keep still and open your mouth."

Freddo, who always resisted taking his worm pills, excelled himself this time by scratching her wrist just as the dramatic and turbulent Verdi Requiem burst forth on the radio. A perfect soundtrack to the violent tussle being enacted in the kitchen. And if Freddo kept on the way he was going the Requiem would be a perfect memoriam for him too.

"Sanctus, Sanctus," bellowed the choir.

Reverting to Plan B, Hannah put him down and dolloped a spoonful of stinky cat food into his bowl, shoving the pills in with her finger in an effort to fool him into eating the little capsules by mistake. As if!

He licked at the offering, stopped, sniffed, licked again.

She growled in frustration. "Eat it, you nuisance. I'm late. I can't waste time with you! I have to finish packing." Freddo's ears flattened against his head and he backed away.

Verdi moved from rousing "Sanctus" to ethereal "Agnus Dei." The phone rang. Dammit! She snatched up the receiver, sniffed suspiciously at the hand holding the phone. "Hello?" Cat food on her fingers.

An unfamiliar man's voice said, "Would you mind answering the door?"

"What?"

"Turn the racket down and open the door, please. I've been standing here for ten minutes." He hung up.

Who on earth was that? Someone connected to Steve no doubt. Of all the times... Hannah, still holding the cat food tin, raced to the front door, remembering just in time to tread carefully on the Persian runner Steve had bought last month in a short-lived spasm of home decorating. The darned thing slipped about on the polished wood floor.

The stained glass panel revealed the dim outline of a blue and red figure. Juggling the cat food she wrestled with the latch, which always stuck a bit, then yanked the door open. A tall, dark-haired man with an expression like the Day of Wrath stood on her doorstep holding a mobile phone.

"Hannah Crawford?"

She nodded. Words jammed in her throat as he studied her with a pair of the most penetrating dark eyes she'd ever seen. X-ray eyes, scanning the inside of her head. "Who are you?" Not a friend of Steve's, she'd remember one who looked like this. Steve didn't have friends who looked like this!

"Jack Rotherford. I've been sent to pick you up. Are you ready?"

"No. Where's Bernard? I thought he was coming." Hannah frowned. Despite the initial, brain disabling rush of attraction, a shiver of alarm made her throat tighten. Bernard hadn't mentioned any Jack something touring with them.

"He's running late, and asked me to collect you on my way. Can I come in? Why aren't you ready?" He moved forward as he spoke...tall, rather angular features, those intense dark eyes still giving her the once over, jeans, tan linen jacket over a black T-

2

shirt. Supercilious manner.

"What's Bernard's other name?" She stood her ground. Just how much protection would a tin of cat food provide?

"Casey, of course, don't you know?" His gaze dropped to the tin in her hand. "That stuff smells terrible."

Reassured, she stepped back although his attitude tempted her to shut the door in his face after emptying Fish Platter over his jacket. If he was here to gain illegal entry, charm wasn't his preferred technique.

"I'm feeding the cat. He won't take his pills so I'm burying them in this. I don't think it fools him, though."

"Will you be long?" Jack stood in the doorway, frowning. Almost glowering. Annoyed, beyond doubt.

"I have to finish packing. Come in and sit down." Ignoring the stifled grunt of irritation, Hannah turned and marched back to the kitchen. Waiting a minute or two wouldn't hurt him. "Close the door, please," she called over her shoulder. Whoops! The rug. "Careful of..." Too late. The click of the front door, a muffled curse and a scuffling noise... "the carpet." A painful, sounding thud. Another curse.

She spun around in dismay. Jack leaned against the wall massaging his elbow. He extended the arm and flexed it several times, grimacing.

"Are you all right?" She rushed forward.

He glared at her and pushed himself upright. "Fine." The word struggled out from between clenched teeth.

Didn't sound fine but from his granite jawed expression he would never admit to pain. A crack on the elbow hurt like crazy. "Come and sit down. I'll get you an icepack." She held out her hand as support, then withdrew it when she realised it was the fishy smelling one.

Jack ignored the gesture. "Just finish getting ready, will you?" He followed her to the living room.

"Sit down." She waved at the couch, then darted to the kitchen to swap the cat food for one of Steve's icepacks. Verdi and company were up to the "Libera Me." Such a beautiful movement. Maybe Jack would find it soothing after his unfortunate accident.

"Can I turn that noise down? Or better still, off?" he called in a voice a long way from being soothed.

"Yes, turn it off. Thanks." She scrubbed cat food from her hands, then armed with tea towel wrapped ice, returned to face the very attractive, but very terse, and decidedly crabby man on her couch.

Hannah skirted round the pair of long legs, taking particular care not to brush against his firm, jeans clad thigh as she bent down. If she did, the mad desire to rub against him Freddo style would take over. To make things worse, up close he had a clean crisp, citrus smell which danced about in her nostrils and threatened total and terminal distraction from the first aid job at hand. Concentrate! He was cranky enough with her as it was.

"Here." She jammed the ice against his elbow. "Hold this in place."

"I don't think I need ice." He winced as the cold registered.

"It'll stop it swelling and reduce the bruising."

"Thanks." Jack gave her a sceptical look but put his hand over the tea towel. Warm, firm, his fingers slipped over hers for an instant. By chance—he wouldn't touch her deliberately, not the way he'd been sizing her up since he arrived, as if she were some sort of looney. "You sound very knowledgeable." Almost grudging. His eyes caught hers, held.

Hannah jerked upright. Was he flirting? Impossible. Her imagination was running amok.

4

Blame the all male, brain fuddling scent. "I'm not. I don't know anything about First Aid. Steve plays football. He uses ice packs all the time because he's always injuring something." Babble, babble, babble. Now he'd think she was a complete nutter.

"Go...and...pack." Jack enunciated each word with slow precision.

Hannah leapt back. "Yes, of course. Won't be long." Freddo, the nuisance, skipped ahead of her as she ran upstairs.

Jack stared around the room he'd been stranded in. This bizarre woman had furnished it with magazines on the floor by the worn leather couch, a pair of sunglasses and discarded mail on the coffee table, a football sock on one of the armchairs and the TV remote and guide on the other together with an open music score.

At least the hideous, deafening music wasn't still bouncing off the walls. He got up and wandered over to the bookcase still holding the ice to his elbow. She certainly had eclectic taste. *A Rose Grower's Companion, Caring for Your Cat*—a book she should read; *Motorbike Maintenance*—horrifying to imagine her loose with a screwdriver near a Harley, but those manuals could be the football sock wearer's; *Home Decorating*—no doubt the inspiration for the trap by the front door. The remaining shelves were crammed with books on music, poetry, novels, a dictionary, an atlas, a few lurid thrillers and a Serbo-Croatian/English phrase book which must be years old by the cover design.

He put the ice pack on the floor and pulled out the phrasebook, turned a few pages. He practised saying, "these socks have shrunk," "I will have to push my bicycle uphill," "he has gambled away his fortune," and "will I need an operation?" in Serbo/Croatian, then put the book back and yelled up the stairs, "Are you nearly ready?"

"Not quite," she yelled back.

She had attractive hair, this Hannah. Unusual colour. Quite striking. Pity she was such a flake. He glanced at his watch and sighed. Bernard had said, "Collect Hannah for me please, Jack. It'll take you ten minutes out of your way." Fifteen minutes wasted already.

He took the ice to the kitchen, left it on the sink, then sat down again. The couch had cat hairs on it. Hadn't noticed before. His nose wrinkled in disgust and he brushed a hand over his jeans. To his surprise a large Ansel Adams print on the dining room wall faced him through an archway. One of his better known. A sensibility of the visual arts must lurk somewhere in this house despite the mess and general lack of discernment in the décor.

A hair-raising screech burst forth from upstairs. Feet thudded overhead. A black and white streak raced past him, shot through the kitchen doorway and disappeared. Moments later Hannah charged downstairs.

"Did you see him?" Eyes wide, hair everywhere in a red-gold cloud.

"I saw a black and white streak," Jack said, being helpful by pointing. "It went through there. What happened?"

"His tail got jammed in a door."

"Oh, good grief!" He shook his head and stood up. At least she was downstairs again. "Are you ready to go now?"

"No." She glared at him as if he'd damaged the animal himself. "Of course not! We can't leave him like this. I have to check he's all right."

"It seemed all right to me." Jack stuck his hands on his hips and glared back. "Sure moved fast enough."

Hannah clamped her mouth closed against a very sharp retort. Boy oh boy! Freddo wasn't number one cat at the moment, but he was nowhere near as irritating as this guy. The least he could do was offer assistance if not sympathy.

"Help me find him." Not daring to look back, she led the way through to the garden and headed for the sprawling, pink rhododendron which occupied the far corner, Freddo's favourite snoozing spot.

"Freddo. Puss, puss." She bent down and peered into the greenery. "Do you think we can get him out?"

A snort of exasperation erupted behind her. Hannah glanced over her shoulder. Jack stood watching, hands on hips, an expression of total disgust on his face. "I'm not crawling in there after a cat." A definitive statement.

"I don't expect you to," she snapped. Just her luck to get stuck with Mr. Charm. And useless to boot. The initial rush of attraction was fading fast. Very fast. Must have been a temporary derangement. "Freddo, come on."

Nothing happened. Hannah grimaced, cursed under her breath. Have to go in. Bugger! She pulled a branch aside. And there was that unhelpful, bad-tempered, increasingly irritating man with a full view of her bottom as she crawled in.

Both knees sank straight into damp, caked leaf mould in the act of turning itself into compost along with other unrecognisable garden things which smelt. One hand went into something soft and very unpleasant. Squashy. It may, or may not, have been a toadstool. One yellow eye glinted as Freddo turned his head her way. Huddled up against the fence, way out of reach, he watched with his habitual suspicion as she attempted to coax him out in her sweetest, gentlest voice.

"Freddo. Come on. Here, puss. Let me see your tail. Come on." Absolutely no response. She crawled further, snagging her hair in a twiggy branch on the way. "Ow. Freddo! Come out."

"Stop messing about and just grab hold of it," Jack called.

"Yes, sir," she muttered through gritted teeth. Freddo rose to his feet. Hannah lunged forward, grabbed his furry black body in both hands and hung on. He growled and hissed, but she struggled out backwards in triumph, clutching him to her chest.

Jack, standing with hands on hips, sighed with an exaggerated and ostentatious, not to mention unnecessary, show of relief. "Thank goodness. Took you long enough."

Hannah ignored him and sat cross-legged with Freddo cradled in her lap as she examined his battered tail. No blood, but it had a strange bend which hadn't been there before.

"Does it look broken to you?" She ran her fingers gingerly along the length of the tail. The ingrate hissed and tried to scratch her hand.

"How would I know?"

Eyes narrowed, still clutching Freddo, she hauled herself to her feet and headed for the house without a word.

Jack followed her across to the back door, past two rickety cane garden chairs on a paved area, and into the kitchen. Did this lunatic know she had a piece of bush in her frizzy hair, and dirty knees?

"Close the door, please and latch the cat flap." She rapped the order out like his primary school headmistress..

He'd had just about enough of this pair. She was obviously one of those frustrated, lonely types who poured all their pent-up emotions on to their unfortunate pets. And thought every man coming to the door was a rapist. Possessed no sense of time, and no idea of its value to anyone else. Perhaps a call to Bernard and tell him to come and get her himself. But it would just be a waste of time for him, and he already had enough to organise.

No. He was here and he was stuck with her. And the cat.

The pair of them disappeared through a side door to the laundry from whence came scraping sounds and thumps and her raised voice telling the thing to keep still. Perhaps he should offer to help? No.

She reappeared dragging a cat travel box and tried to shove the struggling animal in. It tried just as hard to get out until she squashed down with one hand, folded the top with one swift movement and clipped it shut. He watched with arms folded.

"We can take him to the vet on the way." Tossed over her shoulder.

"What? Now?"

She stood up. "Yes. His tail might be broken, and Steve won't be home until this evening." This utterance had an air of finality which dared him to object further.

He returned her glare until she turned on her heel and left the room. "Where are you going?" Much more of this and he'd hog-tie her and drag her to the car.

"To finish packing. You'd better phone Bernard and tell him we'll be late."

"He'll know by now."

Jack exhaled his annoyance and went to slump on the old leather couch. Women! Every time he met a new one she reaffirmed his constantly broken resolve to steer clear of them. Not that he was tempted to steer any closer to this woman. They just walked all over you and left you in a mess on the floor, or created such emotional mayhem it was best to leave in a hurry. This one wore hobnailed boots and created chaos. Jackboots, he thought of them, the special female version.

He'd been wrong to assume she lived alone. This

Steve character, pity help him, who lived with her, played football and read his mail while watching TV. Or maybe she did. Jack dialled Bernard on his mobile.

"Bernard, we'll be late."

"Hannah not ready?" Nothing short of a nuclear blast would perturb Bernard.

"She's packing as we speak. We have to go via the vet."

"The vet?" He sounded almost interested in that bit of information. Perhaps the concept of a vet was foreign to him. No way would Marilyn allow an animal in the house.

"The vet. She slammed the cat's tail in a door."

"How long will it take?"

"I have no idea."

"We're ready so why don't we meet at the motel? Ring if anything else goes wrong." Bernard had adopted his soothing Calm Voice indicating everything was under control and tempers need not be raised. "You should be there in plenty of time. Is she leaving the cat at the vet?"

Jack sighed and closed his eyes. "I have no idea what she's going to do. She operates on a need to know basis and issues the odd order."

"Hannah will grow on you, believe me." Like some sort of fungus? Or a rash?

"I wanted to travel by myself."

"You can after today. Hannah's fine. She's good fun." Bernard's voice took on his 'jolly hockey sticks' tone.

"A barrel of laughs."

Jack hung up and sat in morose silence waiting for good fun Hannah to reappear.

"Nearly ready?" he shouted after five minutes.

"Keep your hair on," came floating back but a minute or two later she appeared, struggling to lift her suitcase down the narrow stairs. He got up to help, and she gave him a smile which startled him with the way it lit her whole face. Dimples flirted in her cheeks, and her blue eyes sparkled as she saw the look on his face when he felt the weight of her suitcase. Laughing at him! She'd tried to remove the filthy marks from her knees because there were darker, damp patches there now instead.

"What have you got in here?"

"Hernias."

Jack gave a surprised snort of laughter. "I'll take it to the car. Have you got anything else?"

"My violin and a bag with music. And a suit bag. And Freddo."

"Oh, of course, let's not forget him," muttered Jack as he went off down the hall, treading with elaborate care when he reached the booby-trapped rug.

Hannah grinned as she raced back upstairs to get the rest of her gear. Crazy and paranoid to think he might have attacked her when she answered the door. This Jack person wasn't too bad after all. Bit grouchy, but he had a nice laugh to go with the incredibly sexy body. Why had Bernard sent him to pick her up instead of coming himself as arranged? She thought they'd be travelling together in the minibus. There was plenty of room for the five of them with their instruments and luggage. Just as well, on second thought, considering Freddo.

She locked the back door, and wrote a brief note for Steve telling him about Freddo's accident. He could deal with the vet, Freddo was his cat, after all. She could only do so much when she was about to go on tour for ten days. Have to ring him tonight and explain how the tail was injured when she was safely out of Sydney...out of range.

Jack had loaded her violin and music into the car. Hannah, carrying restless Freddo in his box, joined him at the well-travelled, far from new, dark

11

blue Volvo parked in the street.

"Got everything?"

"Yes."

"Locked up?"

"Yes."

"Keys?"

Freddo shifted inside the box and started clawing at the air holes and making unhappy noises.

"Yes. What is this? Hurry up and open the door." She bit her lip, frowning. Freddo was a nuisance, but it didn't excuse this guy's attitude. And the poor boy must be in pain and frightened.

"You've got a branch in your hair." Jack reached out a hand to remove the twig. She flinched. "It's all right. I'm not going to pull your hair." His expression made it clear he was tempted though.

"My hands are full. I'll get it in a minute." A branch! Good grief! She must look like the mad woman of...somewhere. Or Birnam Wood coming to Dunsinane. Hope he hadn't noticed her dirty knees earlier.

She waited for him to open the car door, but Jack stepped closer and removed the twig with leaf attached, having to use two hands to untangle it as she stood holding her breath, frowning. He waved it in her face before tossing it into the gutter.

Jack stifled a groan. She was stiff and tense as a plank all of a sudden. Now what? Surely she didn't think he was going to attack her in the street? That's all he needed—a full day's drive with a crazy, paranoid woman. He held the door open for her, scowling as images of the nightmare ahead flashed through his head.

"Get in." Hannah, with surprising meekness, did as she was told and sat holding Freddo in his box on her lap. "Where's the vet?"

She directed him. If you could call getting lost, twice, directions.

"They're only minor mistakes." Her voice was irritatingly unperturbed. "I haven't been to the vet much. Steve takes Freddo for his flu shots and his worm pills."

And all the other fussy things cats, or fussy owners thought they required. Jack gritted his teeth, but when she turned him into a dead-end street he exploded.

"For goodness' sake! Do you know where you're going?"

"Yes! Don't shout at me or I'll get out and walk." Hannah fumbled for the door handle, without doubt forgetting she was still strapped in and hampered by the cat box.

The cat was making some very odd noises, even worse smells and had almost got a paw through one of the holes. If it escaped in the car, she and the cat would be walking. And not just to the vet. He ground his teeth and said with as much control as he could summon, "I'm sorry, Hannah. Sit still. Where should I go?"

"What's this street called?"

"I don't know. You're the one who knows where to go."

"I know where we're going, I just don't know what this street is."

"I know where we're going, too. The vet. I want to know how." His voice rose in frustration again, and Hannah sighed and stared out the window. He moderated his tone to minor annoyance. "What's the address?" He pulled a map out of a side pocket in the door.

"You don't need a map. I know where to go." She peered from left to right several times, as if trying to recognise something, anything. A bus lumbered by with Norton St. on its destination sign. She pointed in the same direction. "This way."

He stuffed the map back into the side pocket,

put the car in gear and drove back the way they'd come with his mouth a grim line. Hannah, whom he suspected had been sending a silent prayer for guidance from above and if she hadn't, should have been, cried, "There, next left. It's about three blocks."

As he pulled into the parking area, he refrained from comment with great effort, but she turned with a triumphant smirk as she got out. "See."

"Nobody likes a clever..." he muttered, but she wouldn't have heard the rest of the remark. She'd already slammed the door with her hip, almost dislocated his fillings, and was now carrying Freddo inside.

Jack waited in the car, fidgeting and listening to a CD until twenty minutes later, she reappeared. He watched her stride—catless, luckily—across the parking lot. Average height, slim, the striking red-blonde hair tending to frizz out around her face, white man's shirt flapping open over a blue T-shirt, jeans and sandals. She'd probably pinched the shirt from that poor Steve. Without asking him.

Hannah opened the door and slid in beside him. "Done!"

"Don't slam the door."

She flashed her cheeky, dimpled smile again as she pulled the door closed with exaggerated care. He grunted and leant forward to switch off the music.

"Leave it on unless you've had enough. I like Miles Davis."

Jack clicked the CD off, then started the engine. "What did the vet say?"

"It's broken."

"You must have really belted the door shut." He grinned.

Hannah narrowed her eyes. What was he smiling about? "I was in a hurry. He always hangs around under my feet. Bites ankles, too," she added in a vague justification for her own initial lack of sympathy for poor wounded Freddo.

A sign for the City West Link flashed by the window. They weren't heading for Bernard's! They should be crossing the harbour not heading west.

"Where are we going?" She only had this man's word for it he even knew Bernard. "Who are you?"

He looked sinister now with his eyes hidden behind Terminator style dark glasses and a secretive smirk on his face. Abduction in broad daylight? Was she about to become a statistic? Horrible things featured in the papers. Would a crazed kidnapper bother to take Freddo to the vet first, though? He hadn't been keen on the idea but he had done it.

"I told you. Jack Rotherford."

"Yes, but why are you here? Why did Bernard send you? Who are you?" The impassive expression on his face did nothing to reduce her alarm. She leaned over into the back seat and groped for the jacket he'd taken off during the wait at the vet's, and which now rested across two bulky-looking bags.

"What are you doing?" he yelled. "Put it back."

Hannah found his wallet. She flipped it open. Driver's licence, credit cards, ID of some sort, a photo of a very pretty woman. Jack W. Rotherford and an address in Glebe on them all except the photo. He hadn't lied so far.

"Are you an investigator?"

"No. A photographer. Put it away." He grabbed for his wallet. Someone blasted their horn as the Volvo slowed and veered erratically towards the gutter.

"Keep your eyes on the road. And you can't pull off here, it's a clearway. Didn't you see the signs?"

Jack cursed and straightened up.

"Just concentrate on driving," added Hannah as she studied the photo of the woman again. A decorative blonde. Figured.

"How dare you?" he growled, but he kept his

attention on the traffic. "Does the word Private have any meaning for you?"

She closed the wallet and slipped it back into the jacket pocket. "Okay, okay, so you're Jack Rotherford, photographer. Now tell me what's happening. Stop mucking around being smart and tell me." What a spectacular pain in the neck he could be. Fish Platter might have been the go, after all.

"Don't shout at me."

Hannah snapped her mouth shut as she heard the genuine, deep anger in his voice.

He took deep slow breaths, in and out. Doing yoga for control?

"Bernard asked me to pick you up. He thought it would save time because I live close but I doubt he realised you would be as..." Jack turned his head to the window, but she just caught the words as he murmured, "hopelessly disorganised, and indulging in cruelty to a cat." He finished in a normal voice, "He expected you to be ready."

She sat up straight but decided with great magnanimity to let the insult go in the interest of world peace. "I understand why you came, you told me before. But why are you involved? We're going on tour for ten days. Country towns of New South Wales, the outback, properties...taking culture to them."

"I'm coming too."

"Why?" What an astounding concept. This man in close proximity for ten days? They'd murder each other.

"Bernard wants me to do a photo journal of the tour, and I want to do my own work as well. It suits us both."

"He never mentioned it to me." Photos! No way! Worse and worse.

"I can't help that."

When Bernard announced this trip, she'd had initial misgivings based on the news his wife Marilyn would be coming along even though she wasn't a musician. To help with the organisation, according to her. Interfere and take control was more like it. But Hannah wasn't in a position to turn down work, and Bernard had managed to wangle a grant out of some Arts body so they'd be paid, which was always the bottom line. Now to go with Marilyn, here was another hanger-on—a bad-tempered, self-satisfied one to boot.

"Why aren't we going to Bernard's?" She frowned at Jack. "We're all travelling together in a mini bus."

"They've already left. We're meeting them in Bathurst." He added caustically, "We're so late, you see."

She ignored the innuendo. "Were you driving on your own?"

"I'd much prefer to."

"What a pity. Sorry."

He grunted, and the dark glasses and compressed lips gave the impression of deep suspicion as he glanced at her.

Hannah wasn't sorry. In fact, she was delighted there was a second car. Travelling for ten days in a confined space with loud, bossy, opinionated Marilyn would be tantamount to slow torture. Violence would be done. Besides she got sick in buses. The only problem might be sweet talking her way into getting Jack to let her ride with him. Didn't look promising so far. Might have to change her approach.

She stretched, reaching into the back, and replaced his coat carefully over the bulky, odd-looking bags he had sitting on the seat." Where's my suit bag? Did you put it in the boot? It has to lie flat."

"No. I took the suitcase and your violin and

music bag."

"We'll have to go back."

"You're kidding! "

"No. It's got my concert clothes." She stared at him. "Why didn't you take it? I told you it had to go out. It was right there."

"I'm not your servant. Why didn't you take it?" He turned into a side street and did a U-turn.

"Lucky there are traffic lights or we'd be sitting at this intersection for days." Arguing, hands at each other's throats. "Good thing we hadn't gone too far." She looked at Jack's white knuckles on the steering wheel. "You need to learn to relax. It's no big deal."

Forty-five minutes later he planted a savage foot to accelerate away from the house for the second time.

"I should call Bernard. Can I use your phone?" Ignoring him seemed the best tactic in the mood he was in.

"Don't you have a mobile?"

"I did, but I mislaid it." And she knew what response that admission was going to get.

"Silly me. Of course, you did. Why didn't you call from the house? You were in there long enough."

"I had to use the loo, I didn't think of it, and anyway, you would have got angry having to wait. Angrier," Hannah amended.

He indicated the mobile phone between them. "No point arguing with your logic, such as it is."

"Bernard? It's Hannah."

"Everything all right?"

"Yep. No problems. We had to go back because Jack didn't put my suit bag in the car." She ignored the hissed intake of breath beside her and gazed out the window as she spoke.

Jack began to construct a tirade to deliver to Bernard when they reached Bathurst. Bernard knew he wanted to be alone on this trip, that he didn't want to be here at all, and had promised picking Hannah up would take him ten minutes out of his way.

"Do me a favour, Jack?" he'd said. "Just collect Hannah, and meet us at my place. Then you're on your own till this evening."

And there was the other thing about sharing a room with someone called Simon, an issue he'd taken up earlier and unsuccessfully with an adamant Bernard. "If you want a room to yourself you'll have to pay for it yourself," he'd threatened.

Hannah said, "No, I don't think so, he's busy driving. Takes all his concentration. See you soon. Bye."

She replaced the phone between them, and relaxed back into her seat with a small sigh of satisfaction which he felt was completely unwarranted given the trouble she'd caused, but they were on the freeway now and traffic flowed along well. Out of the city mayhem he could calm down a bit. As long as she kept quiet. Although a question popped into his head.

"Why did you think I was an investigator? Have you got something to hide?" It wouldn't surprise him to learn she was an escapee from some institution—for the Dangerously Disorganised or the Intensely Irritating.

"No more than anyone else. What about you?"

"I've nothing to hide."

"Why are you so crabby, then? Fight with your girlfriend?" She began rummaging in her massive handbag and emerged with a roll of mints which she offered. "Like one?"

Hannah withdrew her hand quickly when she saw the look on his face. "Oh! Sorry!" She grimaced. Trust her to blunder in. Even this guy would have feelings of some sort.

"She walked out on me yesterday. Not that it's

19

any of your business."

She murmured something sympathetic and she hoped soothing and put the mints back in her bag. No doubt served him right—the girl must have decided he and his boorish behaviour were best left alone. Smart girl.

"Can I have a mint or are they just for show?"

She offered him the roll and he took one without looking at her, muttering, "Thanks."

Cripes! If she wanted to ride with him on this trip she'd better be nice. "I'm sorry about your girlfriend."

"Not your fault." Jack shrugged. "I'm not very good company at the moment."

"No."

"But then neither are you." He crunched down hard on the mint.

Chapter Two

Jack concentrated on the road. If Hannah kept quiet they might reach their destination with his mind and her body intact. He levered some bits of mint from between his teeth with his tongue. Very tangy. Went with her personality.

Did Penny like mints? He'd never know now judging by what she'd said as she stormed off yesterday. Something along the lines of hoping he rotted in hell. Penny was a beautiful woman in every way, she just couldn't understand why he didn't want commitment in the form of a ring. He couldn't understand why she wanted to change what they had—a good relationship, independence, no strings attached.

When a woman began making demands and threats and using emotional blackmail it was time to plan an open-ended, overseas project. Get right away. This time Penny had got in, or rather out first, but it had been a close run thing. Still it didn't ease the hurt feelings and wounded pride. Better to be the dumper than the dumpee and most often, he was.

And there was the added nuisance of finding another model for that arty-farty book when he got back. A pain all round. If he'd known Penny was going to drop out he wouldn't have agreed to this tour, with the deadline so close. He could hardly ask her to go ahead with it now. With any luck Bevan, whose brainchild it was, wouldn't find out until after he got back or there'd be tantrums and heart attacks. Better switch the mobile off.

21

"We can have lunch in Katoomba."

She sounded like an enthusiastic child. Jack glanced at her. "We're not taking the Katoomba road, and I don't want to stop."

"Not even a bathroom break?"

"Must you?" Hadn't she just gone? Was he stuck with a female with a weak bladder, on top of everything else?

"By lunchtime, I will. Anyway we'll need food."

True. Breakfast had been hours ago and he hadn't factored in mucking around with a cat plus driving backwards and forwards in Balmain and surrounding suburbs.

The road wound up into the mountains. Tall, majestic gums towered over the road filling the spring air with the fresh scent of eucalyptus. A tangle of undergrowth carpeted the forest floor, and sunlight dappled through the thick leafy canopy. Hannah wound down the window. Her hair blew in a tangle of red-gold.

"Lovely fresh air up here."

Rather forced enthusiasm, wasn't it? He grunted. A cool rush of wind streamed through the open window and swirled about inside the car.

"Could you wind your window up a bit, please?"

She turned the handle once.

"More."

The glass crept up to within a few inches of the top.

"Thank you."

"I'm feeling a bit woozy."

"Carsick? You get carsick?" Terrific!

"The fresh air helps. I'm okay in a car as a rule. It's the winding road."

Jack gripped the steering wheel and concentrated on negotiating the next bend. "Open the window. Tell me if you need to stop. Before you need to stop!" Cat's urine and vomit, the new fragrance for the interior of the discerning man's car. Perhaps he'd wake up soon from his Alice in Wonderland dream.

Hannah rolled the window down halfway and stuck her nose out.

"I would have thrown up in the bus by now." She turned to grin at him with her hair blowing all over her face in the wind. "Don't worry. I'm feeling better." He stared at her for a moment. Unbelievable!

They stopped in Kurrajong for lunch, high in the Blue Mountains, the natural barrier which for years had prevented the early Australian settlers and explorers from finding a way across to the grazing pastures of the hinterland. Hikers and sightseers had flocked to the area for over a century to gawp at the spectacular views, trudge through or in some cases get lost in the thick natural bushland which stretched for mile after ancient mile over craggy sandstone ridges and deep, secret valleys.

Jack parked in the main street, and they walked back to the nearest café. Hannah would have liked to explore further but one look at his face killed the suggestion before it even made it to her mouth. They sat in an old fashioned, wooden booth along the side wall lined with mirrors. Its elaborate edging featured frosted designs of fruit and flowers. Their reflections sat next to them mimicking their movements. Hannah glanced once and then avoided looking at the messy girl with wild, windblown hair.

"I'm starving." She picked up the menu. "What about you?"

"Should you be eating vast quantities of food?" He took off his sunglasses and stuck them in his jacket pocket. A camera lay on the seat beside him.

Hannah, sitting opposite, looked up and met his dark, cool gaze. Her cheeks prickled with heat and she resumed her examination of the list of food.

Heavens, the man was good-looking! Pity he was such a stinker.

"If I have something light, I'll be all right." She studied the menu as if it contained the secrets of life.

He continued to stare at her. She pushed the menu towards him, flustered. For heaven's sake, get a grip!

A waitress hovered with a pencil, smile and notepad.

"Salad sandwich, please, and cappuccino."

He took a cursory look at the menu. "The same, please. Wholegrain bread."

"Yes, mine too. Thanks." Hannah flashed the woman a grin.

Now she had to repair the damage done by her carsickness revelation. Nothing more off-putting to a potential chauffeur than a nauseous passenger. She'd lost a lot of ground with her admission.

"I don't get sick in the front seat of a car. Buses do it to me. The diesel smell and the swaying..." And being pregnant. A memory crashed in, demolishing the carefully constructed barriers. She'd been sick as a dog...every morning for weeks...but she didn't want to think about it, didn't much any more. Too painful. She'd learned not to. Learned to keep the memories at bay.

"Mmm." An eyebrow lifted. "How were you going to manage on this trip?"

She blinked, focussed again. "Motion pills."

Cripes! She hadn't packed them! Come to think of it, did she have any? And she'd planned on asking to sit in the front. Little likelihood of success there, though, with Marilyn along for the ride. She pulled a face.

"Oh?" His inquiring look switched to a smile of thanks as the waitress slid their sandwiches and coffee on to the table.

"Do you know Marilyn?" She picked up her

sandwich to take a bite.

He nodded and stirred sugar into his coffee with a casual air. "Don't like her?"

Hannah rolled her eyes, unable to answer because her mouth was full of grated carrot and lettuce. A piece of tomato slipped onto the plate. Salad sandwiches were so messy—should have chosen cheese. He'd want to wipe her down before he let her back in his car. She swallowed the mouthful and prepared to tell him exactly what she thought of Marilyn but something in his too-innocent manner stopped her.

"Do you know her well?"

"Quite well." Jack paused and took another neat bite of his sandwich. How did he manage without fallout? "She's my aunt."

Good grief! Hannah shoved the piece of tomato back into the tattered remains of her bread. "So Bernard's your uncle?" Obviously, half-wit!

"Ah...yes."

"Are you related to anyone else on this trip?" Better find out now before she inadvertently insulted his whole family.

"I don't know. Who else is there?"

By the grin, he was hiding vast and petty amusement at her expense.

"Simon Prendergast and Libby McNeill."

Jack shook his head.

"Thank goodness!" He snorted with laughter as she clamped her mouth shut.

Hannah spooned the froth off her coffee and ate it, then stirred the remainder to cover her embarrassment. She couldn't look at him. He infuriated her. He would have sat there and let her insult his aunt, and not even told her if she hadn't specifically asked. Might never have told her! Let her make an idiot of herself so he could continue laughing at her. Then she would never get to ride

25

with him again even if he overlooked the carsickness.

"I'm supposed to be sharing a room with Simon. What's he like?"

She picked up her cup and took a sip. "Great guy. We were students together." Should she mention Simon was gay? No. Completely irrelevant.

"As long as he doesn't snore."

Hannah tilted her head, considering. "I couldn't say. Maybe he's hoping the same thing about you."

They finished their coffee in silence and shared the bill. Hannah disappeared into the Ladies. Jack waited for her on a bench a few metres from the cafe. The sun warmed his face, and for the first time today he began to relax. So good to be away from the city.

He spent as little time there as was possible between projects. Nature was infinitely preferable. Marvellous to spend weeks alone in a tent or an isolated cabin somewhere. Or in a remote village with a handful of locals as company. His last trip had involved snow and ice and Inuits in the far reaches of Canada, and if frostbite hadn't been an issue he'd still be there instead of here playing chauffeur.

He'd expected uninterrupted thinking time about his next project while fulfilling this reluctant favour for Bernard. Not the one he'd lined Penny up for—it was straightforward—a portrait of a woman going about her life. There'd be time to worry about that one later. No. He wanted to think about his big adventure, photographing the world's fast-disappearing wilderness areas. Trouble was, Bevan had made Jack's participation in the other thing a proviso for sponsoring his travels.

This job itself was easy, involving the barest minimum of time with the musicians. Marilyn had suggested with her usual gaiety he regard it as a little holiday. If he wanted a holiday he wouldn't be taking it with a bunch of strangers, let alone classical musicians. His idea of enjoying himself did not involve taking a cat to the vet and driving a carsick, chattering, disorganised, violin-playing woman around the state.

As if on cue, Hannah stepped onto the footpath, and the bright sunlight caught her hair in a flash of copper. She paused to put something in the haversack-looking thing she carted about, her face illuminated for an instant by the halo of shining hair. Her skin had the pale translucent complexion of an angel from one of those mediaeval, religious paintings in Italian churches. Jack snapped off a shot and rose as she came towards him, glowering.

"Did you take my picture?"

"It's my job, remember?"

"I hate having my photo taken."

"Why?" What a complicated piece of work she was. "Do you think I've stolen your soul and trapped it in my little black box?"

"Don't be ridiculous. I just don't like it taken. Let's go." She strode past him.

"That's going to be a problem for you, isn't it?" He grinned at her retreating back. "Hannah."

She stopped. "What?"

Jack caught up to her and pulled out a handkerchief. "Wasn't there a mirror? You've got tomato." He wiped her chin, stuffed the handkerchief in his pocket and walked on. "Come on. We haven't got all day," he tossed over his shoulder, hiding a smile at the sight of her, frozen in place, mouth half open in shock.

Hannah reactivated her limbs and scampered after him, mind whirring. No more salad sandwiches in public. The Ladies only had a tiny blotchy mirror, but how could she have missed a great blob of tomato? They left Kurrajong in silence. She wound the window down, rested her head back, closed her eyes and focussed on enjoying the fresh, soothing bushland sounds and smells wafting into the car. Jack had cheered up a bit, resigned himself to her presence. He wasn't half as crabby. But there's nothing like a laugh at someone else's expense to brighten your day.

How mortifying. Cripplingly embarrassing! Wiping her face in the street like a four-year-old. And he'd taken her photo before he wiped her down.

She hated having her picture taken, hated, hated, hated it. A horrible, traumatic experience. At fifteen. No! Don't dwell. It was behind her, with just the lingering antipathy to being photographed as a reminder. Almost a joke now. Much easier to forget than the other...Adrian, the pain, the despair, the grief...better not...the wave of carsickness had brought it all back...there'll be another baby...Dr Clyde had assured her...and she wanted a baby so much, her own little treasure...don't think about it.

Her breathing slowed. She drifted into a doze. A few minutes later, as if in the distance, she heard Jack slip a CD into the player.

Loud, abrasive Jimi Hendrix! *Hey Joe.*

Hannah's eyes flew open. What an insensitive clod. But what spectacularly emotive lyrics. She'd always liked this song. All about someone shooting their old lady. Did Jack's girlfriend do him wrong with another man? No wonder he was touchy today. Only hope, unlike Joe, he didn't have a gun in his hand.

Hannah glanced at his impassive profile. Without a doubt trying to annoy her, but his infantile effort wasn't going to work.

She stared out at the trees flashing by as images of another guitarist crowded into her mind. Being the girlfriend of a guy in a rock band wore thin pretty fast. Blond, tattooed Paul liked his woman to have no opinions of her own and be there at all times but Hannah had plenty of opinions and things to do once summer holidays ended—a Music Degree to complete, practice and study to be done, more life to live.

"What are you smiling about?" Jack had the vague intention of irritating her with the Hendrix track. Classical musicians, as a rule, were musically very conservative and narrow minded. Hendrix was the loudest and most in your face thing he had in the car. If he'd known, he could've arranged a veritable barrage of heavy metal music. As it was, assuming he'd be travelling alone, he'd chosen ninety percent jazz, his preferred style. And she liked it.

"It reminded me of someone I used to know."

Jack returned to his own black and morose thoughts—starring Penny. Hendrix suited his mood to perfection. If Hannah hadn't been with him he would have turned the volume up even more and sung along, belting out his anger and frustration. After a couple of hours he'd be rid of her. No way would he let Bernard unload any more mad musicians on to him, especially if he already had to share a room with one of them.

"What sort of photographer are you?" shouted Hannah.

"What?" Startled, Jack leaned forward and turned Jimi down.

"What sort of photos do you take? Fashion? Advertising? Kids on Santa's knee? Porn? Are you a member of the paparazzi?" Hannah looked at him, smiling, all phoney innocence.

Jack gritted his teeth. "I freelance. Nature and environment, the odd disaster or war if I'm in the right place." He paused and added, "War is a disaster. I don't photograph people much, although I have one assignment." Scuttled in style by Penny. Another headache he didn't need. "I sell to magazines like *National Geographic*."

She had the grace to look abashed. "You must be very good. What on earth are you doing with us?"

"I'm asking myself the same thing. It's a favour for Bernard." A big favour, getting bigger by the minute.

"And for Aunt Marilyn," added Hannah, turning her head and murmuring something like "Can't forget Marilyn," at the window, so Jack wasn't positive he'd heard correctly.

"Yes. I always travel and work alone."

"It's not my fault I'm riding with you," she snapped. "I didn't ask Bernard to send you to pick me up."

"And if I'd known you weren't going to be ready I wouldn't have agreed," Jack shot back. "I wanted time to myself. To think."

"What about? You can think with me here."

"You can't keep quiet for more than two minutes." Make that two seconds.

"I can."

He restrained an offensive remark with great difficulty. "I like being on my own."

"Could be why your girlfriend ditched you. Women prefer it if their men like being with them."

Now she sounded like a relationship counsellor. "For pity's sake!" Jack's gaze flashed to the thick bushland on either side of the road. Thick enough to hide a body?

"What did you want to think about?"

If he didn't give her an answer she'd never shut up. "I'm going on a tour soon. It's a project I've had in mind for a long time and I've never had enough money or the opportunity to do it. Now I've got the backing of a publisher." Bevan, virtually blackmailing him with the other pictures. If he didn't come good with them things could get sticky on the finance side. "Photographing wilderness areas. It means travelling to all sorts of remote places. It'll take a year at least." He couldn't keep the pleasurable anticipation from his voice.

"Camping?" Hannah wrinkled her nose. "I hate camping. Too uncomfortable. It always rains, the tent leaks or falls down, the ground's lumpy and hard, there are bugs and the food's awful. Most often all the above. Horrible. Give me luxury any day."

"I love it. Fresh air, natural beauty, solitude."

"I imagine it would suit you to perfection, the solitude part." She grinned. "And suit everyone else as well. I'll look at your photos in the comfort of my home, thanks."

He'd seen the comfort of her home, complete with Persian carpet ride and cat's hair. "It's something I want to do. Always have."

"I hate having my picture taken." Such an abrupt switch of subject—had she been listening to his dream at all? Serve him right for lowering his guard. "I wish Bernard had mentioned this."

"Don't worry. I can make anyone look good." He smirked. "Wouldn't have made the slightest difference what you think, the Arts people requested a photographic record."

"Couldn't we have done it ourselves?"

"I think they want something a bit better than happy snaps. You can't take photos and play at the same time." Even if you do know which way to point a camera. "Why don't you like having your photo taken?"

"I always look terrible, I'm really unphotogenic and I hate my hair. In all our family pictures I look like I'm wearing some sort of clown wig."

"Perhaps you've never had a good photographer take your picture." Her hair was her best feature. Apart from her skin and those dimples.

Hannah paused a moment before replying. Oily, slimeball Raoul with his French cigarettes, his whispered promises and his sleazy little studio. To this day Brut aftershave made her want to gag. Her lip curled. "I haven't. No one's that good." And no one would get the chance, not after her teenage exposure on film.

"I am." He looked sideways at her. She knew he wasn't boasting, just stating a fact as he knew it. Why wouldn't he just drop the subject? Insufferable man! And worse still, the way his mouth curved gave her a little jolt of pleasure for which she gave herself a mental kick in the bum. Just because a man had a sexy smile didn't mean anything. A smile can hide a wealth of untapped unpleasantness, and an attractive one was worse because it put you off guard. She knew all about fast talking, superficially attractive photographers. This guy travelled the world even more than Adrian. And if there was one thing she knew for a fact, she would never, ever, fall for another man who didn't come home every night because of his work.

"If you say so."

"I do." And that was that.

****

At ten to four Jack parked in the space next to the white minibus at the Bushranger Motel in Bathurst. Aunt Marilyn, with bouffant blonde hair lacquered into submission, burst out of one of the rooms like a shot from a cannon and hugged Jack while he was half out of the car. Bernard, grey-bearded and distinguished, followed, beaming. He clapped Jack on the back.

"Jack, Hannah. You made it."

"So we did, Bernard." Hannah gave Marilyn a tight smile, which was returned with similar warmth. This chill stemmed from their first meeting, when Hannah had spilled a tiny drop of tea on the cream shag pile in Bernard and Marilyn's living room and commented how lucky it hadn't been red wine. Marilyn was indescribably upset, and carried on about fibres and carelessness until Hannah considered throwing a glass of water in her face to take her mind off it.

"You're later than we thought," said Bernard. "Is the cat all right?"

"Broken tail." Jack jumped in with his curt reply before Hannah could open her mouth. "We had a few delays and stopped for lunch."

"Good." Bernard smiled from one to the other as if he'd achieved a perfect match on a TV game show.

Hannah wanted a word with him. Something along the lines of 'why didn't you tell me?' Later. Right now she needed to wash her face and have a cup of tea. She went to the boot of the car and retrieved her suit bag. Bernard picked up her violin and music.

"Can you bring Hannah's bag in, Jack?" Marilyn's glass-shattering voice bounced around the parking lot as she fluttered about on ridiculous stiletto-heeled sandals. "And you haven't met Libby. Where's Simon?" Bernard shrugged. "He should be here to meet Jack."

Marilyn thumped on Room No 7 and shrilled," Can we come in? Jack's here at last. And Hannah." As if she were a stray dog he'd picked up along the way. She rapped again, short and sharp this time.

"Hi Libby." Hannah grinned from behind Marilyn's sunshine-yellow-clad back as the door opened. Jack lugged her case into the room, muttering about hernias as he lifted it onto the rack.

"This is Jack." Marilyn made the presentation as if she'd invented him.

Libby took Jack's proffered hand. He reacted to her beauty the same way every other man did. A glaze came over their faces but their eyes sparked with lustful light. To be expected. She was gorgeous. And she wasn't interested in anything much other than music and her cello.

"We'll pop around to the venue at about five-ish for a sound check. Concert at eight-fifteen. We can eat something light in between." Bernard rubbed his hands together in anticipation of those delights. "They've organised dinner for us afterwards. Come on, Jack. I'll introduce you to Simon." With one arm draped over Jack's shoulder he ushered him to the door.

"Thanks for the ride, Jack." He had to tear his eyes from Libby to answer her. The dumping girlfriend had just been effectively erased from his memory banks. Out with the old, in with the new.

"No problem." The door closed with a soft click.

Hannah flopped onto her bed. No problem? Liar. He'd been blatant, making it obvious right from the start it was a problem. She was a problem. If she looked like Libby he wouldn't have thought so.

"Cup of tea?" Libby went to fill the little electric jug in the bathroom.

"Love one, thanks."

"Jack's a bit of a hunk. Old though."

"He's one of the most obnoxious people I've ever met. Although—he's Marilyn's nephew so I guess it runs in the family."

"I know all about him." Libby rolled her beautiful, violet coloured eyes and chanted, "He's single, thirty eight, a world famous photographer, has won every award known to man. He doesn't like women much, there's an alleged son whose mother seduced him when he was young and foolish, and he's just been deserted by the latest in a long line of women which stretches around the world and includes the rich and famous and probably even..." she lowered her voice for emphasis, "minor royalty. Their fault, of course. None of them understood his artistic talent, and all were jealous of his success. Marilyn's like a mother to him. His own mother died when he was fourteen which is why he's so independent. His father was a no-good trombonist who seduced his innocent mother, Bernard's sister, and ran off when Jack was three. Hasn't seen him since."

The jug clicked off. Libby poured water into two cups and passed one to Hannah.

"Thanks. Good trip, huh?"

Hannah chuckled as she dunked her teabag but her mind was grappling with one snippet of information. A son? Jack the playboy had a child he didn't care about when she would give anything to have a child? The thought train threatened to derail at this point. She didn't know he didn't care. But there was no photo of a child in his wallet, just the blonde. What sort of father was that?

She tossed the tea bag into the little bin by the dressing table. Still! If only half of the rest were true it's no wonder Jack was annoyed about driving her and Freddo to the vet. Bit of a come down for a jetsetter. Sad for a boy to grow up without a father though, and to lose his mother—and have Marilyn as a substitute. Bound to have some twisted values. Not to mention bizarre impressions of women. And trombone players. But he was a father!

"I bags travelling with Jack tomorrow," said Libby. "To be fair we should share Marilyn around."

"He wants to travel alone. He was pretty annoyed when he got stuck with me."

No way would she let Libby get her shapely foot in his car door. Not with her perfect figure and beautifully behaved black hair, and this was before you even got to know her and discovered she was kind, friendly, funny, smart and talented. The front seat was Hannah's, and she would put up with Jack rather than go in the bus and feel sickened by Marilyn as well as the diesel smell.

Libby continued, "Actually, better still, Jack

should travel with them, and we can drive his car. He's related to them, after all."

"Brilliant! And Simon can come with us."

Libby put her cup on the bedside table. "How do you think this concert will go tonight?" Her smooth brow creased in an anxious frown.

"It'll be fine! I just hope the piano is good."

"You're always so confident." She opened her suitcase and began poking about inside it.

Hannah smiled. "I've been doing it for a few years longer than you, remember. I must have inherited the show-off streak from Mum. But you know, I wouldn't mind taking a break, doing something else. My life seems to revolve around music and my students. I'm getting tunnel vision."

"Like what? I can't imagine doing anything else. Anyway, I can't."

"Oh, be a mother, maybe. Get married again. All the boring stuff." She laughed what she knew was a self conscious sounding laugh and glanced at Libby for her reaction.

"Gosh. I thought you'd be put right off marriage after what you said about your first one." Libby dropped a black dress shoe in her astonishment. "Sorry. I mean, great. I guess, well, for you...you're older than me." She groped about on the floor.

Hannah nodded. "Just the small problem of finding the right guy." And this time she'd make sure he wanted the exact same things she did. Not like Adrian with his upwardly mobile career, and his life-consuming ambition. A home with a man who loved her and lots of babies. Was it too much to ask? Apparently.

"You're one of the nicest people I know. And you'll be a great mother."

Hannah had to turn away and put her empty cup on the bedside table so Libby wouldn't see the tears glistening in her eyes.

Libby held up a black blouse and studied it. "Does this need ironing? I hope not. I'm the world's worst ironer."

Nobody looked at Libby's clothes when Libby wore them. What was she worried about?

Bernard thumped on the door fifteen minutes later. "Come on, girls."

"How do you like Jack?" Hannah asked Simon as they walked to the concert hall. He looked down at her from his imposing height of six feet four inches.

"Seems pleasant enough, keeps himself clean. Why?"

"He wasn't happy about having to share a room."

"I gathered as much from the surly expression on the handsome face. I told him I was a great fan of his work. Praise does the trick most of the time."

"Have you heard of him?"

"Yes, haven't you?"

She shook her head in glum denial.

"You really should get out more."

Jack met them as they approached the concert hall, camera clicking. Hannah gritted her teeth and lowered her face.

"Don't stop, just keep walking and talking. Don't look at me."

"Jack darling, make sure you get the musicians. Not me, I'm just excess baggage." Marilyn's laugh trilled like a manic budgerigar.

Hannah bit her lip and exchanged looks with Simon and Libby, but Marilyn was too close for her to make the obvious remark. Then she realised Jack was still shooting. She'd have to be careful. He wouldn't miss much and would have a memory like an elephant as well.

The concert manager, Fran Scott, neat blue blouse and floral skirt toning artistically with her silver grey hair, met them as they entered the foyer, and ushered them into the hall, talking non-stop. Her committee had arranged sandwiches and light snacks for them after the rehearsal. They'd have dinner at her house after the concert with a few select guests.

Hannah walked on stage to the shiny, black, baby grand piano. "It looks new." She opened the lid and played a few chords. "Nice!"

"We had it tuned just this afternoon." Fran beamed from where she fiddled with a display of flowers and greenery on the front of the stage.

"Absolutely superb flowers, Fran. Very professional," declared Bernard.

"Make sure you get the flowers, Jack," called Marilyn from her seat in the front row. He was studying a light meter in the centre of the stage but nodded a smile at Fran, who was pink with pleasure.

"Can't miss them. They're perfect. Make a good frame."

While they rehearsed, Jack wandered about taking photographs, irritating and distracting Hannah to the point where she made more mistakes than she'd ever made before. He knelt beside her and photographed Libby across the top of her music stand.

"Must you." Hannah's words hissed from between clenched teeth.

"Just doing my job." The camera turned for a close up of her face resting on the violin. She whipped her bow down, furious.

"I can't play with him doing this all the time." The insensitive lunkhead! She'd told him she hated having her photo taken.

Marilyn's voice sliced the air. "It's his job, Hannah. You'll just have to get used to it."

Jack wandered across to the side of the stage and took another shot of the whole group, while Bernard soothed.

"Just a few pics. To get the feel of the rehearsal. Jack won't do it during the concert. Relax. You're just nervous about tonight. It'll be fine." Bernard bestowed his 'reassuring' smile upon her and lifted his violin. "Ready? Last movement?"

Hannah swallowed at least five angry retorts aimed at Jack and lifted her bow. Marilyn, ensconced in the front row, stared at her with contempt, her mouth open ready to join in again, but Bernard gave the downbeat and cut her off with Borodin.

True to her word, Fran and her team had provided a spread of sandwiches, cheese and fruit in the large room backstage. Hannah sat by herself and watched Marilyn monopolise Fran's group of women. Two pink-taloned hands gripped a reluctant-looking Jack by the arm. "He's very well-known overseas, you know, and he's won any number of awards, haven't you, darling? He's my nephew. So sad. His mother passed away when he was a boy..." The bright red lips beamed at Jack. "We're like mother and son. Notice the family resemblance?"

Jack shuffled uncomfortably as they clucked and fluttered. How unusual to see him looking embarrassed. How gratifying. Typically, Marilyn claimed the relationship when he was related to Bernard. But then, as Libby recounted, 'she was like a mother to him.' Hannah grinned to herself as she enjoyed a strawberry. Would Marilyn mention the son?

A chatter of appreciation from the trapped audience greeted Marilyn's next comments. Hannah caught Jack's eye and sent him a big happy grin. He excused himself and came toward her, sat on the next seat, leaned back and sighed.

"Aunt Marilyn hasn't changed a bit." He looked across at her surrounded by the enthusiastic women, and shook his head gently, but smiling.

Hannah ate a cheese cube. Hasn't changed? How on earth did he survive his adolescence? "I haven't known her very long." Tactful.

"I didn't mean to upset you. With the photos."

Startled in mid chew, Hannah struggled to swallow the mouthful of cheese. "I didn't mean to be rude about it."

Sotto voce he said, "Why didn't you tell me Simon's gay?" His gaze swung to where an intent Simon loaded a plate with sandwiches.

"I didn't think it mattered. Does it?" If it did Jack would plummet right off her scale of human decency. He was already teetering on the bottom edge.

"No, of course not. Why would you think it did matter to me?"

"I don't, didn't. Whatever. Anyway, Simon doesn't fancy you."

"Likewise."

"Then what's your problem?"

"I don't have one." He stood up.

"Did you think you'd be irresistible to him?" Is it insulting for a straight guy to be thought unattractive by a gay guy like it is when a woman turns him down? Better not ask. She laughed instead.

"What's so funny?" Jack sat down again.

"Nothing. Calm down. Simon has lived with a guy called Keith for four years and they've got a better relationship than my last one or any of yours by the sound of it." Not surprising Jack's girlfriends departed, the way he was eyeing Libby before the dust had settled behind the blonde.

"Point taken." Jack grinned. "I like Simon."

Hannah smiled. When would be a good time to ask about travelling with him? She could work on it this evening. All signs indicated he regarded her as a companion now. Just needed to ingratiate herself a little more.

"Tell me about Libby."

"What about her?" Hannah's smile faded. The plans took a nose dive.

"Has she done any modelling?" She followed his gaze towards Libby, standing with Simon.

"She wants to play the cello as well as she possibly can. Why do men find that so hard to understand? Just because a woman is beautiful doesn't mean she wants to show herself off all the time. Women can have brains and talent in a beautiful body and be just as dedicated. I thought you didn't like photographing people." Hannah stood up. "I'm going back to change."

She stalked off. Jack stared after her. Why did she always take him for a potential lecher? Why was the wretched woman so prickly and difficult? Had a dud affair by the sound of it, put her off men. He deeply resented her remark about not understanding a beautiful girl with ambition. He, of all people, understood the combination.

Penny was pretty and had an excellent job in TV. The fact she was so independent made it easy to leave and pick up again on his return. A perfect arrangement. She was the one who wanted to start home-making and binding him to her. But Penny had no idea how much his forthcoming trip meant to him, and it was her total ignorance which caused the final eruption and destruction. "Why can't you take pictures here at home?" was her plaintive query. "You could make a fortune doing portrait work, especially with my contacts in the industry."

And another thing annoyed him. Hannah's implication he was bowled over by Libby's good looks. He was a photographer, for goodness' sake! He'd done his share of shoots with stunningly beautiful women all over the world but had also paid his dues doing weddings and anniversaries and family portraits and then some, in the climb to the position he was in now, able to pick and choose his assignments. He needed a non-professional model, a natural woman. Libby might be interested. Simple as that.

Chapter Three

Hannah and Simon walked to the motel together. Hannah's head came to almost level with his chin. Or one of his chins. Could Simon do some subtle investigating re Jack's child? How could anyone not acknowledge they had a child? Hannah frowned. Why did it rankle so much? She hardly knew the man.

Simon said, "I hope the weather stays fine. We'll be outdoors at a couple of the properties."

"Fun." It rankled because Jack was the same selfish, driven sort of man as Adrian. One of those men who did their thing regardless of the effect on their so-called loved ones. They pursued their dream and their women paid the price. And that stinker Jack was the most physically attractive man she'd ever met.

"It's been raining pretty hard further west," Simon went on. "Doesn't bode well."

They turned into the motel just as Jack's car pulled up with Libby, Bernard and Marilyn.

"We should get back there at about seven thirty," Bernard said as they dispersed. "Formal tonight, please."

"What should I wear? Is the peacock blue too much, do you think? For Bathurst?" Marilyn's voice faded as their door closed.

"How come Jack's so nice?" Libby rummaged in her suitcase and came up with black tights.

"He's related to Bernard, not Marilyn." Hannah pulled on her long black skirt. Nice to Libby maybe. Not so nice to Hannah The Nuisance. And with very

43

unpleasant morals. The way things were shaping up she'd have an uphill battle to get into his car tomorrow.

She finished dressing and checked herself in the mirror. Her figure was reasonable—went in and out in the right places—but she'd told Jack the truth about her hair. It wouldn't do anything much but stick out around her face. The clasp and combs she needed to pin it up were still sitting on her dressing table at home. Comb it and leave it.

Libby, elegant in her flowing black skirt and satin blouse, swept her hair into a chic knot. A dash of lipstick, glamour personified. "Done." She put on her shoes. "Are you ready?"

Simon and Jack, waiting, chatting in the parking area, turned as Hannah and Libby emerged from their room. Jack's eyes went directly to Libby, of course. She was beautiful and he was a male. Hannah slammed the door shut with a vicious tug.

"You two look terrific." Jack's gaze washed over Hannah for a second, but she wasn't fooled as to whom he meant even though she smiled and murmured, "Thank you."

"Thanks." Libby wore her politest face.

"We can walk, but Bernard's taking the bus because we'll need it to get to Fran's later," said Simon. He always looked terribly imposing in his dinner suit. Like Jeeves. The sleek cut made him look slimmer, not like his usual sloppy corduroys and baggy sweaters or T-shirts. Hannah brushed some lint off his sleeve. Jack took Libby's cello to carry it. Men were so obvious.

Simon and Hannah walked ahead a few paces, but Jack's voice carried clearly behind them.

"You play very well."

What a line and anyway, how would he know?

"Thank you," said Libby.

"Are you still studying?" was his next effort.

"This is my last year."

Hannah recognised the frigid politeness in Libby's voice. She was waiting for the next move. Men were so predictable.

"Going overseas to study? There's a very good teacher in Vienna. I did a shoot there earlier this year. Heinz Wanhal." He mentioned the name casually. "I suppose you've heard of him?"

Libby's squeak of astonishment matched her own hastily stifled gasp. How on earth had Jack come across an octogenarian cello teacher in Vienna? Wouldn't he have been up a mountain with his camera or wandering in the Vienna Woods? Given his opinion of classical music as displayed by his dismissal of Verdi this morning, it was a wonder he even knew what a cello was, let alone one of its most famous exponents.

"I'm going there next year to study with him!" Libby unleashed a barrage of questions. The pair were still chattering when they entered the concert hall via the backstage door. Simon went to the bathroom. The warm-up room was empty. Hannah played scales to get her fingers moving.

It was obvious who Jack would prefer to travel with. He and Libby hit it off straight away while she and Jack nearly hit each other. And the way he'd taken Libby's cello from her! True, he would've looked a complete pig if he'd let her carry the awkward thing herself, but still...

Hannah practised a few bars of the Borodin Quartet, drawing the bow across the strings with indignation-fuelled energy, facing the corner, her back to Libby and Jack.

Philanderer! Little did he know Libby thought he was old and decrepit, and compared to her he was—sixteen years older. Old enough to be her father. And the sixteen-year-old Jack was sure to have got started early in that department! How old

45

was his son? Her own baby would have been almost two by now.

Simon and Bernard came in discussing the benefits of solar energy in loud voices. Hannah drew a couple of deep breaths and blinked hard before she turned around. Jack had his camera raised. He'd taken her photo while her back was turned. She glared at him. His expression was bland and inscrutable, but he said nothing and pointed his camera towards Simon and Bernard as they unpacked.

Hannah walked on stage with sweaty palms and a churning stomach, and the discomfort had nothing to do with preconcert jitters, and everything to do with Jack. She was a squirming bug under a microscope. Every time she turned around he was there with his eyes and his camera, prying into her mind. She hated it already, and it would go on for the next ten days.

Despite all of which, she still wanted to ride in the car. But only because she got sick in buses and couldn't stand Marilyn, not because she wanted to ride with him. He was the lesser of two evils. All they did was annoy each other, but if she tried very hard—she'd thought this trip was going to be fun even given Marilyn, but now with two of them to contend with...

It was all too irritating and disturbing. How could she stand it?

Hannah took her seat, raised her violin and watched Bernard for the cue to start. Concentrate.

The concert opened with a string quartet by Dvorak, the major work on the programme. They'd spent hours in rehearsal on it, but this was the first public performance and, although no one admitted to it, Hannah knew the others were as tense in anticipation as she—especially Simon, who had some tricky intonation sections he dreaded. Bernard looked each of them in the eye and raised his bow with a confident flourish.

Their work paid off. As they played the last chord, the audience responded with a deafening burst of applause. Gazing out over the crowded hall as they took their bow, Hannah saw Jack kneeling to the side of the stage. The flash went off and spots danced before her eyes. Great—now she wouldn't be able to see anything for ten minutes.

They resumed their seats for the second item, a contemporary piece in one movement by a young Swedish composer. It sounded in some places like Freddo yowling for his dinner and in other places like a car crash, but Bernard had insisted they include some modern works. Hannah and Simon, who both hated it, grudgingly admitted it was a good contrast to the familiarity of Dvorak.

"The Dvorak was superb. Well done everyone," Bernard declared backstage at interval.

"I almost lost it in the ghastly Swedish thing." Simon pulled out a handkerchief and mopped the sweat from his brow.

Marilyn burst through the door, a peacock blue dynamo. "It's going marvellously. The Mayor is there. Did you know? I've been chatting to him. You'll meet him at dinner. Such a nice man. His wife's a bit dull, but then the wives so often are in these places, aren't they?"

Hannah poured herself a glass of water from the carafe on the table to avoid saying something she'd regret. They had a long way to go and patience is a virtue. Jack came into the room with his camera. Should she say something about being constantly photographed? Maybe it wasn't worth it, causing trouble. Marilyn would leap in with all guns and mouth blazing.

Bernard walked across. "All right, Hannah? You look a bit down."

She forced a smile. "No, no, Bernard. I'm fine." He patted her arm. Jack's camera clicked.

She lowered her voice. "Is Jack going to be with us the whole trip?"

"I think so. Does it bother you?" Bernard wrinkled his forehead as if he perceived a terrible problem arising.

Hannah hesitated. This could be delicate, given the family loyalty thing. "You might have told us—at least asked if we minded being photographed non-stop." Or at all.

"I didn't think anyone would mind. It's not as if he's intruding on our privacy. Jack's shooting us as a group to get the flavour of the tour. The Arts people want to use it for publicity. Show how worthwhile the trip is, and how well they spend their money." His teeth shone through the beard, and he beamed as if she were an Arts Council spy he had to convince.

She nodded reluctantly. Bernard added, patting her arm again, "You won't even notice him after a day or two."

Not notice Jack? Sticking his camera in their faces all the time, a constant reminder of the adolescent indiscretion she thought she'd overcome, forever hovering in her consciousness...with that smile and those eyes and that supercilious expression, that acid tongue. Bringing back memories of Adrian.

Jack, out front with his camera after interval, began to enjoy himself. The fascination of angles and light, and the way the players' faces reflected what they were interpreting, the way their bodies moved and their hands and fingers responded to the demands of the music, pushed personal problems from his mind. The memories of Penny's harsh and bitter accusations yesterday, his annoyance at the ridiculous delays and irritations caused by Hannah this morning, faded away. The thought of having to listen to classical music for two weeks became slightly more bearable. He became lost in the task at hand.

Hannah and Bernard walked on stage for the second half of the concert. Their piece must be better than the horrible thing they'd performed earlier. Reminded him of a cat fight.

According to the programme they were playing something called "Vocalise" by Rachmaninoff. Never heard of it. Through his viewfinder Hannah's hair picked up the lights and shone like candle flame as she concentrated on the piano accompaniment to Bernard's singing violin, bringing out all the pathos and beauty of the simple melody. Hannah was absorbed, revelling in the rich, sonorous chords pouring from under her fingers. Her face in concentration looked like a mediaeval angel again. She was a talented woman and quite beautiful sometimes. When she wasn't talking. And from a distance.

Jack turned his camera on spellbound faces in the audience. Bernard, the consummate performer was busy wringing every last drop of emotion possible from his violin. He drew his bow gently across the string for the last soft note, and left it hovering in the air to mingle with the dying chords from the piano. Bow suspended he waited motionless until the whisper of sound died away, then lowered his violin and bowed his head as the applause thundered out.

Hannah and Bernard disappeared off stage. A few minutes later they reappeared with Libby and Simon for the last item, according to the programme, Borodin's "String Quartet No 2." Jack changed lenses and moved closer to the stage. Hannah glanced his way with a slight frown. He lifted the camera and focussed. She looked away. He grinned.

This music was better, he quite liked this. A yawn almost escaped. Long day. How were Hannah and the others feeling? Their playing was fresh and vital, giving no indication of weariness but they'd probably feel it later. Please don't let Simon be a snorer.

The first movement ended and the sparkling dance-like Scherzo began. The melody stirred some memories. An old song. "Baubles, Bangles and Beads." Not bad. This classical stuff had its moments.

Jack went backstage to catch the performers as they came off between bows. Their faces were flushed and smiling, elated by the success of this their first performance. Hannah ignored him as she walked past but he went to offer his congratulations as she put her violin away and she smiled, giving him the full force of her dimples. If only she'd look like that when he had her in his lens.

"Thanks, Jack. Did you enjoy it? I didn't think classical music was your thing."

"It's not but I did. I didn't realise you played two instruments. The Rachmaninoff was beautiful."

"Yes, Bernard is such a ham." Hannah laughed.

Simon, packing up next to them, said, "You know, the original is written for soprano and orchestra but it's such a gorgeous tune everyone has a go at it."

He began to sing "La, la, la" in a high warbly falsetto. Hannah rolled her eyes. "Take no notice, he's an idiot. I love the Borodin. It's our favourite piece. Specially the Nocturne."

Simon swung into "And This Is My Beloved" in a rich, schmaltzy baritone.

Bernard with Marilyn in tow came to chivvy them along. "Fran's expecting us *toute suite*. And there are fans waiting in the foyer for you."

"Do you know where to go?" Libby asked as they

climbed aboard the minibus after fifteen minutes of congratulations and polite chit chat from their enthusiastic groupies. Marilyn's immaculately coiffed head bobbed and craned as she peered through the windscreen at the dimly lit parking area dotted with groups of people strolling away from the hall.

"Follow the Mayor, Bernie," she ordered.

"If I knew where he was, I would."

A silver Mercedes pulled out in front of them. "There's a Mayoral-looking vehicle," Hannah said.

Marilyn shrieked, "Oh yes. There, Bernie! What a divine car. So regal. Don't hit it, Bernie."

Hannah choked on a laugh and Jack, across the aisle, looked at her with raised eyebrows. She immediately composed her face into one of studied innocence.

He leaned towards her. "You're not going to be sick, are you?"

"If I am you'll be the first to know."

He sat back with an impassive expression.

Fran and her husband Reg inhabited a spacious old sandstone house a few blocks from the theatre. Reg, all smiles, open arms, silver-grey hair, false teeth, and stylish maroon cravat, ushered them into an elegant and immaculate living room. Coats and instruments disposed of, he began fussing over drinks.

Fran offered a plate of hors d'oeuvres arranged in colourful patterns. "You all did so well tonight. It was just perfect. Thank you. The Rachmaninoff...oh, simply stunning."

She moved on with her tray. Hannah and Simon sipped champagne and watched the new arrivals. Marilyn attached herself limpet-like to what had to be the Mayor while Bernard was left chatting to a tall woman in a slim-fitting, pale blue silk suit. Libby had been cornered by a group of three goggling men and a jealous-looking young woman clinging with grim fingers to the arm of one of them. Two other elderly couples shared a joke with Reg in the corner.

"Where's Jack?" Hannah asked Simon with casual unconcern. Simon glanced around.

"Don't know. Fiddling with a camera, probably."

"Did you know he was coming?"

"Bernard mentioned it to me yesterday. Didn't you know?"

"Not until he turned up to collect me this morning. I had no idea. I could kick Bernard sometimes."

"Couldn't we all. I'm sharing a room with him." Simon laughed. "Jack's a nice guy, luckily. Excellent photographer."

"How come you've heard of him? Is he well known?"

"He's famous, won an award recently for a shot he took of an oil spill and the effect on the wildlife. It was a bird drenched in oil sitting all alone on the beach, surrounded by a horrible sea of black slime. Don't you remember? It was in all the papers. Earlier this year."

Hannah thought. She did remember the photo. Tears sprang to her eyes as she'd studied it over breakfast.

"Jack took that?"

"Yes. If he can make me look good he deserves another award."

"He told me this morning he can make anyone look good. Oh!"

"What?"

"I forgot to call Steve about Freddo. I'd better do it now."

Reg directed her down the hallway to his study, one hand placed unnervingly low and straying lower, on the small of her back. Wall-to-wall carpet, no treacherous Persian rugs here to trip the unwary visitor. Just a lecherous senior citizen.

"Use the phone in here. Much quieter." A heavy hand rested on her arm and fingers squeezed. "Give you some privacy to whisper sweet nothings to the boyfriend, eh?"

He leaned in closer and winked, false teeth gleaming in the soft light from the lamp on the desk. Hannah blinked and grabbed the phone, whipping the receiver between her ear and his leering face.

Reg left, closing the door with a soft click. She shook her head to clear it of the unsavoury images he'd conjured up, grimaced and glanced at the little gold antique clock ticking away on his polished wood desk. Ten forty-five. Would Steve be home? Doubtful on a Friday night. With any luck she'd get the answering machine and not have to listen to his recriminations. Yes!

She finished explaining to the tape and opened the door. A roar of voices came from the right, but she turned left in search of the bathroom. Mission accomplished, she headed for the living room. Jack was on his way out. Tall and handsome and staring right at her. His smile implied they shared a private joke. Her heart did a leap and a flop.

"Bathroom's down there third door on the right," she babbled as he approached, flustered for no reason at all except they were alone in a confined space. Face to face. Jack paused as he passed her. The tangy citrus scent, definitely not Brut, swept into her nose, the warmth of his body reached out as he crowded her in the passage way. Her feet stopped all by themselves.

"Thanks. I wondered where you'd got to." He didn't move, just stood there looking at her with a light smile curving his lips as she leaned against the wall behind her to avoid having her breasts squashed against his chest.

"I rang Steve about Freddo and got sexually harassed by Reg."

"At the same time?" He looked impressed.

"No, he leered at me more than anything. Poor old chap."

She caught his eye and looked away quickly. There was a print by Tom Roberts on the wall next to him. The one with those bushrangers and the coach. Jack had gorgeous dark eyes. Not so penetrating now, much softer. She knew her cheeks were pink. He'd be laughing at her. She wished she could make her feet move away from him.

"He just told me a joke I couldn't possibly repeat to you," he said. She flicked her gaze back and opened her mouth but he went on, "What did Steve say?"

"Answering machine."

He nodded solemnly. "Just as well. Difficult thing to explain."

Hannah grimaced. Never a truer word spoken. She managed to edge along the wall. "I know. Stevie loves his cat."

"You don't?" Why was he surprised? He couldn't have thought she actually enjoyed crawling about in the garden and going to the vet?

"Not particularly. Freddo doesn't like me. He scratched me this morning and he bites. I quite like cats."

"That can put a strain on a relationship." His eyes never left her face. Hannah nodded, barely able to breathe.

He broke the contact and sauntered on down the hall. She put a hand to her cheek. Hot. She knew it! The last thing she wanted was to let him see the effect he could have on her. He'd revel in it and notch up another one. Men like Jack just couldn't help themselves.

Still, it had been a civil conversation, relative to

some of their recent efforts. Travel plans back on course. She rejoined the crowd. Reg issued instructions to people to help themselves from the buffet as Fran had prepared copious amounts of food.

Hannah sat on one of four elegant, straight-backed antique chairs balancing her loaded plate. The Mayor's wife Cecily, in the blue suit, introduced herself. Contrary to Marilyn's summation she had plenty of interesting things to say and had even seen Hannah's mother in a play several years ago when the production had done a national tour. They were deep in a discussion on single, professional women when Jack reappeared.

"May I join you?"

"Of course," said Cecily in her melodious voice. "I'm so pleased to meet you, Jack. I'm a great admirer of your work. I liked the story you did for the *National Geographic* two or three years ago on deserts."

They began discussing his other projects. Everybody knew about Jack. Everybody had interesting things to say to him except her. All they had in common was Freddo and neither of them particularly liked him. But then she and Jack didn't particularly like each other and she certainly didn't like his callous dismissal of his child. Marilyn must have got 'alleged' from somewhere and she would bet it was Jack, denying his responsibility. Hannah stood up. "Excuse me." She took her empty plate to the table. Bernard and Marilyn were eating standing up, chatting to the Mayor. Bernard beckoned her over.

"Mike. Allow me to introduce Hannah Crawford. She is an indispensable member of our troop of roving minstrels."

"Wonderful concert. Thank you."

"They're all so talented I feel totally useless,"

put in Marilyn and the two men turned indulgent faces her way as Bernard said, "Now, sweetie, you know I couldn't get along without you."

Marilyn batted her eyelashes at him and Mike the Mayor said gallantly or suggestively depending how you looked at it, "I've no doubt you have many talents."

"Hannah. Don't look so grumpy." Marilyn's voice cut through the male laughter. "Hannah sometimes goes off with the fairies," she explained to Mike who nodded and sipped his wine.

Hannah made her lips stretch into something like a smile. "Sorry. I'm tired. It's been a long day, hasn't it?"

"We can sleep in tomorrow. It's not far to Orange. They've organised a barbecue lunch for us," said Bernard. "We'll leave about ten."

Fran announced coffee and dessert were on the table.

Jack appeared beside Hannah as she poured coffee. He held out his cup and she filled it. She had to be polite and interesting and wangle her way into his car tomorrow. And not let him look her in the eye.

"Want some cake?" He added milk and sugar to his coffee.

Hannah shook her head. "I'm too full, more's the pity."

They moved away to allow Libby and Reg access. Elderly Reg had the same smitten look as every other man Libby met although his had more lechery than the average, and his hand hovered over Libby's buttocks as he ushered her forward.

Jack stayed beside her as they drank their coffee. Polite and interesting, polite and interesting. Her head was bereft of conversational gambits. Her tongue was tied.

"So, you're famous," she blurted. That fact

wouldn't change anything. This was still the same man who'd been obnoxious and angry this morning. Explained his general air of confidence and arrogance, though. Now it was disturbing. He was disturbing. He was attractive. That fact was very disturbing. Hannah shuffled from one foot to the other. Be nice!

Jack shrugged. "Not really."

"Cecily knew about you. So did Simon."

"She subscribes to *National Geographic*."

"I've never heard of you."

"I know." Jack smirked. "I've never heard of you."

"I did see your photo of the bird in oil." Hannah employed her most ingratiating smile.

Jack nodded. "A lot of people did." He gazed around the room absently. Losing interest. Should she ask straight out if she could ride with him? He'd laugh in her face. Incredulous.

The coffee was very good, she'd almost finished her cup. Time was running out. Everyone was occupied. Simon and Mike sat on the sofa with Marilyn wedged in between like a kewpie doll and two big teddy bears at a sideshow. Fran and Reg were with Bernard, probably swapping dirty jokes. Libby had been surrounded by men, and Cecily chatted to the rest.

Hannah began formulating ways to frame her question. Jack seemed happy to stand here with her, observing. Now might be a good time. The only time. She opened her mouth.

Crack! The front legs of the sofa gave way. The three occupants slid slowly forward on to the floor, in perfect formation, holding their coffee cups in stunned, arrested elegance before them.

She let out a short burst of surprised laughter but the shocked look on Jack's face made her clamp her mouth shut against the rising flood of giggles.

He shoved his cup into her hand and rushed forward to help his distraught aunt.

Fran shed tears of mortification. Reg flapped about alternately comforting his wife and apologising to Mike who sat in an undignified heap on the floor. Simon lumbered to his feet. The other guests hovered about exclaiming in shocked tones, giving ineffectual pokes at the collapsed sofa and surmising the cause of the disaster.

"Woodworm, do you think?"

"Perhaps the glue dried out."

"This antique furniture is usually quite robust. A crack?"

"A flaw in the wood?"

Maybe it was plain overloaded. Hannah leant against the wall, weak with laughter. Simon passed her on his way to the kitchen.

"Are you hurt?" she managed to gasp.

"I'm well padded." An unaccustomed frown appeared. "Glad you're amused."

"You should have seen your faces! When you slid." She doubled up again.

"For heaven's sake, Hannah!" Jack, almost steaming with rage. "Marilyn's had an awful shock. Fran's terribly upset. Shut up, you insensitive idiot."

Hannah pressed her lips together. She met his furious gaze with what she prayed was a concerned expression. "Is Marilyn all right?"

"Fat lot you care. She's got coffee stains on her dress but apart from that, yes."

He glared at her for a moment, then returned to Marilyn. Bernard assured Reg there would be no repercussions in the form of lawsuits, but they really should leave. Perhaps Reg would get a drycleaning bill though, the way Hannah had received an account for a carpet shampoo. Marilyn should be kept away from tea and coffee. She smothered another little snort of laughter.

Cecily had calmed Fran who was now smiling bravely if a little damp around the edges and clutching a tissue. Hannah approached them.

"Fran, thank you for a fantastic dinner. I'm so sorry about the sofa and..." Fran and Cecily looked at her expectantly. "I'm sorry I laughed. But they did look so funny. They were in perfect formation."

Cecily and Fran exchanged glances. Had she overstepped the mark? Her name was fast becoming mud in Bathurst's social circle.

Fran said in a brave but shaky voice, "I didn't see it. My back was turned."

"I did." Cecily's eyes twinkled.

Hannah sighed. "I'd never be a good politician or a diplomat, I'm afraid."

"You're an artist, Hannah. If you didn't display your emotions you wouldn't be much of a performer. Perhaps just a tad more control off stage." She winked.

Hannah grimaced. "My father says the same thing. constantly." She turned to smile at Fran. "Thank you so much. I'll never forget our Bathurst concert."

"Neither will anyone else," said Fran as Hannah kissed her soft, powdered cheek.

****

Bernard pounded on the door the next morning until Libby roused herself enough to crawl out of bed and open the door.

"Come on, you two. You've got fifteen minutes to be on the bus."

Hannah stayed motionless with the covers over her head as Libby mumbled placating words to Bernard, then stumbled into the bathroom. The shower started. Hannah slipped back into sleep. Next thing the blankets were ripped off, and Libby yelled, "Bathroom's free, Hannah. Get moving! Bernard's pacing up and down out there like Hitler."

59

She emerged from the shower almost awake. Libby had already taken her suitcase out to the bus. Marilyn's voice pierced both the closed door and Hannah's eardrums, complaining they were half an hour late already. Hannah mouthed rude retorts as she stuffed her pyjamas into her bag. She groped about under the bed and found a sandal and yesterday's knickers.

The ride home from Fran's had been a tense affair. Marilyn's ego and bottom were bruised and her dress supposedly ruined. Bernard had his attention fully occupied keeping the bus on the road while comforting her.

She hadn't been aware of Hannah's laughter, fortunately, but Simon and Jack made it quite clear they thought she was childish and tactless by muttering to each other in short indignant bursts, and ignoring her. Libby sat with her eyes closed and said nothing. It didn't seem to be the right time to compare notes on Reg the Rake. And any chance of riding with Jack had collapsed with Fran's sofa.

Hannah dragged the hernia case out the door for an impatient Bernard to heave up into the bus, and went back for her violin and music. Everyone waited, the bus engine chugged, Marilyn fumed. Hannah climbed in and slumped on to the closest seat to the front. She didn't have the energy or the courage to wrangle with Marilyn for the front seat. Not when Marilyn was in the fragile role of disaster survivor.

"I know how you feel," came Simon's raspy voice from his position behind her. "Early night for me tonight." He, at least, appeared to have forgiven her. Dear Simon, incapable of holding a grudge.

Hannah said, "It took me ages to get to sleep. Too much food, too late." And too much excitement. A delayed giggle threatened to erupt as the hilarious image flashed through her mind. She yawned to disguise it, and settled down to continue where she'd been so abruptly interrupted.

Simon said, "Jack set off bright and early."

"I thought he was supposed to film us," said Libby.

"Not all the time, Libby. Certainly not the way you all look this morning. He has his own work to do. An important project." Marilyn's voice cut into their desultory conversation. She, of course, was turned out to perfection, from lavender slacks and white sweater to immaculate makeup and fingers dripping with rings.

"Thank goodness," Hannah murmured with her eyes closed. She'd thrown on jeans and a football jumper of Steve's, waved her hairbrush near her hair and hadn't even attempted to put on makeup, expecting they'd go to the motel before the barbecue lunch.

Jack with his disapproval and his camera was the last thing she wanted to face this morning. "I hope I don't get sick."

"Sick? Are you going to be carsick?" Marilyn's voice hacksawed its way through Hannah's sleep-deprived head.

"I don't know yet. I am in buses. Big ones. I'll tell you if we need to stop. Right now I want to sleep."

They only had to stop once. Hannah hadn't eaten breakfast, so there was nothing to churn around in her stomach, and after she walked about in the fresh air for ten minutes they continued. With a face like curdled milk Marilyn gave up her seat next to Bernard, but even though she said nothing, Hannah knew tomorrow would bring its own seating problems. And every day after. She could picture it now—Hannah and Marilyn wrestling each other to the ground in the parking area.

Libby broke the tension by saying in a casual

voice, "Reg almost had his hand up my dress last night."

Hannah straightened, grinning with delight. "Me too! More the hand on the bum and suggestive leering, though."

"He told me the filthiest joke," said Simon. "Jack, too. Different one, though."

"Did you compare them?" Boys swapping dirty jokes in the dorm at midnight.

"Yes, of course."

"Tell us," said Libby.

"Don't you dare, Simon!" Marilyn's shriek threatened eardrums and windows.

"Never fear, Marilyn," announced Simon, "I am far too much a gentleman to repeat such jokes in mixed company."

"Exactly what Jack said," commented Hannah, as Libby gave a derisive laugh. "He wouldn't tell me, either."

"Oh, Jack is definitely a gentleman," said Marilyn. "I find it hard to believe of Reg. He was very proper towards me, and he seemed so cultured. The cravat always makes a man look distinguished."

"A thin veneer of culture masking a deep layer of smut. His cunning disguise," said Simon. "If it makes you feel any better, he didn't fondle me either. But I didn't fancy him, so there you go."

Bathurst to Orange was an easy drive. Despite Marilyn's fussing before they started, and the unscheduled stop, they pulled into the motel forecourt well before noon. Jack helped unload the suitcases while Bernard sorted out keys and opened doors. Marilyn and Libby disappeared into their respective rooms.

Hannah, clutching her violin, looked at her suitcase and her heart sank like a stone. A boulder. A whole avalanche.

"Where's my suit bag?"

Silence. Simon looked blank.

Jack held up his hands. "You can't blame me this time."

Bernard rejoined them. "What's happened?"

Marilyn, unerringly scenting trouble, popped her head out the door of their room like a desert rodent, nose twitching.

"I left my suit bag behind, I think." Hannah put her violin down with elaborate care.

"What do you mean, you think? Hannah, you are stupid sometimes," Marilyn shrilled. The door closed and she marched towards them. Bernard put a restraining hand on her arm.

"Please, sweetie. What's in it, Hannah?"

"All my concert clothes." Hannah's cheeks burned. "I'm sorry, Bernard. I was in a rush." And asleep. Jack's cynical gaze bored a hole through her brain.

Bernard drew a deep breath. "Well, it's only an hour or so to go back."

"You're not going back for her, Bernard. You can't. You'll miss the lunch and they're expecting you. It's her fault. She's held us up twice already, and it's not even midday."

Hannah's words came out in a rush. "I'll go, Bernard. I'm sorry. It is my fault. Can I take the bus?"

"And how are we supposed to get to lunch? Really! You are so selfish and inconsiderate."

Hannah instinctively leapt back from Marilyn's rage-infested body, out of range of the pink-tipped claws flexing in preparation for attack. A short, uncomfortable silence followed.

Bernard turned to Jack. "I'm sorry, Jack. Would you? Go back with Hannah? The car would be quicker."

"You can't go either, Jack!" snapped Marilyn. "It's a ridiculous idea."

Hannah couldn't bring herself to raise her eyes from Bernard's feet, clad in casual brown loafers and black socks. If she even glimpsed Marilyn she couldn't guarantee the safety of the shrew's teeth and hair. She'd get in a few good blows before the men dragged her off. Think coffee on the peacock blue is bad, Marilyn? How about a black eye and bald patches?

"I could drive myself." She addressed the feet. "But I'd have to take your car, Jack." She looked up at him then, avoiding an eyeful of Marilyn with great care.

He stared back at her and she knew exactly what he was thinking. Disorganised on top of tactless and childish. Let her go off in his car? Hannah? The walking disaster? She must be out of her mind to suggest it.

Chapter Four

"No."

"I don't know what to do, Bernard." She turned to him, annoyed that her voice shook, desperate to maintain a façade of calm in the depths of such humiliation. "I'm sorry. I suppose I could buy an outfit, or squeeze into something of Libby's, but she's tiny compared to me."

"Hopeless!" Disgust from Marilyn.

"I'll drive you back." Jack stared at Hannah, his eyes boring into her brain. "I've done it before."

Marilyn threw up her arms. "It's impossible! You're supposed to be photographing us with these people, not traipsing about the country after her."

Hannah took another step back in case Marilyn was tempted to bite and scratch. She looked angry enough. Someone should stuff her in a catbox. Jack ignored Marilyn but Hannah could tell he was furious, too. It was the whitening around the jaw which gave it away. That and the clenched teeth. Bernard had a satisfied smile. Problem solved.

"If we go now, we'll be back in about two hours. We'll see you there." Jack looked at Hannah, his expression blank. "Ready?"

"Jack..." Hannah blinked rapidly as stupid, embarrassing tears pushed their way to the surface. She spun away, muttering, "Thanks. Give me two minutes." He made her feel like a four-year-old again. First wiping her face, now bailing her out.

She dragged her case into the room, and took her violin from Bernard as he followed her in.

"Don't mind Marilyn, Hannah. She doesn't think

sometimes before she speaks."

"She's right this time, Bernard, I am stupid. Give my apologies to our hosts for me?" Hannah tried to smile. Admit Marilyn was right? She must be going soft in the head.

She nipped into the bathroom for a quick wash and spruce up. Her mouth tasted like the bottom of a parrot's cage, so she scrubbed her teeth, but with too much toothpaste so she foamed at the mouth..

Libby, lounging on the orange-covered bed with a novel, gave her a sympathetic smile. "I'll save a sausage for you."

Jack sat waiting in the car.

"Do you do these things deliberately?" His tone would strip paint. He started the engine and drove out on to the street.

Hannah stared at him in amazement. "Of course not. Why on earth would I? I wasn't even awake when we left and I can't help it if the bus makes me sick."

"Were you sick?"

"No."

"So what was the problem?"

"We just had to stop so I could walk about. It was only ten minutes." Her voice shook with rage at the unfairness of Marilyn's attack. She clenched her teeth and hunched up against the side of the car. "Anyway. Why on earth would I leave my bag behind on purpose?"

Jack shrugged. "No idea."

"Why volunteer to drive me?" Hannah glared at him. "I could have driven myself. I can drive, you know."

"Not my car! I said I'd do it because it would've created problems for Bernard if I hadn't. I'm doing it for him, not you."

"Thanks."

They drove in silence for several kilometres

along the gently undulating highway. Farmland stretched away on both sides of the road with gum trees dotted about providing shade for the sheep grazing contentedly in the warm, spring sunshine. A peaceful, restful scene. She had read somewhere the results of a crucial scientific study, from New Zealand probably, on the breakdown of how sheep spent their day—something like 20% eating, 10% wandering around and the rest of the time staring into space. Thinking nothing. Sheep didn't know how lucky they were.

Hannah's stomach growled. "Have you had breakfast?"

"Yes." He spoke without shifting his eyes from the road. "Hours ago."

"Mind stopping so I can get something to eat?"

He released a long, hissing sigh reminiscent of a leaky valve. "Won't you be sick?"

"Not in the car. I told you yesterday. But I'll start feeling sick if I don't eat."

"If there's a place I'll stop." They were still in the midst of endless, brown, dusty sheep paddocks. Not a building to be seen in any direction. "Didn't you have breakfast?"

"No. Marilyn was furious enough as it was because I slept in and made us leave late, and then afterwards, I didn't want to eat."

"No mints left?"

"You ate them all yesterday." And she wouldn't be so generous with her mints next time. No siree!

A truck stop loomed on the left with petrol pumps and a small café. Jack pulled into the shade of a stand of gums on the edge of the gravel parking area. Hannah leapt out and ostentatiously closed the door with great care. He looked the other way as she grinned back at him through the window. Crabby so-and-so. She could almost smell the scent of burning martyr.

The café had little choice, but she loaded up with muesli snack bars, more mints and fruit juice, and strolled across to the car breathing in the fresh air and chewing on a nut bar. Jack scowled at her as she got in beside him. What was his problem? He'd offered to drive her, the least he could do was be pleasant about it. Not much to ask. However! Better be as nice as possible to raise her chances of travelling with him tomorrow. If she plotted the 'chance of travelling with Jack' curve on a graph, she had the distinct feeling it would be heading down, down, down at the moment.

"Like a drink? Tropical or apple juice."

The engine burst into life. "No thanks."

Hannah opened the small plastic bottle of apple juice and took a swig. Juice ran down her chin.

"Whoops." She wiped her mouth with the back of her hand.

"Can't you even drink without making a mess?"

"You drove over a bump. Anyway it's not on the seat, don't get your knickers in a knot. " Shades of Marilyn and the carpet. She must have trained him to have a pathological fear of stains.

Jack pushed Miles Davis into the CD player.

"What's your important project?" Hannah asked a few kilometres later. Men always liked to talk about themselves, and this one would just love it being so famous. It worked for Simon.

"What important project?"

"Marilyn said you had an important project. Don't you know about it?" She grinned, and gave a convulsive giggle as the image of Marilyn's surprised face sliding to the floor, flashed through her mind.

He turned his head towards her. The Terminator glasses stared, blank, black holes.

"What's so funny?" She mustn't laugh, he'd throw her out of the car.

"I'm sorry, it's just...I keep seeing their faces..."

Hannah clenched her fists so tightly her hands ached. She kept her face towards the window, lips compressed. He might not notice her shoulders shaking. The bag with the drinks and snack bars slid to the floor. She dived down to rescue it, fairly sure the top was screwed firmly back on the apple juice.

"You're such a...a..." Words failed him. Hannah waited, but he obviously couldn't come up with an insult befitting her despicable behaviour. "How could you laugh?"

"Didn't you see?" Under control for the moment, she risked turning her head towards him.

"Yes, I did, as a matter of fact." His lips tightened.

"Jack? Didn't you think it was funny? Not even a tiny bit?"

"If it had been you on the sofa you wouldn't have laughed."

"Yes, I would have." She gave up the struggle and laughed till her stomach hurt.

"Yes, you probably would." His exasperation got the better of him, emerging as a disgusted snort. "And then we could have all had a good laugh at your expense."

"Do you think it was Simon who broke it? The last straw?"

Jack's lips curled the tiniest little bit. So! He did have a mild sense of humour buried below the grim exterior. Some excavation might make their trip more fun.

When they reached the motel with its familiar garish sign, Hannah raced into the office and emerged holding her suit bag triumphantly aloft.

"Better check everything's in there." Now he sounded just like her father.

"It is. I packed very carefully last night so I wouldn't leave anything behind." She grinned at him, but Jack looked away.

"We should be at lunch by two fifteen." He edged the Volvo back into the highway traffic, then glanced at her jeans. "You don't want to go straight there, do you?"

Hannah looked at him. "Why not?"

"I thought you might need to use the bathroom...or something. Women usually do."

"Don't I look good enough?" She narrowed her eyes.

"Suit yourself. Marilyn would probably be annoyed if you turned up in jeans and a Balmain footie sweater."

"Think she supports a different team?"

He shook his head and sighed. She stopped grinning. Enough teasing, she didn't want to alienate him completely. Jack was to be her chauffeur, after all.

"I do want to go to the motel first. To tart myself up."

"Why couldn't you just say so?" His voice sounded very tired. Fed up with her.

"It wasn't as much fun."

"Does what's-his-name, Steve, enjoy your idea of fun?"

"He's known me long enough to handle it." Why was he suddenly so interested in what Steve thought?

"How long?"

"All our lives." Hannah gazed out the window. Jack concentrated on the road. Hannah waited. She snuck a surreptitious glance, but he was intent on driving and his face gave nothing away. "Steve's my cousin."

"Oh." His face remained expressionless. "Poor guy. Does he drink?" he added in a nasty little jab.

"No, he likes me. So. What's your project?" She set her expression to intense interest.

"I told you yesterday. Remember? The coffee table book?"

"Tell me again." Vague snippets of the conversation returned, but she'd been more concerned with being photographed than with what he'd been telling her. Sleazy Raoul and his penchant for naïve, underage teens in their underwear. Hannah shuddered. Camping. It had involved camping, she remembered that much.

Jack glanced at her, hesitated, then said, "I've had an idea for ages about photographing things in the wilderness. Not scenery exactly, more...it's hard to explain...small things in the midst of the vastness of the country and the sky. So many of the small things will be lost forever. Especially in the wilderness areas under threat."

"Sort of...emptiness with life?"

"Exactly! That's exactly what I mean. So many intricate things go on. We miss subtleties and details most of the time."

The surprise on his face was almost insulting. He must have had a very low opinion of her ability to grasp aesthetic, abstract concepts.

"And you'll be tramping about out in the wilds with a tent and a camera. All alone."

"For a lot of the time."

"Don't you get lonely?"

Jack laughed, but he didn't sound amused, more scornful than anything. "No. I like being alone."

"So you said yesterday. Sounds like my idea of hell."

"So you said yesterday. It's my idea of heaven. I've been planning this on and off for years." Jack stared at the road ahead. "Penny thought it was a ridiculous idea." He spoke softly, as if to himself, but stole a swift glance at Hannah.

She spoke to his stern profile. "It's your dream. Dreams aren't ridiculous. We all have them."

"What's yours?"

"Never to have to spend a night in a tent, and never to have my photograph taken."

"I knew you'd be incapable of taking it seriously," he muttered.

"I'm sorry." She even managed to look contrite when his angry face turned her way. "I'm not sure I have just one dream." She frowned. "I want to be as good a musician as I can. Something every artist wants." She paused knowing Jack was waiting for the rest. Be honest. He'd shared. Her voice dropped. All of a sudden this was very real. Intimate and personal. "And I'd like to be someone's mum one day. Several someones'. I really would love to have a family."

"Fortunately, I don't."

"That's obvious." Shouldn't have admitted anything to him. A man, and this man in particular, couldn't possibly understand how a woman felt about these things, otherwise he wouldn't have...

"Why?" His expression when he glanced in her direction, was even more forbidding than when she'd joked about her life's dream.

"Don't you..." Hannah stopped.

"Don't I what?" His voice dropped to a deadly monotone.

Oh, what the heck. She needed to know. What could he do to her? "Already have a child? Marilyn told Libby..."

"It's none of your business." His knuckles were white on the steering wheel.

Hannah swallowed and stared out the window. It was none of her business.

"I'm sorry." Her voice shook infuriatingly. "I just find it incomprehensible not to want a child if you're lucky enough to have one."

Jack said nothing, and they rode in silence for several miles.

"To be a musician you have to interact with other people. I like working alone." The words came out of the blue, but in a calmer voice. "Which is fortunate."

"Yes." Sure was. He must have guessed what she was thinking by her tone.

"No, no. I meant I don't need other people around."

"But you need people to look at your pictures, and display your work, and to buy your books," Hannah pointed out. How had he ever managed to make himself agreeable enough to sell his photos, and to convince a publisher to sponsor his book? And did he have a child or not? Did, by the reaction.

"Yes."

"Not much point taking pictures if no one gets to see them."

"There's an exhibition of my work on at the NSW Art Gallery next month."

"Gosh!" Maybe he really was famous. "I'll come and see it."

"I'll send you an invitation to the opening if you'd like."

"Thank you." Now she was getting somewhere. Never failed. Men just love it when a girl shows an interest in their profession. Even if it's one she has a profound and twisted distaste for brought about by a profoundly twisted exponent in years gone by.

"As long as you promise to behave."

"What do you think I'd do? Embarrass you?" Was he joking? "I am capable of mixing in polite society, you know."

"I saw."

"I'm not an idiot, Jack!"

"No."

Hannah folded her arms across her chest. "Did you treat your girlfriend like that? No wonder she dumped you." Whoops! She sucked air in with a grimace.

He took a deep breath. She held hers waiting for the explosion. It didn't come in the form she expected. "Penny could look after herself." The tone was mild.

"So can I!"

"I see. Explains why I'm driving from Bathurst to Orange for the second time today."

"You didn't have to."

"What would you have done?"

"Rung a courier service or a taxi."

"Expensive."

"Okay Jack. You win. I'm an idiot, and I can't get along without a nursemaid."

"I didn't say that."

"You would have. It's what you think."

"You're impossible!"

"I've already said thank you for doing this. What more do you want? You're already getting the macho warm inner glow from helping a poor little woman."

"I did it for Bernard, not you. I told you before."

They sat in silence for the rest of the trip. Hannah crunched on mints, and didn't offer him one, knowing she was being petty. As soon as they reached the motel she went into her room and slammed the door. He thumped on it. "You've got ten minutes."

"I'll need eight," yelled Hannah.

"Sure," Jack said under his breath and went to his own room where he sat on the bed and called Bernard to check the address. Then he checked his message bank. Penny had texted a 'can we talk?'

There was a peremptory knock at the door, and Hannah's voice called, "Seven and a half minutes, Jack."

The message glared at him. Smothering, claustrophobic—the familiar feeling washed over him, the itch to take a one-way ticket out. He didn't want to talk. Everything had been said. It was over.

"Jack!" yelled Hannah. "Hurry up!"

He flung the door open and glared at her, but the glare turned to amazement as he took in a short blue skirt and tight fitting white top over tempting, full, rounded breasts. Incredibly sexy. And those legs...he hadn't noticed before. Stunning. A leap of desire...

He switched the mobile off.

"Ready?" She'd modified her tone to something resembling polite. He turned to pick up his wallet and keys with a grunt of agreement.

Hannah swallowed. Jack must have been on the phone. Bit aggressive maybe, her greeting just now—and what she'd blurted out in the car had been downright rude. More control off stage, Cecily had suggested. Adrian was always telling her to think first and talk after, until he gave up and left with someone else. But he was fussy and pedantic, on the odd occasions when he was at home.

Jack closed the door. They walked to the car.

She cleared her throat. "I'm sorry, Jack." She buckled her seatbelt. "I shouldn't have said anything about your girlfriend. None of my business. I know what it's like to break up with someone." She paused. "Being dumped. And I'm sorry what I said before. About what Marilyn said. It's not my business either."

Jack started the engine and backed into the parking area. He manoeuvred round and drove out on to the street.

"Here. Tell me where we go." A piece of paper with an address and street names on it was shoved into her hand. She peered at it, unseeing. Her magnanimous apology had gone right over his head. Still mad at her, darn it.

"Hannah? Don't I turn here?"

She looked at the first name on the paper. "Left

75

at Oliver Street."

"Concentrate, will you?" The car swung around the corner with Jack muttering, "See if you can get something right, at least."

Hannah concentrated and got them to the house with no mistakes. He parked in the gutter behind the mini bus and turned off the engine. She unclicked her seatbelt, but Jack didn't move. She paused with her hand on the door latch. His gaze was boring into her again, making her breath come in uncomfortable shallow little gasps.

"Getting out?" Her throat had closed up. Her skin prickled. There was more in his look than anger. An awareness of...what? Her? Her body? What was going on here? Was the playboy warming up for a seduction? If so he must be desperate, to take her on after what they'd said to each other.

Impossible. He wouldn't.

Jack roused himself and flung the door open.

She stood on the nature strip, wiggling her hips to straighten her skirt, smoothing it down with both hands. She swung her handbag over her shoulder, and he came to stand by her side looking at the redbrick house for a moment. It had a neat garden with two birch trees by the front gate just beginning to show fresh green spring leaves.

"Mmm, I smell sausages cooking. Hope Libby saved one for me." Hannah turned to him with a smile. His face was stern with a slight frown. He continued his study of the house but didn't move.

"Jack? Come on." She moved in front of him and peered up into his face to get his attention. Now what? Had he gone deaf all of a sudden? He was acting very strangely. Quite unlike the man she'd travelled with thus far. In fact since the phone call she'd interrupted he'd been particular odd. "Jack? What's..."

"Don't you ever shut up?" Dark eyes stared down

into her eyes for a moment, just long enough for her to draw a quick, startled breath. Then he put his hand to her cheek, slipped his fingers behind her neck, drew her to him and clamped his lips on hers.

An electric shock raced through Hannah's body. Nerve endings tingled which had lain dormant for months, responses activated which she had forgotten existed, feelings were aroused she didn't know she had. His mouth was delicious, his hand on her skin sent shivers of delight rippling down her spine.

Her hands flapped ineffectively against his arms for support as her knees turned to spaghetti. His other arm clasped her round the waist, holding her body against the flat angular planes of his with solid pressure. Surprisingly comfortable, a still functioning part of her stunned brain managed to register. Surprising...

Then the rest of her brain fired into action.

This was Jack the rotter! She'd only just met him, and they'd done nothing but argue. What was his game? Seduction, after all? She'd been forewarned, thought she was forearmed, but he'd slipped through her guard as easily as could be. He must be gloating...

She pulled away, hot and confused. Embarrassed. His hand slid from her neck, and his fingers left a burning trail on her skin. So easily, he did it so easily. He laughed a soft little laugh, holding her eyes with his, then turned and walked towards the house. Stopped, looked back.

"Hannah? Come on." Mimicking her.

Chapter Five

A surge of indignant rage carried Hannah forward. She caught up to him, pushed roughly past, and ran up the front steps to the verandah. The door opened before she could put a shaky finger on the little white bell button. A small, dark-haired woman in jeans and hot pink blouse greeted them, all smiles and fussing and words.

"Hello, do come in. I've been keeping an eye out for you. I'm Louise Swift. Are you ravenous, poor things? We've kept you some food, in fact there's plenty, we've only just finished eating ourselves." Did she really mean it the way it sounded? "You made very good time." She grasped Hannah by the arm. "You must be Hannah. Are you exhausted? And you have to play tonight. You must sit down and rest, and let us wait on you. You too, Jack. I mustn't forget you, I'm sorry. Please come through to the garden. Everyone's making themselves quite at home."

Hannah, still dazed and fuming, bewildered by this onslaught of words and hospitality, allowed herself to be led through the house to the terrace and garden, where a large group of people were doing as Louise had said, making themselves at home.

"At last. We thought you'd miss out on lunch entirely, Jack," cried Marilyn from her position between Bernard and another man on a swinging garden seat.

Not wanting to be embroiled in what was shaping up to be another swipe at her stupidity,

Hannah sidled away from Jack. Her stupidity which was monumental and increasing exponentially. Clearly he'd expected her to accept his advance, and she had. She should have known he'd try it on at some stage. He couldn't help himself. She did know, but she'd underestimated his womanising streak. And how well he kissed.

She strode across to join Simon sitting at the long table surrounded by bowls of salad, bread rolls and sauces. A study in the joy of concentrated eating.

Louise instructed her husband Derek, a tall man brandishing tongs and clad in a Don't Blame Me I'm Only the Cook plastic apron, to put some more meat on the barbecue, then rushed over to offer Hannah a drink.

"I am so sorry to be such a nuisance, Louise, arriving late and everything. I feel like a complete idiot." Hannah's lips tingled. Her mouth wasn't working properly. Jack had kissed her! Of all the brazen, arrogant, conceited...

"She makes up for it when she plays," put in Simon, and Louise trilled, "Oh, I'm so excited about the concert tonight. Hannah, don't you worry about a thing!"

"Thank you. It's very kind of you to have us all here." Jack had kissed her out of the blue. Or had he planned it? Did that explain the odd look? Was his appraisal of the situation 'Give it a shot and see what happens'?

She gazed around the large, beautifully maintained yard. Spring daffodils and jonquils glowed golden against the greenery, and some sort of flowering groundcover ran riot under more birches just starting to show a touch of new leaf. Groups of people sat in canvas garden chairs chatting and laughing on the expanse of well tended lawn.

Louise bustled off to take care of Jack, who had

been trapped by Marilyn. Hannah sighed and leant back in her chair, running her finger up and down the condensation on her glass. And what a dangerous and addictive kiss! Dangerous because apart from all the other obvious pitfalls of a thing with Jack, no way would she become entangled with another man who put his work before his woman.

Derek placed a platter of sizzling cooked steak and sausages on the table before her.

"Thank you very much." Hannah returned his smile. Under his anxious eye she speared a fat sausage, then spooned salad onto her plate. Though how she was going to eat any of it now was beyond her.

Derek, sandy-haired and thin, sat down opposite Simon. He poured himself a glass of beer, and began to tell them in great and tedious detail of the Hamlet staged by their local drama group. Hannah listened with half an ear, and left it to Simon to make the right noises. Louise appeared, clutching Jack by the arm.

"Now you sit here next to Derek and make sure you help yourself to whatever you want. If there's something missing just ask. You've got a beer? Good. Darling, don't bore them with Hamlet, I'm sure they're not interested."

Simon made an indeterminate sound which Derek took as encouragement because he launched into a description of the tantrums thrown by their Ophelia. Jack, his face impassive, sat opposite Hannah, and began piling his plate with potato salad and lettuce. He chose a big steak from the barbecue platter. Not a care in the world. Unless he choked on a piece of cucumber. One could always hope.

"This looks good," he said. "Not hungry, Hannah?"

"Not specially." She hacked into a piece of

sausage as if it were his neck. "Something put me off my food."

"Too many mints in the car, perhaps?" Jack took a big bite of his steak and chewed while studying Hannah with a thoughtful expression. She picked at her mangled sausage. He cleaned his plate with relish, placed his knife and fork neatly together and stood up.

"Excuse me. I left my camera in the car."

Hannah watched him go, sending laser beams of frustrated indignation through his retreating back, but Marilyn's shrill giggle piercing the air claimed her attention, made her glance over her shoulder. The witch stood quite close to the table with her back to Hannah, one hand placed confidentially on some poor man's arm as she waved the other about with extravagant gestures. The voice continued.

"But of course it's such a wonderful opportunity for everyone involved. And we're so fortunate Jack was able to take time out of his tight schedule to come with us. He's in great demand you know, but he's very generous. He just drove one of our musicians all the way back to Bathurst because she forgot something."

The man made a comment Hannah couldn't hear, but Marilyn's next remark came in loud and clear despite the fact she lowered her voice a notch.

"Yes, she is careless but she did this on purpose. Women throw themselves at Jack all the time, and he's too nice to tell them to leave him alone. Mind you, Hannah is talented or Bernard wouldn't have employed her, but such a flaky girl. She'd be number four hundred and forty-seven on Jack's list, I can tell you." A silly giggle accompanied the flow of slander. "I shouldn't say such things. Must be the wine."

Fuelled by sudden and intense rage, Hannah pushed her chair away from the table and, if the back legs hadn't sunk into the lush grass of the lawn, nothing would have prevented her from charging over to thump Marilyn on the powdered nose. As it was the chair fell over, and she knocked her cutlery and empty plate to the ground, plus as a bonus, a basket of bread rolls which scattered in all directions.

By the time she'd grovelled about picking things up, and Derek had righted the chair and helped her to her feet, she was too red, flustered and embarrassed to do more than thank him and sit down to compose herself. Simon eyed her with suspicion.

She didn't dare look at Marilyn, but righteous disgusted resignation billowed out in smothering waves accompanied by little outraged snorts. To make matters take the ultimate nose dive to the absolute bottom of the deepest pit, Jack stood with his camera and a smirk on the terrace, staring straight at her.

****

"What nice people," said Libby in the bus on the way to the motel later. "Anyone get groped?"

"If anyone was going to be groped it'd be you, you lucky thing," said Simon. "I can tell you all about the Dramatic Society's presentation of Hamlet, if you like."

"We don't like," Bernard and Libby chorused.

Marilyn squawked like an indignant hen, "I don't know why you're being so mean. They were lovely people."

"Exactly what I said," retorted Libby.

Hannah gazed out the window. Why had he kissed her? To put her at a disadvantage? He knew she'd be furious? All that and more. Because he was attracted to her? His eyes had slid across to her legs more than once when they'd been driving to lunch.

No. Jack the philanderer was just trying another conquest. Keeping his hand in, so to speak.

He'd discount Libby as too young or accurately read her lack of interest, so Hannah was the sole remaining option. Her feelings wouldn't be a consideration.

To sum up—the girlfriend ditches him, no doubt with very good reason, he sees the potential for a nice little dalliance, then when they return in ten days' time, he goes back to the old one, no strings attached. Was Hannah going to play along? No way, Jose—but it'd be much easier if he wasn't so attractive. And didn't deliver very more-ish kisses.

****

Simon and Hannah sprinted to a nearby café in the rain for breakfast next morning. The place was empty, and a sleepy-looking woman shuffled out from the kitchen to take their order. They faced each other over toast, jam and a pot of tea.

"What's up, Hannah?" Simon selected a little sachet of jam. "All that fuss yesterday—when you got back with Jack you barely spoke to each other." He tore the lid off and picked up his knife.

Hannah studied Simon's plump face as he spread apricot jam. Such a sweet man, with genuine concern for her. She couldn't fool him for long, and he deserved an explanation. Not the real one, whatever it was, but...

"Marilyn upset me. She's so rude and..." Simon's eye caught hers..."she's Jack's aunt."

Simon nodded. "She likes me." He bit into his toast.

"Lucky you. She hates me. It's all because of the dreaded carpet affair." Hannah sipped her tea with the dismal image in her mind. "Do you think she'll let me sit up front?"

"I doubt it. According to her you're faking or at least exaggerating to gain attention. Jack's attention." Simon laughed as Hannah sat momentarily rendered speechless. Did the woman think she was as shallow and conniving as she herself?

"Me!? The absolute...words fail me!"

"Ignore her."

"I would never even think of doing something like that!" Jack had asked her the same thing about leaving her suit bag behind. Maybe Marilyn was right and women did do those things around Jack. Amazing! What must he think of her?

If he assumed she had acted on purpose then the kiss made more sense. He thought she'd fall into his arms in grateful, overwhelmed, swooning delight. She'd dope herself to the eyeballs with motion sickness pills before she asked to ride in his car. Maybe she really would be going a few rounds of wrestling with Marilyn for the front seat each morning.

When Hannah carried her things out to the bus later, Marilyn was so firmly ensconced in the front seat dynamite wouldn't shift her. Hannah plonked down behind the driver's seat and slid the window open a fraction. Marilyn gave no acknowledgment of her presence at all, instead pretending great interest in the dashboard.

Jack came out of his room and exchanged a few words with Bernard in the shelter of the covered walkway. He glanced at Hannah through the window. Their eyes met for an instant before she looked away and rearranged her jacket on the seat next to her. He made her act like a teenager. She glared defiantly back out the window, but Jack had already gone to his car, and she found herself terrorising a startled elderly man as he carried suitcases to his immaculate four-wheel drive.

Bernard took his place behind the wheel.

"Will you be all right, Hannah?" he called, but before she could answer Marilyn snapped, "Of course she will. Don't pander to her."

"Hannah?"

"I'll keep the window open. Thanks, Bernard." Marilyn would not provoke her, and she would not beg to sit in the front seat.

Rain poured down in a thick, drenching curtain. Orange had turned to grey. How would she cope once they got going? If she opened her window more than a crack rain poured in, and the bus was already stuffy. Out on the highway the bus picked up speed. Hannah's stomach, not at all happy with the situation began to complain. Sliding the window open a few more inches resulted in a face full of water, which took her mind off intestinal things for five minutes.

Twenty minutes later she announced, "I'm sorry everyone but I think if we don't stop I'll throw up."

"Better heave to and throw out the anchors, Bernard," boomed Simon, then lowered his voice to a conspiratorial whisper. "Don't worry, Hannah." He winked and leaned over to squeeze her arm. "We know you're not faking it."

Hannah stood up and edged on weak legs to the door as Bernard drew off into a rest stop. She paused on the step and buttoned her light cotton jacket, pulling the collar up around her throat.

"You'll be soaked." Libby stood up and held out her anorak. "Take this."

Marilyn said nothing, eloquently.

Hannah pulled on Libby's anorak and stepped down from the bus into a puddle. She stumbled through rough grass to the relative shelter of a massive old gum tree, and leaned against the gnarled trunk taking deep breaths of fresh, wet, eucalyptus-laden air as she fought to keep the rising nausea at bay. She pressed a clammy hand to her forehead, wiped rain water from her face. Her sneakers were soaked through already. A chill trickle of water ran down her neck and another down one sleeve.

Jack's dark blue sedan splashed into the rest area. Hannah straightened, pushing away from the wet bark of the tree. Bernard must have called him. Now what? Jack taking photos of her being sick? Jack and Marilyn discussing together what a hopeless case she was? A nuisance, holding them up again with her plots to ensnare poor defenceless Jack.

Bernard waved to her through the bleary windscreen and pointed repeatedly at the car. He was mouthing something with exaggerated facial gestures. Hannah took a tentative step away from the tree, but by the time she'd reorganised Libby's coat over her head the bus had started up. A little anguished cry escaped as the tail lights disappeared into the greyness.

What now? She couldn't see Jack in the car about thirty metres away, and he hadn't made a move as far as she could tell. Not that she could see much through the sudden deluge of heavier, slanting rain lashing down between them.

The engine roared into life, and the car rolled forward slowly. Surely he wouldn't leave her here, no matter how furious he was? The car stopped. The window moved down a few inches, and she glimpsed Jack's face through the downpour.

"Are you getting in or what?" he shouted.

She drew the raincoat tighter around her and sprinted across to the passenger side, slipping and sliding and leaping puddles as she ran. She tossed the anorak onto the floor at the back and slammed the door. He turned off the engine with a resigned sigh.

They sat in silence for a few moments until he said, "Are you feeling better?"

What a question. Her feet were soaked, her one pair of sneakers ruined and muddy, the bottoms of her jeans clung like wet newspaper to her legs, her hair was plastered to her head, she was dripping all over Jack's car. Hannah wiped her face ineffectually with her hand. Bernard had driven off with her handbag in the bus. She didn't even have a comb or a tissue.

She looked at him. "Better than what? I'm not sick any more if that's what you mean."

"You look terrible." He pushed a small towel into her hand.

"Thanks a lot." She dried her face and rubbed at her hair. When it dried it would stick out everywhere, but if he thought she looked terrible now, what did it matter? "I'm making the seat wet, I'm sorry. I know how it bothers you."

"Can't be helped."

The rain poured down, drumming on the roof, filling the silence inside the car.

Hannah fumbled with the towel on her lap. It had his initials on it. What sort of man has an initialled hand towel? One with Marilyn for an aunt. She'd seen the same design in Marilyn's bathroom. Maybe she embroidered them herself as Christmas presents. Lovingly, by hand, for her dear boy Jack.

"Should we go?" Her voice came out in a sort of croak. She cleared her throat.

"Do you feel well enough?"

She nodded. He turned the key in the ignition.

"I'm sorry about this." Now her voice worked better.

Jack shrugged. "You can't help it." Peering to the right through the sheeting rain he eased the Volvo onto the highway.

"Marilyn thinks I can."

"Marilyn thinks a lot of things."

Maybe he wasn't so cross after all. "I meant to pack travel sickness tablets but..."

"You didn't," Jack filled in.

"I got distracted by Freddo and you turned up early."

"I wasn't early. Don't blame me for your inefficiency."

"If you hadn't been sitting there yelling at me to hurry up I would've packed the tablets and a raincoat and an umbrella as well. Maybe even gumboots!" she finished extravagantly.

"Hah!"

"If I'd remembered to buy them I would've packed them. If you and Freddo hadn't flustered me."

"What?" Jack burst out laughing. He never had a problem laughing at her.

"I'll get some tomorrow. Don't worry, I won't annoy you anymore." Those lines around his mouth when he laughed were making her insides turn to jelly.

"Good. The extra petrol is costing me a fortune."

"I'll reimburse you." Expenses hadn't occurred to her at all. No wonder he was cross with her on top of everything else.

"Bernard is reimbursing me. He wants you to ride with me."

"I don't need to ride with you, thank you." She knew what his game was and she refused to be another of his statistics, and prove Marilyn right into the bargain. "If Marilyn let me sit in the front seat I'd be all right in the bus."

"She won't."

"No," Hannah agreed. "But you want to be by yourself, you've made it very clear."

Jack's voice rose in annoyance. "I've offered you a ride. Do you want it or not? Why do you have to be so difficult?"

"Bernard offered me the ride," she corrected. "I'm not difficult and no, I don't want to ride with you." Now she'd done it. Idiot! How had that happened?

"Suit yourself."

If it was physically possible to kick herself, she would. Hannah peered through the windscreen at the rain. The wipers struggled to keep up with the onslaught. Pale watery headlights from oncoming cars appeared and disappeared at infrequent intervals. Sane people stayed home in this weather. Occasionally a large truck swished by showering them with muddy, greasy water, temporarily blinding them, and making the car shudder in the slipstream.

"It's getting heavier."

"The forecast said it's supposed to keep raining all week, and there are flood warnings in some areas." Jack flexed his hands on the wheel.

"I'm not surprised. I haven't seen rain like it for years. But we might drive out of it, mightn't we?"

"I don't think so. The forecast said the whole of NSW and Southern Queensland were affected. It's been raining for days further west."

"We're supposed to be playing out of doors at a few places."

"They'll put you in the woolshed with the sheep."

Hannah giggled. "Marilyn can go in the cow shed with..." Then she remembered. "Whoops, sorry."

He pursed his lips but said nothing. She leaned down and pulled her shoes off. Her socks were sodden and stuck to her feet. So much for keeping her sneakers dry.

"You'd better take those socks off. I'll put the heater on." The voice of the long-suffering parent.

Hannah rubbed her feet vigorously with the towel until they tingled. She stretched out her legs and wriggled her cold toes.

"My jeans are wet too."

"You can take them off if you like." He glanced at her.

"Only from the knees down." Her damp jacket proved awkward to remove but she succeeded after a brief struggle, and tossed it over the back of the seat on top of his camera bags.

"Is your jacket very wet?"

"The sleeves are. The anorak's on the floor." Fuss, fuss, fuss.

"My stuff is valuable. It mustn't get wet."

"It's not wet." She enunciated the words with excessive clarity. "You remind me of my ex. Pedantic and fussy."

"I'm not pedantic. I want to protect my gear, that's all. Being organised and careful is different from being fussy and pedantic. Would you leave your violin in the rain?"

"Of course not! What a stupid question."

Jack said nothing.

"I'm afraid I'm not a very organised person," she admitted after a minute or two.

"Really?"

Chapter Six

"Warm now?" asked Jack a short time later. "Can I turn the heater down?"

"Yes, thanks." Now. How to take back her dense and rash statement about not wanting to ride with him. He'd actually offered! Think first, talk after. Why was it so difficult?

"Tell me about you, Jack."

He sent her a very suspicious look, but she returned her friendliest smile.

"Not much to tell. Grew up in Sydney. Started taking photos. Decided it was my lot in life. That's it. I travel a lot. All the time in fact. I haven't been in Australia much in the last few years."

"Must be hard for girlfriends." Neat gloss over the child, Mr. Rotherford.

The suspicious glance again. "Women don't like it when I travel. It has its advantages though."

"Easy to ditch them?"

"Yes. I don't like to be tied down to one place and not many women want to follow a man about. Give up their own career for him."

"Compromises can work, you know, Jack."

"I won't compromise my work. I can't afford to and I don't want to. Never have, never will. I have to travel and I like it."

"Well, you can't expect to have a satisfactory relationship then, can you?" So. There was the answer cut and dried. The mother of his child wouldn't have stood a chance.

"I know. I agree, remember?"

"Maybe you haven't met the right woman yet. I

91

think if you did you would do anything to keep her."

"The right woman? There's no such thing. Romantic claptrap. Any woman who would traipse around the world after me would be such a spineless type I wouldn't be interested. She'd get in the way."

"What if she had a mobile career? If she was a photographer, too?" A girl scout would be ideal. Always prepared, able to cook over a campfire she'd lit using one match, or no matches at all, with one collapsible saucepan, catch fish with hairpins and string, tie knots, use the sun as a compass, paddle a canoe down a waterfall. She'd have to be a big, strapping girl able to carry his equipment for him, and hike up and down mountains. And she'd have to not want children.

"That would be different. Perfect. Unless she was better at it than me."

"I hope you're joking. So you'll end up a lonely old man? With a camera. In a tent."

"Probably."

"How sad. I don't want to end up the same as you. I won't end up a lonely old woman with a violin. Somewhere out there is my perfect other half. I just have to find him or he has to find me. Whichever way it works."

Jack grinned a most supercilious grin. "How will you know?"

"We'll know," she said with a confidence she didn't feel. How did you know? She'd fallen for Adrian, and he'd turned out to be totally wrong, with different goals and different priorities not only from hers but from what she thought were his initially, as well.

Her mother had always told her to find another artist because only he would understand her. "But Dad's not an artist," Hannah had protested. "He's in the Navy."

"Your father is an exceptional man," said her

mother. "We were destined for each other." Maybe that's where she'd got the idea, from Tildy.

"Pity if he doesn't realise." Jack laughed. "Hope he's more prepared to cope with you than I was or he'll get a nasty shock. He's in for a nasty shock, anyway."

"He will be." No way was she letting him in on any secret doubts. "That's why he's my other half and you're not."

"What utter rubbish!"

****

They reached Dubbo late in the afternoon. Rain fell in a relentless torrent and gutters, choked to overflowing, turned streets into swirling lakes of muddy water. Jack kept to the centre of the road as much as he could and said, as they sat at a traffic light watching a red plastic garbage bin sail serenely by in the flood, "I never thought I'd be so glad to see the main street of Dubbo, even if it is a river."

The light turned green, and they edged their way across the intersection towards the bright red glowing sign advertising the motel, just visible in the murky light a block further on. The thunder on the roof of the car ceased abruptly as Jack pulled in under the covered entrance way. A small sign reading Office was stuck to a screen door.

"I wonder where the others are?" Hannah peered about the parking area with its forlorn array of dripping cars. "They must have got here before us. This is the right place, isn't it?"

"If you'd been in charge of directions I'd be doubtful, but yes, it is. We would've passed them if they'd had an accident or broken down. I'll check."

While he was in the office Hannah gathered up her wet socks and stuffed them into the sneakers.

"You're in eight and I'm in eleven." Jack slammed the door.

"The others are here. Bernard must have taken

the bus somewhere."

Libby let Hannah in, exclaiming over the weather.

"Bernard's out checking whether we can go on after tomorrow." She took in Hannah's bare feet, damp jeans and armful of anorak and wet footwear. "What have you been doing? Paddling?"

"You mean he might cancel the tour?" Hannah dumped the things on the floor. "My feet got wet. Thanks for the anorak, otherwise I'd have been really drenched." She handed it to Libby, and began peeling off her wet jeans.

"Might not have any choice if this rain keeps up. " Libby took the dripping anorak into the bathroom. Hannah opened her suitcase. A hot, steaming shower and dry clothes. Luxury. What did Jack do in a tent in weather like this? Too horrible to contemplate.

Later, Libby and Hannah sat cross-legged on their respective beds, drinking tea. "What about dinner?" Hannah asked. Thunderous knocking sent her to the door before Libby could open her mouth to reply.

"We come bearing gifts." Simon, brandishing a packet of chocolate biscuits. Jack stood beside him, hands thrust into his jacket pockets. Simon walked in. "Afternoon tea time. I see you started without us."

"But we'll start again," said Libby. "Where did you get those? Tim Tams, my favourites."

"He's got a stash of them in his bag," said Jack. "Eats them in bed." Midnight snacks as well as dirty jokes in the dorm.

Simon and Libby fussed with the tea things while Jack sat down on the bed next to Hannah. He was overwhelming here in the confines of the room. More so than in the car for some reason. The kiss loomed between them.

"Dry now?" A soft, gentle query.

Hannah couldn't take her eyes off his lips. She nodded. Dumbstruck. His hand reached out, a fingertip touched her hair. He smiled. Hannah held her breath. What was going on? Surely he wouldn't kiss her here in front of the others? Teasing her by being nice to her. Confusing her by being friendly. She frowned and edged away. If he kept looking at her with such tenderness she might throw herself on him and be disgraceful.

"Tell Jack and Libby your umbrella story." Simon plonked himself down on Libby's bed, munching his biscuit.

"Simon!" Hannah snapped back to attention. "I wish I'd never told you!"

"Go on. It's such a good wet weather tale," he urged. "We're all your friends here."

Jack raised his eyebrows. "Would this be another Hannah misadventure?"

"No!" She screwed up her nose, considering. "Well, yes. But it could've happened to anyone."

"Tell us," ordered Libby.

Hannah glanced at Simon. He grinned and nodded. Might as well, wouldn't get any peace otherwise. "It was raining and I had my umbrella with me..."

"So you do own one?" interrupted Jack.

She ignored him. "And I was coming up out of the subway at Town Hall. It was crowded on the steps, but I put my umbrella up as we came into the rain and I...got one of the spikes stuck in a man's hair in front of me. It came off. The hair, I mean. I got such a fright! A hairy, brown thing dangling down." She stopped, laughing, as Libby and Jack collapsed, and Simon gave a hoot of delight. "It was very embarrassing."

"I bet!" said Jack.

"What did you do?" gasped Libby when she could

speak.

"I couldn't do anything. He snatched it and ran away. Stuffed it into his pocket. I remember thinking it looked just like a little animal peeping out." Hannah met Jack's laughing eyes, and a flash of lightning crackled between them. With a stifled gasp she jumped up to put her empty cup on the tray.

****

The next day the rain had eased by the time they finished the performances for several hundred high schoolers. It held off overnight as they performed for a more appreciative audience in the civic theatre, and the sun played hide and seek with billowing clouds as they assembled in the motel parking lot the following day, preparing for departure.

Hannah struggled out of the room with her suitcase. Had Jack meant his invitation to travel with him? More importantly did he remember her refusal? She was prepared to grovel rather than spend a whole day in the bus.

Jack wandered about with a camera, snapping off shots as they loaded the bus.

"I hope you're not going to hold us up again, Hannah, with your nonsense about feeling sick." The tone of voice belied the sickly smile plastered across Marilyn's hot pink lips. "We've a long way to go today."

Hannah gritted her teeth and let go the case near Marilyn's foot, causing her to step back hastily and cannon into Bernard, who was just stepping down from the bus. The woman was a hot pink vision today from fingertips to designer tracksuit to lipstick. Like a giant boiled lolly.

"I'll get my suit bag." Hannah turned and rushed back to the room. "If the bus doesn't make me sick Marilyn will," she muttered to Libby.

Libby looked out through the open door. "Aren't you going with Jack? He's putting your bag in his car. Either that or he's stealing it."

Hannah grabbed her suit bag, music case and violin, slung her handbag over her shoulder, and joined Jack at the blue Volvo.

"That everything?" He took stock of her laden figure with an amused grimace.

"Yes. I thought I said..."

He cut her off. "You did. Have you got everything?" His gaze met hers square on. Hannah thought before she spoke.

"Yes."

"Sure?"

"Positive."

"That's what you said last time. Go and check."

She frowned and bit back a hasty retort. Jack treated her like a child. He took her violin and suit bag and music and stowed them in the boot, laying her clothing bag flat across the top. She went to the room. Libby came out of the bathroom with a toothbrush.

"This yours?"

Hannah grimaced. Guilty. Too late to pack it—into her pocket. "Thanks."

She walked over to Jack's car and got in, pondering the conversation she'd had with Libby last night as they got ready for bed.

"Jack likes you," Libby had said.

"I don't much like him," returned Hannah, hoping to nip the conversation in the bud.

"I mean really likes you as in fancies you." Libby hopped into bed and pulled up the covers.

"I don't think so! He's known me for two days, and we've done nothing but argue and annoy each other."

"Haven't you heard of love at first sight?" Libby's grin had a cheeky edge.

"Libby! Jack's the type who falls in love, or probably lust, at the drop of a hat. He's a graduate with Honours of the Love-em and Leave-em School."

"Oh well." Libby thought for a moment. "Doesn't mean he can't fancy you."

"Jack's first sight of me was brandishing a tin of cat food at him. Hardly the stuff to unleash unbridled passion."

Hannah switched out the light. Libby said, "Jack asked me to pose for him but I said I was too busy. Got my final recital coming up. Pity, because he's the most interesting man I've met for a long time. It's so nice he doesn't hit on me, probably 'cos he's seen so many models. Way too old for me, though. Just right for you, Hannah."

"Thanks a lot. Just wheel me off with the geriatrics, and we can compare dentures and give each other our adrenalin shots."

Libby giggled. "You know what I mean. But do you fancy him?"

"I'm not in the market."

"Neither am I. Nothing like a man to get in the way of what you want to do."

The words revolved in Hannah's head as she watched Jack and Bernard peering at a map and discussing the route. Jack said, "We'll meet you at this turnoff."

He walked to the car, got in, slammed the door, and turned to Hannah. "Ready?"

"Yep. Can we stop at a shop first?"

"What for?"

"Food. Marilyn said it would be a long drive."

"I suppose so. If we must." A snort of laughter made her frown.

"What?" Surely Libby would have told her if she had toothpaste on her face or something.

"Nothing." But he had a smirk on his face which made her very suspicious.

"Thanks for letting me come with you, Jack."

He looked at her with narrowed eyes. "Beats driving back and forth to pick you up. At least I can keep you under surveillance this way."

"Why do you have the idea I'm incapable of looking after myself?"

"Experience."

"How unfair! You hardly know me."

"True. But on recent form I've got a pretty good idea."

"You're so smug! Haven't you ever made a mistake?" Apart from a gigantic life-producing one.

"Perhaps I've just made one offering you a ride."

"Too late and too bad, buddy!" She sent him a wide, gleeful grin.

His fingers tightened on the steering wheel, but he didn't respond. A couple of blocks later, he slowed to indicate a small supermarket. "Will this do?"

"I'll be five minutes." Hannah bundled out of the car. "Wait here."

"Where am I likely to go?"

Jack watched her run across the parking lot. He shook his head as she disappeared through the self-opening doors. Here he was sitting, waiting for her again. Would he live to regret this?

The woman had a way of insinuating herself into his consciousness he just couldn't ignore. What was it about her? Maybe it was the excitement of keeping up with her mental gymnastics. She wasn't boring, that's for sure. And she was showing a decided resistance to his charms, which in itself was intriguing, and offered rather a challenge on an otherwise unchallenging trip. Very nice legs too, she should wear short skirts more often. Very nice lips, surprising, the effect of that spontaneous kiss. On both of them.

But she wasn't a woman to become involved with beyond mild flirtation. Her agenda was common to many a female closing on thirty. Secure herself a man and breed. Not in his agenda at all. Jack heaved a deep sigh and closed his eyes. Why on earth had Marilyn blurted out the private and very personal information about Carol and Richard? Good grief she had a tongue. Why couldn't she just let it rest the way they had?

He squinted up at the sky. Leaden and grey. More rain on the way. Hurry up Hannah! Maybe he had made a mistake agreeing to offer her a ride, but Bernard had been keen to make good time in the slower bus, and she added hours onto every journey with her messing around.

Hannah spent fifteen minutes plundering in the supermarket. She strode back to the car with two bulging plastic shopping bags.

"This should keep us going." She dumped it all on the back seat, pushing his camera bags aside to make room.

"For a week at least. Careful with those."

"I am being careful. I got a loaf of bread and some sliced meat and cheese so we can make sandwiches. And fruit and chocolate and juice and mineral water. And prewashed lettuce."

"You forgot the kitchen sink." Jack started the car and edged back onto the road.

"You'll thank me later." Hannah unperturbed, continued. "They'd run out of umbrellas strangely enough, or I would've got one."

"I've got one."

"And where was it when I was standing under that tree in the pouring rain, may I ask?"

He shrugged. "No point both of us getting our feet wet. Yours were already soaked."

"Because I stood in a puddle when I got out of the bus."

"Exactly. The umbrella wouldn't have helped at all."

"Pain!"

Jack wore his annoying smirk again. Hannah turned her head away. Slugging the driver of a moving vehicle was not a good idea. Tempting, but unwise.

"You know what happened to me in there?" she asked a few minutes later.

"How could I know?"

"I was looking at the chocolate shelf deciding what to get, and one of the assistants came up behind me and said, "What do you think you're doing?" in a really aggressive voice."

"What were you doing? Taste tests?" Jack laughed.

"No! I turned around and said, 'I'm choosing chocolate' because I didn't know what else to say."

"And?"

"She was really embarrassed because she mistook me for someone else, some friend." Hannah looked across at Jack and laughed, and then looked away because he was just too attractive, and she wanted him to kiss her again. And he was a despicable man with the morals of an oversexed alley cat.

The highway headed west through miles of grazing land. Every creek they came to was swollen and spreading out across its banks in a brown lake. In one place rushing water almost swirled over the road. Jack slowed to a crawl, and they ploughed through, leaving a plume of spray in their wake.

"If it starts raining again that's going to close the road," he commented.

Hannah scanned the sky through the windscreen, lowering grey clouds covered the earlier blue patches. There was no sign of the sun now, and the wind had picked up, tugging at the trees and buffeting the car. She gave an involuntary shiver.

"Cold?"

"No but it looks very threatening, doesn't it? It's going to rain again for sure."

"Would you mind if we stop occasionally for a photo?"

"Of course not. Be interesting."

"It's not exactly riveting viewing."

"Is this for the coffee table book?"

"No." His expression was so forbidding she decided not to say anything else.

Jack pulled the car to the side of the road as they topped a small rise. The land fell away gently, then rose again in a series of undulations stretching into the misty distance.

"Won't be long." He collected one of his cameras from the back of the car. The swirling masses of grey-white clouds did look threatening. Very primal, the rawness of nature and the elements.

He picked his way through the long, wet, straw-coloured grass to the fence. His shoes would be soaked. A huge gum tree towered overhead, and several more grew scattered across the sodden paddocks, their branches waving regally in the increasing wind. A number of miserable, sodden sheep stood huddled together down the slope a distance away. They must be in the 70%-no-thought part of their day. Jack wandered about, lifting his camera to his eye, changing the angle, squatting down, standing, leaning forward. Trying to capture the vast storminess of the sky contrasted with the small dejected mob, Hannah decided. When he returned he wore a satisfied expression.

"I think I got it." He closed the door against the chill rush of air.

"Colour or black and white?"

"Black and white for this sort of thing."

She nodded. "I remember the bird in the oil photo. It was very powerful in black and white. Made me cry over my breakfast."

"Made me cry when I saw it and all the others. Horrible! They ought to ban oil shipping."

Hannah couldn't imagine the horrors he must have witnessed during his career. How shallow and selfish she was. His art was a far cry from Raoul's, not that those porn shots were art. Was she being unfair lumping them together in her mind just because they were photographers? Attractive photographers? Most likely, but Jack wasn't Mr. Pure either.

Twenty minutes later they spotted the little white bus parked at the intersection of the highway and a secondary road. Libby and Marilyn were walking about and waved vigorously when they saw the car. Marilyn's pink extravaganza provided the one bright jarring spot in the uniform soft brown, grey and blue-green of the landscape.

"What happened to you?" she demanded when Jack wound down his window. "Was Hannah sick again?"

Hannah gritted her teeth. Jack said, "No, I wanted to stop for some photos."

"Oh, marvellous. You must make sure Hannah doesn't interfere with your work, though."

"It's starting to rain again," said Libby in a strangled voice. Hannah didn't dare catch her eye. "See you when we get there." She turned and ran back to the bus.

Marilyn waved and hurried after her.

"I'll have a word with Bernard." Jack rummaged around in the back seat. "Where did you put the umbrella?"

"I didn't touch it. It's your mess back there, not mine."

He yanked the umbrella out and opened it. "Your food was on it." The rain started again with a vengeance as Jack dodged puddles on his return. The bus started up and pulled out onto the road.

"He gave me the directions in case we get separated again. I told him not to worry about us because we'll be stopping a bit, but I think we should stay with them as much as possible."

They travelled slowly now. The narrow road was half flooded in places, and visibility decreased almost to nothing as the rain bore down.

Hannah peered through the windscreen with an anxious frown. Could Jack see the road at all? "How far along here do we go?"

"About seventy kilometres."

"That'll take hours."

"Yes."

"Hungry? I am."

He glanced at her. "Do you want to stop? I don't want to lose sight of the bus if we can help it."

Two red pinpoints of light and a blur of white shone through the gloom up ahead.

"No. I can make a sandwich as we go. Do you want one? Or a banana?"

"A banana, thanks. We can stop later."

Hannah hummed under her breath as she handed Jack his banana. She built herself a lettuce and cold beef sandwich and munched, staring out at the drenching rain. They came to a small bridge with a roaring torrent of water under it. Jack slowed to a halt.

He wound down the window and clicked off a few shots.

"I can't see the bus anymore."

"No, but it's okay, we've got the instructions. Here." A crumpled piece of paper emerged from his pocket. She looked at it. Bernard had written the name of the property and then the name of the small town closest to it—Goolabri.

"How far is it to Goolabri?"

"I don't know."

"Have you got a map?"

"Should be one in the glove box." She clicked the button. A first aid kit, a torch and a spare pair of sunglasses. A few coins.

"There isn't."

"Oh. I was sure... We can ask if we get lost."

"Who?"

"Someone at the next town."

"There might not be a next town."

"Ring Bernard if you're so worried."

"I'm not worried. Phones wouldn't work out here anyway." She began to hum "Baubles, Bangles and Beads."

Jack shot her an exasperated look, and she stopped. They drove in silence.

"Hey, that sign said Goolabri." Hannah's head whipped around as a white post went by, dimly visible in the downpour.

"Which sign? I can't see anything through this rain."

"Stop! Back there. Turn around."

"I can't turn here."

Jack slowed the car to halt, peered over his shoulder, then reversed at snail's pace to the signpost Hannah had glimpsed. Sure enough it pointed off to the right. "Goolabri 88 kilometres."

He sucked in air through pursed lips. "I thought Bernard said less. That road looks even worse than this one." His brow creased, considering. "If it turns to gravel we might have to give up. Don't want to get bogged."

"We should try it at least. We can always turn back."

"I don't know. He didn't say we should turn off. Let me see the instructions."

"It says go to Goolabri. See." Hannah pointed at the piece of crumpled paper. "Goolabri. The sign says Goolabri. We don't know where we'll end up if we stay on this road. Not having a map," she added.

105

"Make up your mind, driver, or we'll never catch Bernard."

"All right." But he still sounded doubtful. "Here goes."

The side road had only been sealed for the first hundred metres, and parts of surface had washed away in the recent downpour. Jack edged the Volvo around huge potholes filled with water. The rain was so heavy he had to strain forward to see the road ahead. After twenty exhausting kilometres of muddy corrugated dirt he slowed as they came to another small wooden bridge with brown water lapping almost at road level. Small branches had already jammed against the bridge supports, creating a damming effect.

"What do you think?"

She peered through the grey murk. "Go for it. They must have got across and if we wait we'll get stuck on the wrong side. It's not very wide."

"Makes sense. Hope you can swim."

Hannah held her breath as the car crept over the creaky bridge. Any minute now it would collapse and plunge them into the flood. She let out a relieved whoosh of air as they reached solid ground, and realised she'd been gripping the seat with both hands. Jack sat back and loosened his grip on the steering wheel. He drove on cautiously until a cleared area, used by roadwork teams to coordinate their equipment, appeared on the left. A pile of gravel loomed through the downpour on one side, but the surface wasn't boggy and was clear of deep puddles. Jack pulled in and stopped the engine.

"I need a break." He unclipped his seat belt and stretched his arms over his head.

"Want something to eat?"

"Yes, please."

Hannah twisted around and knelt on the seat to lift both her grocery bags into the front. He pulled out the orange juice and took a swig.

"Good grief, look at the time!" Hannah's gaze landed on the clock. "Three fifteen. Is that right?"

"Must be. It's taken forty-five minutes to do twenty kilometres. No wonder I'm hungry. And tired." He rubbed his eyes.

"It's very dark. Where does all this rain come from? Australia is supposed to be a dry continent."

She handed him a thick sandwich and found another bottle of juice.

"You make a good sandwich, Crawford."

"Glad I can do something right," she said, tilting the bottle too fast so apple juice slopped forward and overflowed down the sides of her mouth as she drank.

"Aah." She laughed, holding the bottle out in front of her as it dripped onto her legs. "Not again."

"And we're not even moving this time. Don't get juice on the seat." He removed the bottle from her grasp with a muttered, "Dopey," screwed the top back on and dropped the offending article into one of the bags. Then he sat and watched as the juice ran down her chin. Hannah fumbled desperately in her pocket for a tissue, knowing he was about to make some remark about her messiness, and wipe her down with his Marilyn-embroidered towel.

Instead he leaned over, grabbed her face in his hands and kissed her with fierce passion.

His mouth tasted of orange juice and lettuce, sweet and delicious, his hands held her captive. She closed her eyes and savoured the exquisite pleasure. She really did enjoy kissing him. Everything else slipped into the background. A kiss couldn't hurt. No...it wasn't anything—she knew what he was up to, could keep this under control... Why not? Her hand stole around his neck of its own accord, and he deepened the kiss. Her body responded with an instantaneous rush of heat. She moved her other arm for more support, and the toothbrush in her pocket jabbed into her groin. She started back with a cry, realising at the same time what she'd been doing—losing control. He let her go abruptly.

"Sorry, my mistake." Breathing hard he stared out the windscreen although it was so misted up there was nothing to see. "Don't know what I'm doing, kissing you," he muttered.

"Meaning?" Her voice rose on a wave of indignation.

"I don't need more female complications. Especially a female like you."

"What makes you think I'll be a complication? Do you think because you kiss me I'll be falling all over you? Do you think you're irresistible? Smart Libby had the sense to turn you down before you could get started. What an ego. Good grief!" Hot tears threatened to undermine her rage. "What's wrong with kissing me, anyway? What's a 'female like me'?" Furious, Hannah flung the door open and leapt out of the car.

"What are you doing?" Jack's startled voice rang in her ears as she scrambled to get away.

Humiliation blinded her to the drenching rain, and she stumbled a few steps as the onslaught hit her before heading for the flimsy shelter of a clump of gums. The car door slammed. Jack was coming towards her, with his umbrella this time. Wouldn't want to get himself wet.

Hannah stood with her arms wrapped around her, back turned to him. What was she doing? Jack made her do crazy things. It was all his fault. He should warn her before he kissed her, then she could prepare herself. What an unbelievably insulting thing to say! He placed a coat over her shaking shoulders and held the umbrella over their heads.

"Come on. Back to the car."

His voice was firm with vast amounts of

suppressed rage. Hannah let herself be led back and shoved into the front seat again. Jack folded the umbrella and put it on the floor behind the front seat as he took his place behind the wheel. He glared at her. "Well? What was that lunacy in aid of? Have you been dropped off on the wrong planet? Hasn't anyone kissed you before?"

"They don't usually say they wished they hadn't." Hannah stared back, matching his chilled anger. "They're not usually so insulting."

"You're a complete maniac. Now what are you going to do? You're soaking wet."

Hannah drew a deep breath. "I'm sorry." She sure was! These were her new Dubbo sneakers.

"You're the one who's wet, not me. Except for my shoes, thanks to you." Jack stared at her as if he'd never come across such a cretin in his life. He reached around to pick up his umbrella again, opened the door and went to the boot, returning in minutes with a towel and a bundle of clothing which he dumped in her lap.

"Take those things off and put these on." Hannah hesitated. "Now!" he barked. "Strip right off! I don't want to be lumbered with you sneezing all over the place."

Hannah pulled off her sodden sweatshirt, wriggled free of her jeans, and towelled herself as well as she could while sitting in the cramped space. What had possessed her? It was colder today. Her T-shirt had wet patches on the shoulders, but she couldn't take it off in front of him. She was already sitting all goosebumpy in her knickers to dry her legs. She dragged the track pants up as fast as possible. No free show for him!

"Take it off, Hannah. You'll get pneumonia. I won't look." He sounded exactly like her generally mild-mannered, imperturbable father when his two giggling, little daughters had stretched his good nature to the limit. Except Jack didn't have a good nature.

She waited while he turned his head, then quickly swapped the wet T-shirt for his dark green, wool sweater. It was big and came almost to her knees. The socks came halfway up her legs. The pants were several sizes too big, too, but all the clothes smelt of Jack. Like being hugged by him.

"Ready."

"We'd better get going." He started the engine, turned the heater up.

"Jack? I'm sorry." Now he would think she was a complete flake, and she didn't want that. She wanted...she didn't know what she wanted in relation to Jack. Why couldn't she say the toothbrush had stuck into her? Too late now, he'd think she was making excuses. Weak ones. Especially after what she'd said last time!

"Stupid fool thing to do!" His own action or hers? Avoiding flooded potholes he navigated back onto the winding, slippery road.

They travelled in uncomfortable silence for an hour, and covered maybe thirty kilometres. Then another flooding river blocked their way. A larger torrent than the first, the water already flowed in wild abandon over the road way. The flood level indicators on the roadside showed the water was almost one metre deep and rising fast. The sides of the submerged wooden bridge stuck up out of the flood, white, isolated and incongruous twenty metres away. As they watched a tree washed down and jammed against the crossbeams.

Jack stopped well back from the muddy brown, swirling water. "Well that's that."

"What can we do?"

"I'll try the phone." He pressed a button. "No signal."

"We'll have to go back."

"The other bridge will be covered by now. We're stuck."

Hannah gulped. "Did you notice any side roads or anything? Any houses? I didn't."

"No, I was too busy keeping us on the road."

She stared at him, wide eyed. He stared back, blank faced, then turned to study the flood. "I'll move us a bit further on to higher ground. The water's rising pretty fast."

He parked the car close to a stand of gums which gave some shelter from the driving rain. "I suppose we could walk across the paddocks in search of a house." He sounded about as keen as she was on the idea.

"We? It's your umbrella," she reminded him.

Ignoring her, he continued, "Except we don't have the slightest idea where to go. We'll have to stay put until either the river drops or someone comes from the other direction."

"What could they do?"

"Nothing I suppose, but at least they'd know we're here."

"Is it worth driving back in case we missed a turn off?"

"I suppose so."

He started the car and reversed until the road widened enough for him to do a very cautious three-point turn. They travelled for several hundred metres back the way they'd come, but there was no sign of any habitation at all. Not even sheep thinking about nothing, just endless undulating paddocks of tussocky grass dotted with gums, grey and dismal in the gloomy afternoon. The road dipped down and turned through a grove of trees. Jack trod on the brakes, causing the car to slide in slow motion sideways and come to rest inches from the trunk of a gigantic tree fallen diagonally across the road. The roots thrust muddy and twisted at least two metres in the air on one side of the road, and on the other the branches spread out over the fence and surrounding area in a tangle of foliage.

Hannah stared in horrified amazement at the newly fallen giant. "It could have landed on us!"

Jack changed gears and the car edged away from the remaining trees, slipping and sliding alarmingly as the tyres fought for grip on the muddy, greasy surface.

"Don't want one of them dropping on us in the night."

"In the night?" squeaked Hannah.

"I can't see us getting out before night, can you?" The handbrake came on with a firm click. He'd be about as keen on spending the night in the car with her as she was with him.

Chapter Seven

The clock on the dashboard read five twenty-three when Hannah focussed her panic-stricken gaze. Darkness wasn't far off in this gloom laden weather.

"Maybe someone will come." But it was a forlorn hope. This was worse than camping, this was a nightmare come true in 3D and technicolour. Correction—black and white.

"How? Both bridges will be impassable."

Hannah pressed her lips together. She didn't know, and the full impact of their predicament dawned on her as she sat watching the rain drops sliding in hypnotic patterns down the windscreen. They were isolated, marooned, cut off, stranded. She and Jack Rotherford stuck in a car together in the pouring rain for who knew how long? Days? Weeks? Sitting cramped in the car, arguing and insulting each other. She put her hands over her face and rubbed her eyes.

"Don't start crying. That's all I need."

"I'm not crying, I'm rubbing my face." She turned towards him to prove it but Jack wasn't looking, his head rested on the seat back, eyes closed. He wouldn't care. He loved this sort of thing. Did it all the time. Went out of his way to have experiences like this in countries no one had ever heard of, then took photos of it.

Hannah watched him for a moment. Frowning. Withdrawn and uncommunicative again. Just as well. It'd prevent him starting another fight. But it could get awfully boring if he wouldn't talk to her at all. For weeks.

Her legs needed stretching but the rain was far too heavy to get out. The best she could do was slide the seat back and straighten herself as much as possible. Then she leaned forward and touched her toes, almost banging her head on the dashboard. Sleeping in the car would be horrible. Uncomfortable in the extreme.

She studied the dozing figure. Even though he'd kissed her twice, and despite his reputation, she doubted he'd force himself on her, rape, harass or attack her. She couldn't see herself having to flee across the sheep paddocks pursued by a maniacal Jack intent on molestation and murder.

Spend the night in the car with him? There were worse people. Marilyn, for instance. Would the bus have got through all the flooding? Where were they? Maybe they were stuck too. What a hoot! Stuck in a similar situation with Marilyn. Poor Simon and Libby. She smiled. There's always someone worse off than yourself, her Dad said.

But if they had got through they'd be in a panic when they realised what had happened. Marilyn would be gibbering with worry over her precious Jack, convinced it was Hannah's fault. Kidnapped him, would be the theory. Simon and Libby would be concerned. Bernard would make phone calls to the police and emergency services and try to calm people down.

Hannah wriggled her bottom on the seat. She'd have to get out soon. She reached around to grab the umbrella from the back seat, but the handle accidentally whacked Jack on the head.

"Ow! What are you doing?" He rubbed his head, scowling.

"Sorry. I need to go to the loo."

"You shouldn't be allowed to have an umbrella. It's a lethal weapon in your hands."

Turning her back on his grumbles she opened the door a crack to stick the umbrella out. Rain dashed in on to her legs. "These pants will fall down if I stand up."

"Take them off before you go," He said it as if it were the most obvious thing in the world." I don't want my track pants dragged in the mud. You might have brought enough clothing for six months but I didn't."

She had no choice. The matter was fast becoming urgent so she swallowed her remaining shreds of pride and pulled the warm pants off together with the socks. Her bare feet went into her sodden, muddy sneakers, and she made an undignified and awkward trip with the big, green jumper serving as the sort of dress which had never been fashionable and never would be. She returned to the car to find Jack fiddling with a camera.

"You didn't take my photo, did you?"

He shook his head. "I'm not a voyeur and you're not what I'd call model material. Give me the umbrella."

Hannah passed it, dripping, across to him, and he got out and disappeared in the direction of the fallen tree. She caught glimpses of him as he poked about in the branches, but lost sight of him, and after pulling the track pants and socks on, leant her head back, eyes closed.

He slid into the driver's seat.

"It's getting dark."

It'd be pitch black soon with the dense, low cloud cover and no lights of any sort.

"Perhaps we can listen to the radio and get a weather forecast," she suggested.

Jack turned on the ignition. She scanned the frequencies for a clear signal. A staticky news report of an overseas crisis, music, the end of a report stating flooding was widespread in North Western

New South Wales.

"Rain continuing overnight and most of tomorrow, easing towards the end of the week," the announcer said.

Jack switched it off. "How much food have we got?"

She investigated her bags. "Bread, cheese, lettuce, chocolate and mineral water. Half the juice. Two apples and a banana."

In the dim light she saw the flash of his teeth. "Thank you."

"What for?" The smile was more surprising than the words.

"You said I'd thank you later. Well it is and I am."

Hannah lifted a smug eyebrow. "You didn't think of food, did you, Mr. Expert Camper?"

"I didn't expect we'd be stuck, and I can manage on very light rations if necessary."

"You might have to if we're trapped for a week." The thought made her voice shake. She clamped her lips tightly together.

His voice was calm, very reminiscent of Bernard, but with a far more patronising edge. "Look on it as an adventure. We're not in any danger. The road's way above flood level here. Thanks to you we've got plenty of food. We're warm and dry."

"Like camping out?"

"Exactly!"

"I hate it."

"I know. You prefer luxury." He grinned, plainly enjoying her discomfort, leaning his back against the side of the car casually so as to face her. "This car is a luxury vehicle, you said so yourself. Elderly, not very spacious but waterproof."

She peered out through the fogged-up window, clearing a space with the sleeve of his sweater. "It's stopped raining or at least it's not as heavy now."

Hannah wiggled in the seat. Her bottom was getting numb from sitting down for so long.

"How are we going to sleep in here, Jack?"

"The seats lie right back."

"It'll get cold, won't it?"

"There's a blanket under all the stuff on the back seat."

"The seats won't go completely flat. I can't sleep sitting up."

"I can. I can sleep anywhere."

"Well, don't snore." Arms folded she glowered at him.

He laughed. Without a doubt he was having the time of his life at her expense. "I'm hungry. How about making a sandwich," he said when he'd stopped laughing.

They ate in silence and shared the drinks. Hannah was careful not to slop juice down her chin again. She gave him chocolate, and divided an apple in half for dessert with scrupulous precision.

The rain stopped by the time they'd finished eating. Jack opened the door and got out. He looked back into the car.

"Coming?"

"Where are you going? You can't see a thing out there."

"There's a torch in the glove box."

Of course there was, she'd just forgotten for the moment. She grabbed it and joined him, clutching the waistband of the enormous pants. The beam danced over the fallen tree. "Maybe if we stand on the trunk we'll see a light somewhere."

They walked closer, stepping carefully through the branches and leaves to where the trunk was low enough to scale. Hannah held the light steady while Jack grasped a branch and hauled himself up on to the wide surface.

"Turn the torch off for a minute," he ordered.

She stood fidgeting while he shuffled round to look in all directions.

"See anything?"

"No. Shine the torch at my feet so I can get down."

She flicked the beam back on. The pants slipped down her legs and she grabbed for them. The light shone straight into Jack's eyes. He lost his balance as the glare seared into his retinas, and flinging up an arm in defence, staggered back to crash down off the trunk on the other side of the tree.

"Jack!" she screamed. "Are you okay?"

No sign of him at all. What if he'd killed himself? He'd fallen into a black hole. Sucked in without a sound. Not even a curse. The trunk was too wide for her to lean over, so she waved the torch in frantic arcs in the general direction of his last appearance, and the beam went slicing through the darkness. The gigantic baggy pants were around her ankles getting wet and hobbling her. Jack's disembodied, angry face suddenly materialised in a shaft of light.

"Hold that damned thing still!"

A monster, mud-streaked and furious rose up and clambered over the tree trunk. Hannah frantically yanked at the track pants and struggled forward to help.

"Leave me alone." He slid down to land at her feet and pushed her arm away.

She stepped back, holding the torch as steady as she could while keeping her clothing under control and her footing solid in the debris-strewn area. She aimed the beam on the ground at his feet. He took a cautious step forward, wincing as the leg took his weight. Hannah held her breath and edged backwards. Mud, leaves, loose tangled branches clutched at her feet in the dark. Her sneaker caught.

He grabbed her arm.

"Careful!" They clung together in torturous silence until their feet trod clear ground and he released his grasp.

Covert observation revealed Jack wasn't limping and no blood poured from his body. Visible blood. Bruises and wounded pride most likely. Dark stains spread from ankle to knee of his jeans, the front of his shirt had a rip plus streaks and clumps of clay-coloured mud. There was even a gum leaf in his hair. Put plainly, he was a mess. She must look even crazier in her outsize clothing. Enough to frighten the horses. Suppressed laughter burst out in a series of little snorts.

"Gee, Jack." Hannah bit her cheek hard. She plucked the leaf from his hair and waved it in his face.

"If you laugh I'll murder you," he growled.

They reached the car. He popped the boot open and disappeared, to return in grey track pants and a black, long-sleeved T-shirt.

His voice was grim, not a flicker of friendliness. "You could get your own clothes now. I only brought one warm sweater. You must have at least some warm clothes, judging by the weight of that thing."

She leapt out of the car. It never occurred to her he gave her his clothes to avoid rummaging in her suitcase. Lucky she'd brought a heavy sweater too. She stripped off behind the car and piled on several layers of T-shirts, the navy wool sweater, her own track pants, and with two pairs of socks and his green sweater in her hand, returned to the front seat. Like a great, waddling blimp.

"Sorry. Here's yours."

Jack pulled it over his head. Scent of Hannah. He breathed long and slow as the wool passed over his face.

"Where's the seat thingy?" She found it before he

119

could answer. Her seat collapsed backwards with a jerk. He adjusted his own seat and spread the blanket out. Though why he would bother sharing his blanket with her... His eyes closed while his tired mind took stock of the aches and bruising in his body.

The fall had shaken him. So unexpected and stupid. He was too old for that kind of caper. Hannah was a complete disaster area. Fancy shining the torch right in his eyes! And he was positive she was busting with laughter as they walked back to the car—like a child. He yawned. The air temperature was dropping fast. But she wasn't a child. For a few moments when he kissed her juice-flavoured mouth, he knew she was responding as a woman, a passionate, exciting woman. But what was her crack about Libby supposed to mean? Did she think he would try it on with a girl her age?

Now she was worried, uncomfortable, scared even, about their current situation. He smiled to himself. Good. Put her at a disadvantage for a change. He'd told her the truth about their not being in danger. This could prove entertaining. Pay her back for the cat, the Persian carpet ride, the countless extra miles he'd driven on her behalf, the wet shoes, laughing at Marilyn's fall although he'd been hard pressed not to laugh himself, laughing at him when he fell just now, and above all, being crazily attractive. Who'd have thought it? What an insane situation.

Hannah drew her legs up to curl into a ball. She pulled on her part of the blanket. He hung onto his half. She tugged harder. He resisted.

She turned on to her other side and then back again. Jack grinned to himself. The seat was reasonably comfortable but bulged in the wrong places. He'd slept in better spots, but he could cope with just about anything now. It was going to be a long, long night for her. She'd pinched most of the blanket with all her fidgeting about. He gave it a vicious tug. She resisted.

****

Hannah slept in short patches through the endless night, waking finally and completely at dawn. She sat up and readjusted the seat. Jack slept beside her uncovered. She'd hogged the whole of the blanket during the night. He'd never know if she draped it over him now. An arm moved, but he didn't wake.

Jack looked vulnerable, asleep. His features still had strength and confidence, but the cynical, world-weary look had gone. Too attractive for her own good even with rumpled hair and stubble on his chin and cheeks, lips full and half parted in sleep. Those lips...she leaned closer. His breathing altered, he shifted, turned his head.

She jerked upright and opened the door to step out into crisp fresh morning air. The dawn chorus had begun. Magpies chortled and warbled as the sun rose, breaking briefly through the clouds with a tantalising glimpse of pink and golden light before disappearing behind banks of billowing grey. She couldn't remember being up at dawn. It had a certain attraction. The air smelled different out here in the country.

Hannah stretched and took deep breaths of eucalyptus-laden air. Her body was stiff and bent into an unnatural and awkward shape by the carseat bed. Joints cracked and creaked as she reached up then curled over to try for her toes. Should go back to Tai Chi classes. She felt like an eighty-year-old arthritis sufferer this morning. Someone had been at the insides of her eyelids with sandpaper, too. Better not look in a mirror.

She went behind a tree for a minute, first checking for prickles or crawling things, and when she re-emerged Jack was standing in the road beside the car stretching his arms over his head. Grimacing as he rubbed his lower back. What a delightful sight.

"Good morning." So. Not as comfortable as you thought, eh?

"Morning. Sleep well?"

"Are you kidding? No!"

"I did." He had the audacity to smirk.

"You had most of the blanket."

"You're wearing enough clothes to keep an army warm. Share the banana for breakfast?"

Hannah eyed him speculatively. He seemed very cheerful this morning. Maybe she looked even worse than she felt. She walked back to the car.

"How are you feeling? Break any bones last night? Perhaps a few bruises?" With any luck.

"Probably. I haven't looked." He took a swig from the mineral water bottle and passed it to her. "It's lucky I didn't break anything or you'd be in trouble."

"What would you do? Sue me?"

"No, don't be ridiculous. I meant you'd have to take care of me out here all by yourself. Go for help across the paddocks after splinting and bandaging and doing First Aid."

Girl Scouts knew about all those things. Definitely the partner for him. "You'd be in trouble because I don't do First Aid." She broke the banana in half and handed him a piece.

"No, you just make it necessary."

"I said I was sorry. My pants were falling down. I got distracted."

"Okay, okay." Jack held up his hands, his mouth full of banana. He swallowed. "I surrender. What do you suggest we do now?"

She stared around. Nothing to see except tussocky brown grass hills, gum trees, clouds and the muddy road snaking away towards the flooded bridge.

"We could see if the bridge is still underwater."

"Walk? It's only about a kilometre. Two at most. I've been sitting in the car too long."

"Me too. Want some bread and cheese? We'd better start rationing soon, though."

"Yes. Don't want to have to eat each other." He took a slice of bread.

They walked along the road. Hannah carried the umbrella, and Jack had one of his collection of cameras slung around his neck. Now and again he stopped to squint through the lens, and despite Hannah's protests, took a shot of her walking away from him up a slight incline, dwarfed by a towering eucalypt on her right, and the emptiness of the paddocks stretching to the horizon where they met the wild, stormy skies.

Hannah topped the rise and gasped in dismay at the floodwaters stretching out in a vast lake before her. The top of the bridge appeared and disappeared now in the swirling torrent, and the road emerged drenched and forlorn on the far side at least eighty metres away.

"Phew! It'll take days to go down." He sounded pleased! Didn't care about her feelings. Too busy enjoying this!

"What are we going to do?" She stared at him, breathing hard, fear rising like the floodwater. Would they really be stuck out here in the wilderness? People died in the outback. Would they have to wander aimlessly about in search of food like the early explorers? Most of them died. Slow and dismal deaths from starvation and thirst. Tragic Burke and Wills. And Leichhardt who disappeared without trace. No one ever knew what happened to him.

"We're not going to die out here, Hannah, calm down."

"I know!" she snapped, and turned away, but not before she caught sight of the huge grin spreading across his face.

"We can climb over the tree and walk in the other direction in case we did miss a turnoff," he called as she marched down the road. "Or go to the top of a hill and have a look. There might be a farmhouse close by. Could be a whole town just over the ridge. Or a holiday resort."

"Don't humour me, Jack!" Her pace increased, her foot slid on the greasy surface.

"I'm not. I'm serious." He gave a spontaneous shout of laughter as she flailed her arms in a wild attempt to stay upright.

Hannah faced him, furious. "What are you laughing at?"

"It's not so funny is it, now? When it's you who nearly falls over?" He didn't even try to hide the huge grin, swinging his camera by the strap as he approached. "Pity I didn't get a shot of that!"

"I only laugh when things are funny. Not when people are frightened. I don't humiliate people and make fun of them. I'm not a sadist!" She whirled about and continued on her manic way.

"Hey!" Jack ran to catch up and grabbed her arm. "I'm sorry. There's no need to be frightened. We'll be fine." He held tight as she struggled to free herself, wrapping both arms around her and hugging her hard against his chest.

Hannah stood stiff as a board within the circle of his embrace, tempted to collapse against him, but unwilling to give him the satisfaction. She lurched backwards, breaking his grip with the sudden surge of energy. He let go of both her and the camera strap.

The fragile instrument hit the rough gravel of the road with a sickening crash and the unmistakable sound of cracking glass. Jack let fly some colourful language as he bent down and picked it up. Two pieces of lens dropped to the ground and landed in a puddle. Her horrified gaze flashed to his face.

He spat his fury at her. "Don't say a word! Not one word."

When they reached the car, he went straight to his bulky equipment bags in furious silence broken only by the occasional *sotto voce* curse. Hannah sat in miserable silence in the front seat with the door open and her feet on the road. How did she manage to do it? Every time. Why didn't she just accept his embrace for the comfort he offered? Why didn't she think?

Jack appeared. "I'm going up that hill. You wait here and don't touch anything."

She nodded meekly. Don't touch anything? As if she weren't to be trusted. She didn't dare object, although she wanted to go up the hill too. She watched him pick his way through the long, wet grass by the roadside and clamber through the fence. Without so much as a glance her way he ploughed on up the hill making a beeline for the highest point. A good half hour's walk by her very inexperienced calculation. More big rain drops began to tumble down.

Lucky Jack had taken the umbrella. Hannah sat in the car and peered up at the hillside searching for the bright blue speck. Was that a glimpse of colour half way up the slope? A heavy shower reduced visibility to the roadside fence. It eased off ten minutes later. She got out and stared across the paddocks. Where was he? Maybe he'd found a farmhouse just over the hill and was sitting in a warm, friendly kitchen having a hot cup of tea. Leaving her here in the rain while he relaxed in comfort.

She stomped to the edge of the road and scanned

the hillside. A few lone gums waved their branches in the wind. His green jumper would blend in like camouflage but the umbrella wouldn't. If he had it open, of course. With great effort she clambered onto a solid old fence post to balance, wobbling, with one foot on the wire and the other on the post. There he was. About a third of the way up and in a slight hollow where the land dipped. Invisible from road level.

Sitting down. Why was he sitting down? His bottom would be all wet. She waved both arms over her head and almost fell off her perch.

"Jack! What are you doing?" Her voice sounded tiny and sailed away in the wind. She tried again. "Jack! "

His tiny arm waved, and she waved back, straining to hear if he was shouting to her. The wind stole his voice too so she hear a faint, lost cry. She climbed down from the fence ripping her jeans in the process. Her knee was bleeding. She hobbled back to the car and unzipped her pants to study the injury, then dabbed at the scratch with a mineral water soaked tissue. Not too bad, but didn't people get tetanus from things like this?

Jack! Sitting on his bum in a sheep paddock. Did he want her to go to him? What was he shouting? Go away or come here? Did he need help or did he want solitude? He'd told her to stay in the car. But why sit down in the middle of a paddock on the wet grass? And in the rain.

Did he need rescuing? By Hannah? Oh yes, please!

She paced up and down the road in a fever of thinking. The answer sprang into her mind. Obvious. Go.

She struggled through the fence and stumbled across the wet tussocks. The place was riddled with holes. Rabbit holes. And sheep poo. Who would do this for pleasure?

Jack sat with his legs stuck out in front of him, the umbrella by his side and his camera around his neck.

"What are you doing?" she demanded at the same time as he said, "What took you so long?"

Hannah, panting and hot from the climb, stuck her hands on her hips and stared at him. "I'll go back down if that's all you can say."

Dark, angry eyes squinted up at her. "I thought you might have come a bit earlier. Help me up."

"It was raining and you've got the umbrella, remember? And you told me to stay there. I was doing as I was told." She frowned as he drew his right leg in under him and attempted to stand up. He lurched, couldn't put any weight on the left. She stepped closer, offering her arm, and he leant on her as he steadied himself. "You fell in a rabbit hole, right?"

"I didn't fall in one. I stepped in one," he corrected. "The top caved in as I came over the rise. Could've happened to anyone."

"Oh dear, oh dear." They began a slow and lurching descent. "And here's me with no First Aid."

The rain started again.

Chapter Eight

"It needs ice and rest." Jack stopped to hoist the umbrella over their heads. "It's not too bad. I've had worse."

"Make a habit of it, do you?" Hannah grunted as all his weight landed on her, while he juggled the umbrella and his camera.

"Skiing accident, and I fell off a horse once."

"And you think I'm accident prone?" she managed to gasp. Her foot caught and she stumbled. His fingers dug into her shoulder, the umbrella dipped. Cold water dashed into their faces, and icy drops ran down the back of her neck. "Can't you hold that thing steady? I'm getting soaked. I can't believe this is happening."

"Some nurse you are."

"I told you I don't do First Aid."

Grumbling and muttering, they staggered towards the car, which to Hannah's cranky eyes never got any closer, but sat like a little blue toy deliberately tantalising with its promise of shelter and warmth. Wet, cross and exhausted, they reached the fence. She placed a foot on one wire and struggled to lift the next as high as it would go to let Jack crawl through. He handed her the umbrella, and she held it awkwardly aloft as he hopped through the gap, wincing and exclaiming as his injured ankle bore the brunt of his weight. She squeezed through, and they hobbled as fast as possible to the car.

"I'll have to change again," Hannah wailed. She peeled off her damp sweater and threw it onto the back seat. "Why did you have to go and do a stupid thing like that?"

"I didn't do it on purpose!" He spread the towel under his wet backside.

"You shouldn't have gone off on your own."

"If I hadn't you'd be strangled and buried in a shallow grave."

"Thanks very much! I'll leave you out there next time."

"Believe me there won't be a next time." Jack spoke with great finality. He finished unlacing his boots and examined his ankle. Hannah peered at it. Larger than it should be and puffy.

"Swollen."

"Dr. Crawford now, are we?"

"Does it hurt? I've got some painkillers in my bag." She squirmed around and lifted her handbag over to the front seat, then handed him two tablets which he washed down with a mouthful of mineral water.

"Thanks."

"I cut my knee, do you think I'll get lockjaw?" She poked at the sore spot through the rip in her jeans.

"We can but hope. I need to elevate my foot. I'll have to put it on your lap." He twisted in the seat so his back was against the car door, and lifted his leg to stretch it over to Hannah's side.

"Are you ticklish? Let's see."

"Cut it out," he snapped with such anger she pulled a face and let her hand drop. "It hurts."

"Sorry."

She closed her eyes. What a horrible day, and it was still the morning. She hadn't been up at dawn before. Ever, that she could remember. Marilyn would be impressed. With a little chuckle she slipped into a doze with Jack's leg heavy across her thighs.

When she next opened her eyes, the blanket was

129

draped across their legs and he was asleep beside her, propped against the door. How could he sleep in such an uncomfortable position? The car was warm and the windows had misted up. Rain still drummed on the roof. She slept again.

"Anyone there? Hey. In the car. Anyone alive in there?"

Hannah's eyes flew open. Jack was still asleep. Easing herself from under his leg which had made her thighs go numb from the weight, she flung wide the door. The rain had stopped.

Two people on horses were at the fence staring across at the car and now Hannah, with unrestrained interest. A muddy cattle dog ran towards her until a sharp whistle stopped it in its tracks. Tail down it scurried back and pushed through the fence.

"Hello. Am I glad to see you!" She floundered through the wet grass to the fence.

Teenagers, dressed alike in waterproof riding coats, hats, boots and filthy jeans. A girl sat with relaxed grace astride a grey horse and a boy perched high on a black giant of an animal. Both horses had muddy legs and streaks of mud along their bellies and flanks. Breath steamed in gentle coils from their velvety nostrils. They pricked their ears and turned soft, inquisitive, brown eyes towards Hannah.

"You stuck, are you?" the girl said.

"Yes."

"How long've you been here?" asked the boy.

"Since yesterday afternoon. The bridge is flooded."

"Yeah, we know."

They sat on their horses and stared at her. The dog stared too, sitting on its bottom panting with its red tongue hanging out. She didn't trust that dog. Definitely looked mean.

"Can you get some help for my friend, please?

He's had a fall. His ankle is swollen."

"There's no doctor around here." The girl's thin face showed no sign of sympathy. "Even if there was he couldn't get through. Roads are all cut. Phone's off, too."

The boy looked at the girl. "S'pose we could take her home." He made it sound a novel idea to have visitors at their house. Perhaps it was. Perhaps these two had a family of crazed, inbred hillbilly people...

"It's a man." Hannah reined in her bolting imagination. "Could you perhaps get someone with a car to come? Is it far?"

"Three kilometres over there." The girl waved an arm behind her in a vague gesture. "Ute might get through." Her horse fidgeted at the sudden movement and tossed its head, backing away with delicate, prancing steps. She didn't seem to notice. The dog scampered out of the way. "Quicker to take him on Pepper."

They looked at each other and came to an unspoken decision. The boy slid off the giant horse and handed the reins to the girl.

"What's your name?"

"Hannah. My friend's name is Jack."

"I'm Tony and that's my sister Linda."

Tony climbed through the fence and strode towards the car. Hannah hurried after him. Maybe she'd seen too many movies but she didn't entirely trust this pair. They might slit their throats and rob them. No one would ever know. Linda was decidedly odd with that thin, suspicious face and blank expression. Cold blue eyes.

Maybe she was just being paranoid, but she managed to get to the car ahead of him.

"He's asleep. Let me wake him, please."

Tony stopped. Hannah opened the driver's door forgetting Jack was leaning against it with his leg across the seat. His eyes flew open as he fell, his hands grabbed at the steering wheel. Heavy shoulders cannoned into her stomach as she darted forward to support him. He weighed a ton.

"Hannah! What are you doing?" Struggling to right himself, wincing as he dragged his injured ankle over the gear lever and handbrake, he turned to glare at her.

"Sorry, sorry. There are two kids here on horses. They said they'll take you home with them. On the horse." Hannah stared at him, willing him to understand her fears by her expression. She couldn't tell him she thought these two were potentially murderous abductors, with Tony standing right behind her.

Jack's furious gaze slid past her then he grinned. "G'day."

"G'day, mate," said Tony. "Reckon you can get on the horse?"

"With a bit of help." Jack got out of the car and stood swaying for a moment. Tony stepped forward and steadied him.

"Twisted ankle. Did that meself last year."

"I did it before, too. Came off a horse." They made their way to the fence.

"Yeah, that's what I did, except it was in the rodeo. Cracked me collarbone, too." Tony put one booted foot on the wire and held the top strand up to let Jack through. Much stronger than Hannah, he lifted the wires apart with ease. The dog sniffed at Jack. He rubbed its head roughly, prompting the tail to wag two or three times.

"Geez, we laughed," said Linda. "He stayed on about two seconds." Her face lit up for a second or two at the memory.

"That's Linda."

"Hello, Linda," said Jack. Hannah struggled through the fence on her own, catching her torn pants leg on a twist of wire, and hopping about trying to untangle herself. She fidgeted from one foot to the other, twisting her fingers together while they discussed how to get Jack up on Pepper.

"Jack?" He turned to her. "Will you be okay?" She tried to communicate her doubts again through her expression, but she wasn't as good an actress as her mother, and he just grinned.

"I'll try not to fall off. I'll ask someone to come back for you."

He had no qualms about going off with two complete strangers. Injured. At their mercy. Plus leaving her here alone. Divide and conquer, the oldest trick in the book. Separate your opponents and pick them off one by one.

"You won't be frightened here all alone, will you?" He looked down at her with a tiny smile.

"Why would I be?"

He shrugged. "All by yourself in the great outdoors...who knows? A kangaroo might attack you."

"Kangaroos don't atta-..." The smile widened. "I can take care of myself," she said.

"Want to go on the horse? I'm happy to wait here for the car."

Nothing would get her on to that enormous and terrifying horse! "You're the injured one, not me."

"Sure? See you later, then."

The boy was grinning behind him. Hannah forced herself to smile, as well.

"Ready, Jack?" Tony cupped his hands and squatted so Jack could put his right foot on the support, then boosted him up onto Pepper's broad back. Jack swore when his ankle banged onto the back of the saddle, but he stayed upright and settled himself. Tony swung up behind him.

They waved as they rode away. Would this be her last sight of Jack? In movies you could always tell when a character wasn't coming back. The foolish one who volunteered to investigate something on behalf of the group always got eaten by a lion, or fell down a crevasse.

"Be about an hour," called Linda. An afterthought.

Hannah watched them go until, dramatically outlined against the white clouds, they disappeared over the brow of the hill. She turned in glum solitude to wait in the car. It was mid afternoon, but felt like six in the evening. Her stomach growled so she ate the last of the bread and cheese and the apple, and drank the rest of the water.

Pepper was a huge horse, so far from the ground. What if he didn't like two people on board? He was so big he may not even notice. But Tony would know what to do if Pepper got stroppy. If he cared. What if they were taking Jack away to dump him and then come back to get her? Hannah held her breath, but let it out in an exasperated rush of air.

"Don't be ridiculous! They're normal kids. Helpful and caring."

She sprang from the car, went to the boot and took out her violin. Practice to fill in the time instead of imagining horror story scenarios. Her fingers felt stiff and cold. The sound was quite different outside, disappearing off into the surrounding paddocks and up into the waving branches of the remaining gums.

Later she managed to clamber onto the tree trunk for a better look around, only taking a bit of skin off her forearm in the process. Linda's hour stretched into two. She ate the last of the chocolate while listening to the news and weather forecast on the radio, learning motorists should be wary of encountering loose stock on the roads in flood-affected areas.

"I haven't even seen a sheep," she told the

announcer, "but if one comes along I'll be very wary of it."

She picked up her violin again and leant against the car playing the "Vocalise" Bernard played so beautifully. A magpie joined in from a nearby fence post, warbling and carolling along with her.

The sound of an engine stopped her mid phrase. Coming across the hill, bouncing and swaying, was a white utility. The magpie flew away. She laid her violin in its case. The ute skidded to a halt, and a young man in jeans and red-checked flannelette shirt jumped out and slammed the door.

"You Hannah?"

She grinned and looked around the otherwise empty landscape. "Yes."

"Guy." He climbed through the fence and stuck out his hand. She grasped the workworn fingers and he flashed a wide expanse of teeth, gleaming shiny white in his dark-skinned face.

"Thanks for rescuing me, Guy."

"That's all right. Lotta people stuck in these floods."

"Will the roads be open soon?"

"Can't tell. Gotta stop rainin' first. Got much gear to take?"

Guy had the ute loaded in no time. Hannah sat beside him, clutching the seat belt with two hands as they bounced and slid their way over the paddocks. The interior smelt of sheep and dogs and had bits of a machine rolling around on the floor, pummelling her feet and ankles with every bump. A dirty coiled rope sat between them on the seat.

"Where you fellas goin'?"

"We were heading for Goolabri and then a property called Jamieson Downs."

"What you on this road for?"

"Isn't it the road to Goolabri?" Good grief! She'd directed them down this road. Insisted on it.

"Yeah, but it's the back road. Lot further and rougher. Only about sixty kilometres from the turnoff. Over eighty this way."

Hannah gaped at him in disbelief. Dreading the answer she had to ask, "Is that road closed?"

"Don't think so. No bridges." He shouted with laughter. "Big mistake, eh?"

"Very big mistake, Guy. Don't tell my friend."

"He already knows. Linda told him." Eyes sparkling with laughter met hers. She realised he'd already had a laugh at Jack's expense and wanted another at hers.

"Did he laugh?" Not a chance.

"Nuh." This brought a roar of delight, accompanied by the slapping of his hand on the steering wheel.

"Whose place is it?" Perhaps she could divert his attention from city slicker's silliness.

"Harvey Beddowes. Linda and Tony are his kids. Twins they are."

Explained the apparent lack of verbal communication between them. "How old are they?"

"Sixteen."

"Shouldn't they be at school?"

"Yeah, they've been sick. They board in Dubbo and come home at weekends. Can't go back now."

"I don't suppose they care."

White teeth flashed in another grin. "Nuh."

"Is there a Mrs. Beddowes?"

"Sure is! Pat. She's lookin' after your mate. Good as a doctor, Pat."

The truck jolted across an open paddock, slipping and sliding on patches of wet bare earth. Hannah clung on, white-knuckled, and hoped her violin, which she had wedged between her knees and up off the floor, would survive intact. Imagine opening the case to find a pile of wooden pieces like one of those model aeroplane kits. They bounced onto a track which Guy said was the driveway, and after a few minutes crested a rise.

A typical Australian homestead lay before them—a low, sprawling, white-painted, dark-green-roofed building with wide verandahs on three sides, fenced yard around the house enclosing a lawn and flowerbeds, and probably vegetables at the rear. Several large pine trees provided shelter from the blistering summer sun and winter's wind and rain.

The drive led up to the house gate and made a circle. Off to the left squatted a smaller cottage and another building with wooden railed yards. To the right sat large sheds, and further away stockyards and a shearing shed. It all looked neat and prosperous. They drove past the cottage. Guy said, "My place."

A woman carrying a baby came to the door and stared.

"Is she your wife? With your baby?"

"Yeah."

They pulled up outside the wrought iron gate to the main house. Linda appeared on the verandah with a woman. Pat was taller than her daughter, but they both had thin tanned faces, wispy brown hair and angular, bony figures.

"Take the bags down to the shearers quarters, thanks, Guy." Pat came closer. "No room in the house, sorry." She gave Hannah a brief smile.

Guy swung the case down and carried it and Jack's bag across the yard as if they were empty. He disappeared inside what looked like a shed. Shearers' quarters? Were the shearers there?

"I'm Pat Beddowes. Come in. You must be dying for a wash and something hot to drink." Clear blue eyes assessed Hannah. Not unfriendly. Weary.

"Hello, Pat. Thank you so much for this. You've no idea how glad I was to see Linda and Tony. Not to mention Guy, just now."

She smiled at Linda who looked back at her with those blank blue eyes. Gripping her violin and handbag Hannah followed Pat who had turned towards the house.

"How's Jack?"

"He's all right. Just needs ice and rest until the swelling goes down."

Pat led her up the steps and across the verandah, opening a screen door to a hallway running through the house to the kitchen. A large living room opened on the left with a big old squashy couch and armchairs, and Hannah guessed there would be bedrooms down a passage on the right.

"I expect you'd like a wash. Bathroom's right next to you. Here. The shearers' bathrooms are a bit spartan. No hot water at the moment down there." No shearers either, hopefully. "You're welcome to come up to the house."

Pat flung open the door of a spacious bathroom. A hot shower and clean clothes. Luxury.

"Come to the kitchen for a cuppa when you're ready. I'll leave you to it," she said. "Shall I put this in the living room for you?" Strong fingers grasped Hannah's violin case.

"Thanks." Fabulous! Hot water, soap, shampoo. Hannah closed the door and jumped back in fright when she caught sight of herself in the mirror over the basin. No wonder the twins had been wary and Pat took one look and banished her to the shearers' quarters. Jack hadn't told her she had mud on her face, and her hair looked like it belonged to one of those witches in Macbeth! She'd have to borrow a horse brush to get the knots out.

Clothes! Guy had taken her bag away. She washed her face and hands, then went out the front door and picked her way across the muddy yard. The shearers lived about a hundred metres from the house.

The fly screen door squeaked despite her cautious opening. All quiet. The door banged shut behind her. She stood uncertainly in the pale green passage way. Tobacco-coloured linoleum covered the floor, and the place smelled of stale cigarette smoke and beer. Like a pub but damp and unused.

Where was Jack? She walked along the corridor peering into the open doorways as she went. The four side rooms had either double bunks or single beds in them. No bedding, just thin, lumpy, grey striped mattresses on those terrible wire bases that sagged. School camp all over again. One short, unpleasant step removed from camping.

At the end of the corridor was a communal living area with ancient lounge chairs and dining tables. Not a shearer to be seen. No Jack either. Three more doors opened off this room. One was the bathroom with four shower cubicles and several brown-stained toilets and urinals, at sight of which she did a swift about turn.

The next door revealed a kitchen and the last another bedroom. This one had a double bed in it. For a married couple? This one also had the suitcases and Jack in it. The cases sat by the door. Jack was asleep. He'd claimed the best bed, the only bed with bedding. Where was she supposed to sleep? With him?

Hannah stepped closer and studied him with hands on hips. His face looked pale but peaceful, his lanky body sprawled under the pink chenille bedspread. Harmless, asleep. Share a bed with him?

She drove him mad, and he wanted to strangle her. He was patronising and rude to her, treated her like an incompetent child then kissed her, and made thinly veiled advances to Libby shortly thereafter. If only he wasn't so handsome, didn't have that way of looking at her which made her insides go weak, those lines near his mouth when he smiled, didn't electrify her with his kiss. The same way he affected multitudes of women.

No point in even thinking of an affair with him. She wanted everything Jack patently didn't, and she wasn't about to invest any emotional capital in a man who wouldn't provide what she wanted. And all without even taking into account his unwanted, unloved child. Whatever explanation, whatever excuse, nothing he said could mitigate the fact he had a son he didn't care about while she had lost a child she treasured. The two events were separate, she knew, but nothing could possibly reconcile two people with such opposite opinions on one of life's basic issues—the love of a parent for a child.

Jack's breathing altered, but he didn't wake. She studied his face, taking in every detail of the strong, angular features.

"You're a selfish bastard, Jack," she whispered. He stirred and shifted, grimaced, but his breathing resumed its steady rhythm, his expression relaxed.

Hannah opened her suitcase. A complete change of clothes was a necessity. Pat had left towels on the bed and she took one, headed back to the house and spent the next fifteen minutes washing off two days of stale grime.

Jack smiled when she returned to the room.

"Hello."

"How do you feel?" She dumped her filthy clothes and fussed with her hairbrush and wet hair. He was barelegged under the bedclothes because his dirty track pants lay on the floor at the foot of the bed. Her mind kept straying to his body...

"Sore but okay apart from that." His eyes tracked her movements like radar. "What about you?"

"Better now I've had a shower."

"You look wonderful." Hannah's cheeks grew warm. Flattery? What was he after?

"Pat's making a cup of tea, I think. Do you want one?"

The radar gaze switched off, replaced by a smile and a nod. "I'll get up. Hannah?"

"What?"

"This is a double bed." His face was impassive.

"I know." Her eyes narrowed. "And you bagsed it before I even got here."

"We can share it."

"We can not!"

"There's plenty of room. Why not?" A grin spread across his face as indicated the expanse of unused bed next to him.

"I'm not getting into a bed with you!"

"Would you prefer one of those bunks?"

"Totally irrelevant because you'll be sleeping in one, not me."

"You're shorter than I am. I won't fit, they're too small."

"The shearers manage and I bet some of them are bigger blokes than you!"

"Too bad. I got here first." He sat up. "I'm getting up now, if you don't mind..." A hand flapped at her, indicating she should leave. Hannah stomped out the door. She'd have to ask Pat for more bedding, and pick the least revolting of those beds. What a mean, selfish so-and-so he was.

A tiny and traitorous part of her brain, however, registered a tremor of disappointment there wouldn't be any advances from Jack tonight, or any other time apparently. He'd made a token, teasing offer and her virtue was safe with him. She was more worried about her own instant reaction to the idea. Would she have been able to keep her hands off him if they had shared a bed together? The whole night.

Pat was in the kitchen preparing dinner. A pile of potatoes sat on the draining board and a big saucepan waited on the stove top. She poured steaming water from a kettle into a tea pot sitting ready on the bench.

"Mugs are in that cupboard, Hannah." Pat pointed behind them. Hannah found three coloured mugs and set them down on the large wooden table. It was a typical farmhouse kitchen big enough for the whole family and more to eat in, the meeting place of the house, the nerve centre.

"Pat we're really grateful to you for putting us up like this. I've no idea how we can ever repay you."

Pat glanced up as she poured the tea. "To tell you the truth I'm glad to see some new faces." She sat down. "You'll be stuck here for a day or two."

"Do you think Jack will be all right?"

"Yeah, there's nothing much the doctor would do except x-ray it."

"Guy said you were as good as a doctor."

"Not much choice. We have to shift for ourselves out here. Can't go running off to the doctor with every little scratch like city people." Better not mention her wounded knee. The Band-Aid she'd found in the bathroom would have to do.

Jack hobbled in using a walking stick as a crutch, wearing one shoe on his good foot and a sock on his swollen one. How did he manage to get across the yard without floundering in mud? Pat poured him a cup of tea.

"You're looking better. Stick your leg up on a chair and we'll ice it again." She went to the refrigerator, took out an icepack, wrapped it in a tea towel and handed it to him.

"The sleep did me good. I didn't think I'd be able to with the pain, but I must have been too tired." He grimaced as the cold seeped into his skin.

Pat sipped her tea and eyed Hannah speculatively. "What's in that case you've got?"

"A violin. I'm a musician and Jack's a

photographer. We're supposed to be on a concert tour with four other people but got separated. Oh!" Hannah gasped and put her tea down too fast. Liquid slopped on to the table.

Jack and Pat stared at her. Dreading the reaction, Hannah said, "Jack, I left your camera bags in the car. I'm sorry."

Jack's face darkened. "Hannah!"

"I'm sorry. They'll be all right, won't they?"

"They valuable?" asked Pat.

"Very." Jack glowered at Hannah. "Except one."

"Never know who'll come along." Pat stood up and went out the back door. "Tony," she called. Her voice faded as she walked across the yard.

"Hannah, how could you? You remembered your violin." His voice was icy with rage. She'd never heard him so angry, even when his camera broke.

"I didn't think of them. I only looked in the boot and I'd been practicing, so my violin was out. I'm not used to thinking about other people's cameras. You didn't either."

"I was injured, remember? On a horse? You're so selfish."

And who's so selfish they bagsed the best bed? Trembling with fury, she stood up. All those words and accusations were too familiar, too hurtful. He sounded just like Adrian, and more recently, Marilyn. "I knew it was a mistake to get involved with you!"

Jack glared at her in astonishment. "Involved? I'd hardly call a kiss or two involved. And you weren't involved as far as I could judge. I may as well have kissed your cat. You're the last person I'd want to be involved with."

Hannah drew a deep, angry breath and wiped her eyes with both hands. Don't cry in front of him, he'd love that.

"Your stupid cameras will be all right. I locked

143

the car. Who's going to take them? A thieving magpie?"

He was about to speak, when the outer screen door squeaked open.

"Tony's going down now. He'll want the keys." Pat gave Hannah a tiny sympathetic smile. She had to have heard the raised voices if not the words.

"I'll go with him." Hannah fled from the kitchen, ran to the shearers' room to grab the car keys and across to meet Tony waiting in the same battered ute she'd been rescued in.

"Thanks, Tony. I'm sorry to be such a nuisance."

"S'all right," he said. "I like driving."

He accelerated the ute down the muddy driveway. Darkness came with stealthy swiftness out here and the headlights bounced crazily from the tussocky grass to the sky. They topped a hill. A paler thread indicated the road away down the long slope. She gripped the seat belt and held her breath as they careered down the paddock, letting it out when the ground levelled at the bottom. Tony grinned at her as he put on the brakes and parked the ute next to the fence.

"Scared you, ay?"

"No." She glanced at his eager boy's face and grinned back. "Yes, you horror."

Tony held the fence for her to climb through. The car was as they had left it, of course. A surge of rage at Jack's nastiness choked her. Hannah hoisted the two bulky bags over her shoulder, had a quick look around the interior and the boot to check for anything else she may have missed. Her suit bag. Would Jack think that was funny? Very unlikely. Sourpuss.

"What's in the bags?"

"Cameras. Jack's a photographer."

"What's he photograph?"

"He's a freelance nature photographer but he

144

does soft porn as a sideline."

"Yeah? Nude stuff?" His eyes nearly popped out of his head.

"Yes. Girls in and out of their underwear." Just like rotten Raoul had taken of her. For all she knew it could be true.

"Think he's got any with him?"

"Don't know. Ask him at dinner."

Smiling, she stowed one of the bags on the seat between them and clutched the other on her lap with the suit bag. Amazing how Tony knew where to go in the dark, but he was a very confident driver, and they roared along with him whistling tunelessly between intermittent bursts of conversation.

A tempting and mouth-watering smell permeated the house when they returned. Roast lamb. After two days of cheese sandwiches and water she'd never looked forward to a meal more.

They lugged the bags to the living room and left them by the couch. Hannah hung her suit bag over the back of an armchair and went to wash. She peered at herself in the bathroom mirror.

Her hair was everywhere as usual. Maybe if she had it cut short? Or shaved her head. She poked her tongue out at herself and left the room to tackle the roast lamb dinner, with the possible bonus of witnessing Jack field Tony's inevitable questions. With any luck he'd choose a most inappropriate moment.

Chapter Nine

Everyone sat around the big wooden table drinking beer. A heavyset, ruddy faced man in a blue shirt and brown work trousers lumbered to his feet and offered his hand when she entered the kitchen.

"Harvey Beddowes."

"Hannah Crawford." Grasping the callused hand she gave him her best smile. Jack raised his glass and took a sip, watching her over the rim. Still angry.

"Get you a beer, Hannah?"

"No, no," Pat said with a quick, frowning shake of the head. "Soft drink."

She flicked an apologetic glance at Hannah and lowered her voice. "Jack told us about your...you know...problem."

The only problem she had, namely Jack, was drinking his beer and wouldn't meet her eye. So! That's how it was.

"Soft drink is fine, thank you." Little did he know she didn't like beer.

"Jack says you're a musician." Harvey placed a glass of lemon squash in front of her.

"Thank you. Yes. Violin and piano."

"You could play for us later," he suggested, but it was more like an order.

"I'd love to."

"Do you live off it?" Linda broke her long silence.

"Yes. I play the piano for people, accompanying them in recitals or for music exams and I also teach. I prefer to play, though."

Linda digested this information. "Did you go to a

146

college or something?"

"Yes. I did my degree at the Brisbane Conservatorium of Music, but I started learning when I was little."

"Hannah loves to play for people," said Jack. "She's a real show off. Get her started and she won't stop."

"We'll have a music night. Get Guy and Lalla to come over after tea," stated Harvey. Hannah caught Jack's eye. He smiled. She glanced at Tony, sitting listening, staring at Jack. Her time bomb ticking away innocently. What foresight!

Pat stood up. "Dinner's about ready."

"I'll help." Hannah jumped to her feet.

"Set the table, please, Linda. Jack peeled the potatoes for me earlier," Pat said.

"Have another beer, Jack, you don't want to go doing too much of that domestic stuff." Harvey leaned back in his chair. "Watch the women work."

"Have you had much flood damage?"

Harvey began to explain the problems the weather had caused the new lambs and his crops, finishing with, "Mug's game, this farming. Trouble is I can't do anything else." He drained his glass and got up to switch on the radio, waving aside Pat's protest they were about to eat.

"Just want to catch the weather forecast, love."

The announcer was in the middle of a report on overseas investments. Tony started asking Jack about his work. Any minute now...Hannah grinned to herself as she spooned steamed broccoli into a serving dish.

Harvey shushed everyone as news of the flooding came on.

"Heavy rain has caused major flooding in northern New South Wales and there are reports of minor damage and stock loss from other parts of the state. Many roads are still closed but the Newell

Highway has reopened. The situation should ease if there is no further rain overnight. Motorists are advised not to travel in the affected areas."

"Let's eat," said Pat but Harvey said, "Hang on. Listen."

"...believed to be travelling in the Dubbo area with a female companion. Jack Rotherford is best known through his work for *National Geographic* magazine. He recently won the Sylvia Harden Award for environmental photography."

Anything else he may have said was drowned in the clamour.

"Is that you?"

"What did he say?"

"What was the first bit?"

"Are you famous?"

"We might catch it on the TV news." Harvey stood up and led the charge for the living room.

They didn't have to wait long. Footage of swirling floodwaters, people wading knee deep through front gardens and looking in despair at their ruined homes. The vision cut to the newsreader with a picture of Jack behind him holding a camera, and an inset of the bird in oil photo. Tony and Linda gasped with excitement.

"Photographer Jack Rotherford is still missing in the flood areas west of Dubbo. He and a female companion failed to arrive at their destination two days ago. His aunt, Mrs. Marilyn Casey says he often took detours looking for photographic opportunities, and she is concerned his constant search for the unusual may have contributed to his fate. Police advise Mr. Rotherford may be safe but cut off by flood waters. They urge either him or his companion to contact Dubbo police as soon as they are able."

Jack caught Hannah's eye. "Marilyn!"

"Dinner," said Harvey.

"Is your phone working yet?" Jack asked as they trooped back to finish their neglected meal. "My mobile's out of range here."

Pat picked up the receiver of the wall phone in the kitchen. "Dead."

She served the roast meat onto plates and passed them around the table but gave Hannah, whose mouth was watering in anticipation, an odd look. "You won't be eating the meat, Jack said."

"Why not?" demanded Harvey in his booming farmer's voice. "That's prime lamb, that is."

"Hannah's a vegetarian," announced Jack. "Can't see the appeal myself. This roast smells delicious, Pat."

"But it's all right, Hannah, the lamb was a vegetarian." Harvey laughed as he spooned broccoli on to his plate.

"Why are you a vegetarian?" asked Linda.

"I'm not." Hannah gave Jack the evil eye. "I don't know where he got that idea." Beer was one thing, roast lamb another. No way was she going to miss out on this scrumptious meal. Nice try, Jack.

"Must have been something you said. I misunderstood." Jack helped himself to baked potatoes, then sent an innocent little glance at Hannah.

"He often gets long words confused." Hannah turned to Harvey. "Are we cut off here?"

"Our driveway comes out on a different road to the one you're on but it's cut, too." Harvey shovelled roast lamb into his mouth.

"So there's no way to let them know we're okay?"

"No." He chewed on unconcerned by thwarted travel matters.

Afterwards Hannah helped Linda and Tony wash dishes. Jack limped out of the kitchen.

Ten minutes later Hannah went to the living room to collect her violin. She stopped short as she entered the room. Jack was standing by his bags with a thunderous look on his face and the broken camera in his hand. Perhaps she could offer to replace it, although knowing her luck it would turn out to be either a family heirloom or a rare model made by a now deceased artisan from Transylvania, or some other equally obscure place. Or the one he'd won that prize with. Her sins just kept on piling up.

She picked up her violin and suit bag in silence and backed out to stumble across to the shearers' bunkhouse in the dark. Heavens knows what she was treading on, the ground squelched squashy and slippery with every step, but she didn't remember seeing anything earlier which needed avoiding. She wiped her shoes on the mat and switched on the outside light for Jack. But only because he was injured.

The chill, damp air inside smelled just like a cave. Her nose wrinkled as a shiver ran down her body, She switched on the corridor light. Dammit, she'd forgotten to ask for more sheets and blankets. Would Jack really make her sleep in one of those bunks? Yes, he would.

Where was her toothbrush? Must be in her case.

Jack's voice startled her. "Hannah, I'm sorry I was angry with you. Thank you for going back."

He could move with surprising stealth for a man with one functioning foot.

"You should thank Tony." The gentleness of the apology made her breath catch in her throat.

"I did."

But this was Jack, she couldn't trust him. "Nice trick, the alcoholic bit. Shame about the vegetarian thing not working for you. And thank you for suggesting I play tonight. I'm exhausted."

"You'll manage." He hobbled closer. His expression changed. "I'd like to be involved with you, Hannah," he murmured. Her heart thumped like a pile driver, she couldn't drag her eyes from his. "And I'd much rather kiss you than Freddo."

She gave a little snicker of laughter. He smiled and his arms slipped around her waist. Hannah closed her eyes and rested her forehead on his shoulder. How did he do this to her so easily? Manipulate her. If she lifted her face now he'd kiss her for sure, and she'd let him. In fact, she'd kiss him, and where would that lead? Hannah with a broken heart. For once she was thinking ahead.

"But I don't want to be involved with you, Jack." Her voice was firm but she didn't move. Couldn't. The arms around her were too comforting, safe even. At least she could pretend they were. His chest was warm and solid, the sort of chest a girl could curl up against when the going got tough. If its owner stayed around long enough.

"Because of what I said?"

Jack's arms slid from her waist. Hannah looked up into his face. Big mistake.

"Yes. No. It couldn't work." Not a convincing tone at all. She dropped her gaze. Was this the time to go into murky areas? No, she had to perform tonight.

"Why not?" He hopped to the bed, sat down and swung his leg on to the pink chenille cover.

"You know perfectly well you don't want to get involved with me, and I certainly don't want to get involved with you. I have it on good authority, namely Marilyn, you thrive on short-term affairs. You told me yourself you've just been dumped. It's fast, even for you, to move on to the next woman. I'm not in the market for a quick fling. I'm not that kind of girl." If he had any sense he'd leave it there. She opened the suit bag. "The least I can do is dress up for them tonight."

"Maybe I find you irresistibly attractive."

"Hah! For about five minutes until the next girl

comes along." Did he? How could she possibly tell? Why was she even giving the idea brain space? Hannah slipped him a sidelong glance, just to see the expression on his face. Frowning.

"How do you know I don't want to get involved with you?" His eyes narrowed. "Why do you always think you know what I'm thinking?"

"Because you think mainly about sex. It's obvious."

"That's ridiculous!"

"No, it's not. You're a man. You all pretend you're interested in something else, but you're not. You're no different. Especially with me. How do I know? Because I annoy you and have done since you first laid eyes on me. Contrary to popular opinion I'm not a complete idiot. I know when a guy is spinning a line." She held up a dark red blouse, smoothing its wrinkles with her free hand.

"You had a tin of cat food in your hand when I first saw you." Jack grinned. Catching his eye Hannah had to grin back. "I thought you were going to empty it over me," he said.

"So did I."

"I'm glad you restrained yourself."

"I don't usually, that's what annoys people—my ex, for example." She searched for tights.

"What annoyed him?"

"Me."

"He's an idiot. You take a bit of getting used to, but I think I'm getting the hang of it now." He lay back on the bed with his patronising face on.

"Don't start, and don't get comfortable there," she said. "I want to change."

"Go ahead. After what we've been through I can't believe you're modest?" He clasped his hands behind his head. "I'll never forget you in your knickers drying yourself, with your gorgeous legs everywhere. Or wearing my sweater and nothing else."

She glared at his smiling face. "If you don't leave you'll have two sore ankles and a black eye."

"Okay, I'm going."

She handed him his walking stick. "Here you are, grandpa."

"What will you play?" Jack asked as he hobbled to the door. Could he be remorseful?

"I've got a few party pieces."

****

"What's on first?" demanded Harvey. "Come on. Let's get this show on the road."

He took a pull at his beer. Settling in for an evening's entertainment with copious liquid refreshments. Jack lolled in the doorway with his camera and an interested face. Tony, sitting on the floor by his mother's feet, mustn't have had the opportunity to question him yet. Harvey, Pat, Linda, Guy and his wife Lalla lounged on the couch and in various big, old armchairs.

The tired old piano had turned out to be a disaster. The few experimental chords Hannah had struck were so out of tune as to be virtually unrecognisable. She plucked and tuned the violin strings, intent, listening, while her audience watched, fascinated.

"I'll play part of a Bach "Unaccompanied Suite for Violin."

Eyes closed she pictured the music, lifted her bow.

Jack watched from the doorway. Perhaps he shouldn't have pushed her into it. But no, served her right for leaving his cameras behind. Any guilt was immediately squelched. The others were amazed, he could see by their faces. He snapped several quick shots of their rapt expressions. They'd never have heard a live classical player of her calibre. This was what the tour had been all about. She had an ex? Ex-husband or ex-boyfriend? Should have asked Simon.

Hannah finished the "Gigue" with a flourish and bowed to the applause. She began the beautiful "Vocalise" Bernard performed at their concerts.

"Cool," breathed Linda when the last note died away into the silence.

"Give us another tune, Hannah. Something we can sing along to," Harvey cried. "Classical stuff's all right, but we've heard enough of that."

Hannah stood with her violin still tucked under her chin. She wiped her palm against her jeans. Nervous? Doubtful. More likely stumped by Harvey's request.

What would she do now? She was a classical musician, probably couldn't play anything else. No telling how Harvey would react if she refused or couldn't play what he wanted. Might turn ugly with a quantity of beer under his belt. Jack pursed his lips, ready to intervene if necessary. Such a stupid joke without asking her first. He stepped forward. Hannah sent him a blank look over their heads.

She said, "How about this?" and launched into a fast and furious version of the "Irish Washerwoman."

"This is the stuff." Harvey jumped up to swing Pat around the room, endangering everyone's feet and sending Tony diving to catch a lamp as it rocked on the mantelpiece.

"Where'd you learn that?" asked Linda when it finished, and her father had collapsed panting onto the couch.

"I played in an Irish band for a few years," Hannah replied. "This is one of my favourites, and I know Jack likes it, too." A sweet and highly suspect smile came his way. "He just loves to sing, don't you, Jack? *The Londonderry Air*, or you may know it as *Danny Boy*."

"Sing, Jack," demanded Harvey.

Jack improvised a desperate response as Harvey's eager red face swung towards him. "I'm afraid I don't know all the words." Sing? And he was feeling sorry for her?

"Doesn't matter. Pat's got the music here, you can read them." Hannah held out a piece of sheet music with a smile which on closer examination was of sheer malice.

"Come on, Jack," cried Tony.

"I..."

"Sing something you do know," suggested Pat.

"Yes. What do you know, Jack?" Hannah continued to smile. He knew he should have strangled her when he had the chance way back in the Blue Mountains where the bush was thickest.

"My throat is very sore." A little, raspy, throat-clearing noise offered proof.

"What a shame." Hannah studied him with narrowed eyes.

"Play it, anyway," roared Harvey. "We'll sing."

Hannah patiently played tune after tune from Pat's song books while they bellowed along in tuneless enthusiasm until Harvey stood up, yawned, belched and announced it was time for bed. Pat and Linda followed him out the door.

Guy and Lalla said goodnight. "Come and visit tomorrow for a cuppa," Lalla said to Hannah.

Jack and Hannah were left alone in the living room with Tony. Hannah headed for the bathroom before the trek to the shearers' cells. And she had to catch Pat about the extra bedding. As she left the living room Tony said to Jack, "Have you got any of those photos?" Not as spectacular a result as she'd hoped but still... The scores were just about even.

When she returned with an armful of bedding Jack stood in the hallway with an incredulous expression.

"Porn?" He stepped out and held the door wide

for her. They began groping their way across the yard towards the pool of light cast by the single bare bulb outside the bunkhouse door. A few spots of rain fell.

"You mean it's not true? Wonder where I got that idea?" She grinned in the darkness.

"I wonder." He lurched into her, and she stumbled and nearly dropped her blankets.

"Careful, you'll have us both out of these trousers."

"Sorry, my stick got stuck in the mud." Using her as a support he regained his balance.

"It's a lucrative sideline, so I believe. For the photographer, at least."

"How do you know?" His most scathing tone.

"I was told when some scumbag took my pictures when I was fifteen. Perhaps he's a pal of yours. Raoul Conti?"

"Really? You were a porn model?"

"No! I was a stupid, naïve teenager who was taken advantage of by a creep."

Jack opened the door and switched on the inside light. Enlightenment visited him at the same time as the feeble light from the unshaded bulb.

"Aah—now I understand."

"Do you, indeed?" She pushed passed with her bundle of linen.

"We're not all like Raoul, Hannah."

"I know. But it left a nasty stain." Hannah dumped the bundle on the double bed.

"I bet." Jack smiled. "This is my room, remember?"

"Don't panic. I'm just going to find the least unsavoury of the beds." Hannah turned with hands on hips. "If you were any sort of gentleman you'd let me sleep in that bed."

"But I'm no sort of gentleman at all. I'm a purveyor of porn and a lecher." The bed bounced and sagged as he flopped back onto it with a laugh, "You're welcome to join me any time you like." He swung his injured leg up, winced.

"Is it very painful? Do you need more painkillers?" She could be a nurse if necessary. His face was pale.

"Pat gave me some, thanks. They're pretty strong. Industrial strength. She probably gives them to the horses. The ice helps a lot. Swelling should be down by tomorrow."

He lay back and closed his eyes. Hannah glared at him ferociously for a minute, then went to investigate the bed situation. The first room had the biggest Huntsman spider in it she'd ever seen in her life. She knew they were harmless, knew they ate flies, knew they kept to themselves up on the ceiling or high on the wall, but she was not sleeping in a room with a spider the size of her open hand.

She slammed the door and tried the next. Something had died in here. Died or was in the process of decomposing under the floor. Two left. The next seemed reasonably safe. Hannah gave each of the mattresses on the four single beds in the room a suspicious examination. Most were stained and all were thin and lumpy. Shearers would be so exhausted after work they wouldn't care where they slept. Like Jack. So much for his boast! Pinching the best bed while she had to rough it with spiders and rotting corpses.

She marched back to collect the bedding. Jack was sprawled across the bed asleep already, snoring. Too bad if he woke up cold in the middle of the night. Back in the other room she threw the sheets and blankets on to the closest bed, then went to find her pyjamas. Backwards and forwards half the night, finding a bed, making the bed, changing...all while he snored.

When she returned to hang up her blouse and

skirt, clad in her silky, pink pyjamas with white clouds on them, she stood for a moment with hands on hips staring at his peaceful figure. The big selfish lump. She switched off the light in his room, scampered back to her narrow, spartan bed, clicked off the light and dived in, shivering in the darkness. As long as the Huntsman didn't have friends lurking in this room.

Rain came pelting down in a sudden onslaught, deafening on the corrugated iron roof. The water gurgled down the drain pipes and dripped from the eaves. Soothing. Loud but peaceful in its constancy. The bed began to warm up and she drifted into sleep. Some time in the middle of the night she woke.

Cold. Damp. She lifted her head. Water splashed on to her cheek. She sat up.

Water? It was still raining outside. Now it was raining inside! Her groping fingers found dampness. Her pillow was soaked and so was the sheet and mattress. Hannah flung back the covers and fumbled her way across the room in the dark for the light. Please don't let that spider be sitting on the switch. She trod in a puddle on the floor.

The light revealed several leaks, one directly over her bed. What a nightmare. Now what could she do? Her bedding was wet so even if the fourth unexplored room was by some miracle uncontaminated by spiders, smells or water she couldn't sleep there.

Nothing else for it. She crept, shivering, down the hallway in the dark and felt for the light switch in the living area. By its dim sixty-watt glow Jack was visible still lying sprawled where she'd left him, taking up most of the bed.

"Jack." She prodded his thigh. "Jack!"

He moved his head to the other side. She knelt on the bed next to him and shook his shoulder.

"Jack. Wake up."

He produced an indeterminate muttering noise. She growled and shook him harder. "Move, Jack!" He rolled over, turning his back on her.

"For heavens sake! Jack!" She hissed viciously, "Let me go to bed, you selfish sod."

She lifted the edge of the covers, crawled into the cramped space and curled up. Gave a helpless ineffectual tug at the blankets. Gave up. The bed was dry, warm and all she wanted was sleep.

Jack woke an hour later, cold and uncomfortable. Groping about in the dark, still half asleep he discovered Hannah sound asleep beside him. Smiling, he removed his shirt and clad in T-shirt and jockey shorts, slipped under the covers beside her, snuggling close to the warmth of her body, breathing in the sweet scent of her.

Hannah woke and lay in a warm stupor. Her brain slowly registered where she was. In bed. A delicious, cosy, soft bed. At the Beddowes. Daylight filtered around the edges of the blind but it wasn't bright sunshine. Softer light, more like rain again. Cloudy anyway, and extraordinarily quiet after the tremendous downpour last night. Marvellous sleep after that horrible start and when Jack had...Jack?! Her eyes snapped wide open and she rolled over to find his face inches from her own. His eyes were shining with a dangerous light, and he watched her with a smile on his lips.

"Good morning," he murmured. "Glad you changed your mind."

Hannah said nothing. She couldn't because his hand was gentle on her cheek, holding her face and his mouth was on hers. A brief flutter of doubt was eclipsed by the awareness of how his lips moved against hers, stalling her brain, paralysing her limbs, focussing every fibre of her being on the point of contact. Soft, insistent but not forceful, giving her room to object. If she chose... If she... He shifted, rose higher, slid his hand behind her neck, deepened the kiss.

Hannah's mouth opened and he took that for the acquiescence it was. Had to be. Couldn't think straight when he kissed her. No reason why not. Why not? No reason. Endless kiss. Best ever. Best...ooohhh.

The other hand slid over her breast, caressing, teasing. She groaned deep in her throat. Sparks ignited, shot through her body, melting her from the inside out. She should object but...her arms wrapped themselves around his neck, drew him closer...his unshaven cheek rasped on her skin as his mouth left hers and trailed kisses along her jaw, down her throat. Head thrown back she sucked in air, desire surged, hot, insistent. Had to have him. Now.

The pink pyjama top somehow became unbuttoned, was hurled out of bed. His T-shirt flew after. Skin against hot skin. Her breasts craving his touch. Her mouth wanting his. More of him. All of him. His body hard and demanding. Hannah matching him. Urgent. Reality telescoped into a series of moments, sensations—searching lips, tongues, fingers and clamouring bodies—to the ultimate. A crashing, exhilarating rollercoaster ride. Freefalling. Whirling.

Chapter Ten

"See." Coming from where he lay beside her in the wreckage of the bed, his voice held a wealth of satisfaction. Lips kissed her cheek, stubble prickling gently, then his head dropped back onto the pillow. "Now we're involved."

Hannah lay silent—stunned and exhausted by the onslaught, the overwhelming strength of the passion they'd unleashed. Was sex with Jack always like this? Could it be this way? She'd had no idea. Then the reality of what had just occurred seeped into her brain. The reality and the ensuing complications, or rather the implications as he would see them. A conquest. Add her to the list.

"On a very superficial level." She groped about in the bed with her feet for her pyjama bottoms, and accidentally kicked his leg.

"Ow, Careful! My ankle's still sore," he growled. "These what you're looking for?" He held the pink pants out over his side of the bed.

She leaned over her side to the floor where the pyjama jacket lay in a crumpled heap, slipped it on and buttoned as fast as she could while trying to avoid his melodramatic, leering gaze.

"Can I have those, please?"

"Come and get them," He waved the pants about like a flag, grinning like an idiot.

"Jack, please."

"Don't know why you're being so coy all of a sudden. You can't pretend you didn't enjoy what we just did. All I can say is, it's a good thing we're so far from the house. I like a girl who gets carried away."

"I'm not pretending I didn't enjoy it, but I don't want to give Harvey an eyeful when I go to the bathroom."

"Then come over here and get your pants." He continued to grin that irresistibly sexy grin. The one that ought to be banned. He should be banned.

Hannah sat up and turned her back on him. Why on earth had she allowed it to happen? Now he'd be insufferable. His little scheme had fallen into place like a dream, and she'd gone along like the idiot she was. Rational, controlled action had never been her strong suit. And he knew it. Jack who planned every move he made and figured things out in advance. What a coup for him.

The bedclothes rustled as he moved towards her. The mattress bounced up and down. His fingers caressed her shoulder, squeezed, moved to lift the hair on her neck.

"Hannah?" Soft, cajoling. "Come back to bed. I'm sorry." A kiss pressed through the silky fabric of her pyjama top. Her spine sagged. She closed her eyes. Mustn't give in again. Mustn't! Lips nuzzled her neck.

She sprang off the bed, snatched the pyjama pants from his hand before he could react, and pulled them on. Jack collapsed onto the tumbled pillows grinning at her through lust-slaked eyes. From now on she would be just as calculating and cool as he was. She would think before she spoke and think twice before she acted.

"If we have to spend another night here you're in with the spider," she said. Planning ahead.

"What spider? What's up with you all of a sudden?" He heaved himself to a sitting position and regarded her with an amused, smug expression.

"You took advantage of me. I was asleep and I'm not very good in the mornings."

"I thought you were. I thought you were

terrific." Jack's voice took on a slight edge. "I didn't take advantage of you and you know it. Your eyes were wide open." He gave a little snort of laughter. "Most of the time."

"I didn't want to do that with you, Jack."

"Not what it felt like to me." He had such a self-satisfied smirk Hannah seriously considered throwing her hairbrush at him. "Just because I was in bed with you didn't mean I wanted to...do that."

This time it was a shout of laughter. "What was I supposed to think? Why did you get into my bed?"

"Because there was a gigantic spider in one room, something dead in another, and in the middle of the night the roof leaked and my bed got soaked. I had no choice. You were the lesser of multiple evils."

"Oh and here was I thinking it was my charm." Still with a silly wide grin. "Didn't change the result though, and you know I didn't force myself on you. Hannah?" His expression changed. "Did I? If you'd said no I would've stopped. Instantly."

Hannah bit her lip. She'd never been a good liar either. "I know. I'm not accusing you of rape or anything. I just don't want to..." She met his gaze.

"Make love, you mean? Why can't you say it?" His eyes bored into hers.

"Because, Jack, there was no love involved." At least on his part, which was the worst thing of all, the sneaking suspicion in the back of her mind that maybe she was falling for this smug, handsome hunk of ego. Just the way he expected and just the way she didn't want. "This was just sex, and yes, I admit I wanted to as much as you did, but it was just sex."

"It was pretty amazing for just sex. But anyway... Does it matter?" He spoke slowly, staring at her. His eyes exerted a strange, hypnotic effect. She blinked, broke the rabbit-like trance. What a question!

"It does to me, but you wouldn't understand."

He continued to gaze at her with a thoughtful expression. Or was he assessing her, deciding whether she was worth the bother of pursuing further?

Hannah frowned. "Look, Jack. This was a mistake. Let's not turn it into a disaster. We both know we have absolutely nothing in common and can't agree on anything. As soon as we get back to Sydney you'll heave a sigh of relief and go off to the wilderness, and I'll stay home in my comfortable house and resume my life. There's no point pretending any different."

"Me thinks she protesteth too much." Jack's eyes gleamed with dangerous light again. "Come over here and say it all again. We've got more in common than you think."

"You heard what I said."

"Come on, get back in."

"I don't collect people the way you do, Jack. Do you have a photo album with all your girls in it? A little black book with pictures?"

"And I thought you were a romantic." Jack sighed.

"I am, that's the problem. You're not. You're just a guy looking for some action, and I'm sad to say I provided it in a weak moment. I want much more from a relationship than you're capable of providing, Jack."

Hannah grabbed her towel off the chair and flung the door open to slam it with a very satisfactory crash behind her. Then she had to open it again because she hadn't picked up any clothes to put on after her shower, or shoes to wear up to the house.

He lay in bed and laughed at her as she picked up a T-shirt and underclothes at random. She had no clean, dry socks. Her feet would freeze in sandals.

"Can I borrow some socks?"

"Won't they be too big?"

"I don't care."

"Help yourself. I can't believe that in your gigantic suitcase weighing about ten tons, you don't have socks."

"Guy didn't have any trouble lifting it. He carried both our cases." She took a pair of black socks off the top of his bag and left the room with his infuriating laughter ringing in her ears.

****

Hannah sat at the kitchen table watching Pat make a cake. Jack appeared, smiling and relaxed.

"Sleep well? How's the ankle, Jack?"

"Much better, thanks, Pat. I can put weight on it today. Are the roads still closed?"

Pat slid the cake tin into the oven. "Don't know yet. The twins rode down earlier to finish checking the fences, so they'll be able to tell you at lunch time."

"Will Harvey clear the tree out of the way?" He sat down.

"Might get time later. Not much point until the bridges are clear. Cuppa?"

Hannah filled the kettle. She put toast in the toaster. "I promised to visit Lalla and meet the baby."

"Go down after lunch. The others will be in soon. You two certainly had a good sleep in," said Pat.

"I can only sleep properly in a bed." Hannah avoided Jack's eye. "The night in the car was murder."

"I can sleep anywhere," boasted Jack. "And have."

Oh, really? Try the saggy wire bed with the lumpy wet mattress for size tonight, Jack.

"I suppose you go to such strange places you'd have to," said Pat, which encouraged him to relate

165

bizarre experiences on assignment. Sleeping in a cave wrapped in a smelly horse blanket, in an igloo on soft warm furs, on a train in India jammed in beside people cooking pungent dinners on little gas stoves, on South American buses with goats and pigs stuffed under the seat, and on and on.

Hannah spread marmalade on a piece of toast, listening with half an ear. What a terrible way to pass your time. But what about the explosive and spontaneous burst of passion this morning. How on earth had it happened? She'd been so convinced it wouldn't, that he would never take that step, and she would never respond. But when he kissed her it was all over bar the shouting, so to speak. She was hopeless at hiding her feelings and in such a situation, half asleep and defenceless, with attractive and sexy Jack intent on marauding, forget it. How was a girl supposed to resist? And it looked as though they'd be stuck here another night. It wouldn't happen again!

Hannah set her cup down with a small clunk. "Can I do some washing, please, Pat?"

"Of course."

She rinsed her cup and plate in the sink.

"I'll come with you." Jack followed her to the bunkhouse. Hannah scooped up a bundle of dirty clothes, but he grabbed her around the waist when she turned. "What will we do while the clothes are washing?" He snatched a kiss before she could escape.

"Not that." She pushed him away, dropping damp smelly socks on the floor.

"Spoilsport."

"Jack..."

"What?" He tried for another kiss, but she stepped back.

"This isn't a good idea, you know."

"I think it is. Your socks stink."

"You know what I mean." She scooped up the socks, wrinkling her nose. He was right about the smell, a mixture of mud, mould and wet sneaker.

"We're both adults, Hannah. No harm in enjoying ourselves. And we did, didn't we? It's not as if we're making some great commitment to each other."

She gripped the stinky clothing. He didn't have a clue.

"No," she agreed. "Absolutely not. Which is why I don't want to get into this any further. I told you before. Anyway you're the last person I'd choose when commitments were being made."

His voice rose in exasperation. "Me too. So what's the problem?"

There it was in a nutshell. "If you don't understand, it's hopeless for me to even try to explain."

****

"The river's dropped," said Tony at lunch. "You should be able to get to Goolabri tomorrow."

"Think the others are there?" Hannah looked at Jack.

He concentrated on the piece of bread he was buttering. "Might have gone back to Dubbo."

Sounded like he was sulking now. Big baby. Just because he didn't get to continue on his way with her.

Jack wandered into the living room after lunch and took out one of his cameras. He sat on the couch to load a roll of film. What on earth would he do about the "Natural Woman" photo series thing? Time was ticking away. Bevan would be beside himself if he knew about Penny. He'd be beside himself anyway, thanks to Marilyn's dramatic announcement on national TV that he might be drowned. Lucky the phones were down. Messages would be knee deep when his mobile was back in range.

There was Hannah. No, impossible. She'd never agree, and the idea of working with her on a project this important was frightening. She'd grab any and every opportunity to sabotage it, deliberately or otherwise. He couldn't afford to mess up because Bevan had given the clear implication it was an 'I'll scratch your back, you scratch mine' deal. The thought of losing the backing for his dream trip was simply...well...unthinkable.

They filled in the afternoon wandering about the sheds and stockyards wearing borrowed rubber gumboots and carrying umbrellas. Mid afternoon the sun struggled through the clouds with a few feeble rays. Hannah insisted on taking a photo of Jack, overriding his objections with, "I bet there aren't many pictures of you around."

"It's not that. I'm afraid you'll drop the camera, and I can't afford to keep replacing them."

"It was your fault before, but if you're so worried about it I'll buy you another one." Good grief, what was she saying? It'd cost a fortune, the Transylvanian special.

"Done!"

"Give me the camera." Hannah held out her hand, and he passed it to her as if it were the Holy Grail. "Which button do I press? This one?"

"No! Don't touch anything." He grabbed it, adjusted some settings and handed it back to her. "I'll stand here and you make sure it's in focus by moving this. See?"

"Okay. Stand still. Try to smile." She squinted through the viewfinder at Jack leaning on the wooden railing of the horse yards with a curious horse peering over his shoulder. Click.

"What a winner. Make sure you put it in your exhibition."

"We'll see if it's in focus first. Or if you put your

thumb over the lens."

"Ha, ha, ha."

They visited Lalla and her baby, Veronica—curly dark hair, her dad's beaming smile and her own chubby, sweet face. Jack crawled about on the floor snapping pictures as she played with her blocks. Hannah and Lalla drank tea and laughed at him. He sat up, smiling.

"Kids are great. Totally unselfconscious. I'll send you some prints, Lalla."

Hannah cuddled Veronica on her lap, the baby giggling and smiling as Hannah pulled faces and generally played the fool, trying not to pretend the baby was hers.

"You got any kids?" Clearly, Lalla meant them together as a couple.

"No." Hannah kept her voice level. "We're not married. But Jack has."

"What you got, Jack? Boy or girl?"

"Boy." He stared at Hannah with an expression similar to the one he'd worn on her doorstep that first day. "But he lives with his mother. I don't."

"Seemed like you two were married," said Lalla. "Gettin' married?"

"No," said Jack. "Hannah doesn't want to."

Hannah shook her head. "Certainly not to him. But Jack doesn't want to be married either, to anyone."

"Shame." Lalla, smiled her lovely, shy smile. "You both be good parents and you go good together."

"We'd fight all the time," said Hannah.

"Bit of fightin' doesn't matter."

"Making up's fun, eh, Lalla?" Jack winked at her. She giggled and put her hand over her mouth.

"I'd love to have babies one day." Hannah bounced Veronica up and down on her knee. "Jack's too busy tramping about the world with his camera to bother with his family."

"You like doin' that?"

"I do, but Hannah doesn't know what I want or what I think." Jack smiled at Lalla. "She just thinks she does and passes judgement."

"What do you mean by that remark? Hannah passes judgement," she demanded as they walked to the main house." You have a son you don't see and you told me yourself you'd end up a lonely old man in a tent with a camera. It was a reasonable observation, I thought."

"Did I say it was what I wanted?" Did he? Hannah frowned. "And my relationship with my son has nothing to do with you even though you think for some reason you're qualified to judge."

"You're being pedantic."

"You make all sorts of assumptions about me."

"Such as?"

"I don't want a family, I'm pedantic and fussy, I'm incapable of loving someone, I'm not romantic..."

"You're definitely not romantic!"

"I can be."

"You think my other half thing is romantic claptrap."

"It is." Jack snorted his disdain.

"Rubbish."

"I can be as romantic as the next guy."

"If the next guy's Harvey."

"I can be romantic when the woman inspires me."

"So I don't make you feel romantic. Now there's an extremely romantic thing to say. I'm in a swoon already."

"Do you want me to be romantic with you?" Jack raised an eyebrow.

"It would test your credibility to breaking point, but as you'll fail dismally, it's academic."

"Will you admit I can be romantic when I am? You have to be fair."

Hannah studied him for a moment. Was he being serious? Looked that way. Bruised ego. "Yes."

"And then you'll go to bed with me again." He leapt aside as she swatted at him with the furled umbrella.

"You haven't got a hope."

Hannah went to the laundry to collect the washing. She dumped Jack's things in a pile on his suitcase, and folded hers in neat piles in her own. Then she headed for the kitchen to help Pat with dinner and to prevent Jack making any more suggestions as to her diet. He was sitting at the table with a glass of beer in his hand laughing uproariously at a story of Harvey's.

"Harve says the bridge is clear," said Pat.

Hannah picked up a knife to help chop carrots. "We'll leave in the morning. Thank you, Pat. I'll never forget our stay."

A loud burst of laughter covered Pat's reply. She shook her head at the men.

"And then there was old Kev," said Harvey. "Never did have much luck with his teeth. Reckons the trouble started when he was seven and his brother jumped off the shed roof and landed on him. Jarred something loose, and his teeth went all chalky and brittle from then on. Kept breaking them on things, and by the time he grew up he had a couple of false ones in the front. Well, one day he was leaning over tipping the last of a bag of chaff into the bin for the horse, and the horse had his head in the way. A couple of Kev's kids were tossing a tennis ball about. One of them threw it and hit the horse in the flank. He tossed his head up real hard and banged Kev in the jaw. Kev reckons when he came to from seeing stars and the world spinning around, he realised his false teeth were missing. They looked everywhere, round on the ground and in the feed bin, then one of the kids says 'There they

171

are Dad,' and points at the horse. He had Kev's two front teeth stuck in the top of his head."

"We'd better get dinner on the table," Pat said to Hannah when she could be heard over the laughter. "Harve'll go on all night with stories like that."

****

Hannah woke as dawn light seeped through the blind, rolled over and leapt straight out of the double bed. Jack was sleeping like a baby right there next to her, and she hadn't even realised he'd got in. He was supposed to be sleeping with the spider!

Jack opened bleary eyes as she stomped about collecting clean clothes, making no attempt to keep quiet.

"Do you mind? Some of us are still asleep."

She paused mid-stomp. "What are you doing sleeping here?"

"What? Even if I was properly awake I couldn't answer that."

"You're supposed to be sleeping in one of those bunks."

"Who says?" His laugh was smothered as he rubbed his face.

"I do—I must have forgotten to tell you. How did you get in?"

"I opened the door." He yawned displaying most of his teeth and tonsils. Hannah turned to examine the door handle and its lock. She hadn't thought to check if it worked. It didn't.

"I meant to lock the door."

"Too late now." His eyes closed. She sent him an impotent glare and went to the bathroom.

****

The sun shone bright and warm in a cloudless sky today and if it wasn't for the puddles and mud everywhere the idea of rain seemed impossible. The family gathered in the yard after breakfast to say goodbye. The dog approached Hannah wagging his tail and she patted his head.

"Group photo, please," called Jack. He began organising them into place. She stood to one side with the dog by her feet, watching them, all self conscious, as they joked and laughed and smiled, while one of the world's best photographers took their picture. They insisted on including Hannah in the next one. Then Guy took one of the Beddowes with Hannah and Jack. Then it was done. Time to go.

Hannah threw her arms around Pat. "Thank you so much."

Pat hugged her in return. "Come and see us again."

Hannah turned to Guy and Lalla while Jack made his farewells to Pat. Tony and Linda had already raced off on the horses with the shouted intention of beating them to the car.

They squeezed into the ute beside Harvey to churn over the sodden paddocks. It didn't seem to take nearly as long this time. Tony and Linda trotted down the long slope to the road, the blue heeler dog racing beside them. Jack's car sat abandoned in the distance, the sun sparkling off the windows.

Hannah sniffed as they got into the car and Jack, in the passenger seat because his ankle was too stiff for him to drive in safety, looked at her in surprise.

"You hardly know them and you're crying?"

"I am not." She sniffed again, hard, and turned the key in the ignition. "Hope this old bomb starts." The engine roared into life.

"You can drive, can't you?" Jack threw her a quick look as they lurched forward towards the fallen tree. "We have to turn around. Can you manage, do you think?"

Hannah ignored him, lips pursed, concentrating

on the three-point turn in such a cramped area. There'd be no end of it if she bogged the Volvo in the mud on the edge of the road.

"Just checking," he murmured.

At the bridge which had thwarted them that first day the level had dropped, but water swirled, muddy and swift beneath the wooden supports. Branches and debris piled in a messy tangle against the length of the bridge, but it looked solid and safe. Hannah drove straight across without hesitation.

"Harvey said Goolabri was about fifty kilometres," said Jack. "This isn't the main road."

"I know. Guy told me. He thought it was hilariously funny, especially as the other road was open. I'm sorry." Best to get in early and forestall him. Strange he hadn't mentioned it before.

"Why? It's not your fault we got stuck."

"I made us go on this road and I made us go over the first bridge."

He reached out a hand to touch light fingers to her cheek. "No, you didn't. We decided. I saw the signpost too, and I wouldn't have driven over the bridge if I thought we'd be stuck."

Hannah smiled. Was his attempt at being romantic making a shaky start already? He'd have to do better than that. But admitting he was partly to blame would be new to him. The caressing fingers almost made her purr.

"You don't make the decisions in this outfit, anyway," he said.

"Oh, yeah?"

"Yeah." But he was grinning and so was she.

In the Goolabri pub, an orange-haired woman, jovial and large with multiple wobbling chins, told them their friends had gone back to Dubbo two days ago. But the phones were working.

"Who should we call first?" Jack paused, finger poised to dial.

"Bernard. Then the police."

Hannah listened in as Jack made the call, her head close to his as they shared the receiver. Within seconds Bernard lost the phone to an hysterical Marilyn. Jack held the phone away, shaking his head.

Interpreting the squawks, Hannah said, "Don't tell me, let me guess. Hannah made us take the wrong road, got the car stuck, pushed you down a rabbit hole, and didn't nurse your injury. And tried to drown you."

"Isn't that right?" Grinning. With his hand over the receiver.

"Better ring the police or you'll be reporting an assault and battery as well."

Next, Hannah rang her parents in Brisbane while Jack lounged against the bar.

He straightened as she hung up. "Are they worriers?"

"Not Dad, but Mum's hyper emotional. She's an actress, very theatrical both on and off stage."

His expression implied she'd explained a lot. "What's her name?"

"Tildy Crawford. She mostly does theatre work in Brisbane, but a few TV shows and minor roles in movies. Shall we go?" Hannah swung her handbag over her shoulder.

"I'd better ring my publisher."

"I'll wait outside." She strode towards the door as he dialled.

"Bevan? Jack. I'm fine. I'll be back in town in a day or two. I'll call." Either an answering machine or Bevan didn't have much to say.

He followed her to the car and climbed in beside her. "What does your father do?"

Hannah accelerated on to the road. "Retired Navy." Goolabri receded into the distance.

"You must've travelled a lot with postings."

"Yes. All the time. Now I want to stay put. I moved from Brisbane to Sydney a while ago and I'm not moving again."

"How did your mother manage her career?"

"She did bits and pieces wherever we were living. I couldn't live the way Mum did. Dad was at sea all the time. But they've been in Brisbane for years now, since I was in High School. It's very unfair for one person's career to stifle another's."

She hadn't see it with such clarity before Adrian, being blinded by love. Now she knew.

Jack shifted in his seat. "You were the one talking about compromise before. They must have discussed it. They must have decided they loved each other enough to put up with the travel and separations. It can work."

"Hah! I can't see that applying to you. You told me yourself you wouldn't compromise your work for a woman."

"True. I wouldn't, but it doesn't mean other people can't."

Hannah stamped her foot harder on the accelerator making the car lurch and bounce over the pot-holed road.

He glanced across with raised eyebrows. "Slow down. Or Marilyn might truly have something to blame you for. My wrecked undercarriage."

Hannah eased her foot in case he was right and the car suffered some kind of injury. "What did Bernard say?"

"Not much before Marilyn came on. They've abandoned the rest of the tour. Too much flood damage. Have to finish it later. Next year probably."

"Where are they?"

"In Dubbo, but they'll leave for Sydney straight away. No point waiting, we'll be two hours yet."

The sign post that had started them off on their adventure appeared ahead. Hannah slowed to stare down the side road, innocuous and attractive now in bright sunshine, winding peacefully through the paddocks and lined with gum trees all new washed and shiny leaved.

"Amazing to think what happened down there," Jack said.

"It looks so...innocent. You didn't come out of it too well. Twisted ankle and a broken camera."

"You're forgetting the best part. Two nights in bed with you. And a morning."

"Yes, well, you can forget it." Funny how it kept popping back into her mind at the most inappropriate moments.

"Why? I enjoyed myself, brief though it was. So did you."

"It won't happen again."

"How do you know?"

"Because I'm half of it and I say so." She frowned. "We've had this conversation. Stop playing games with me! You know it and I know it. I don't want to fall in love with you. You don't want to fall in love with me. That's assuming of course, you're even capable of falling in love."

"Did I mention falling in love?" More raised eyebrows and innocent face. "And you're making assumptions again."

Hannah was silent. He hadn't, of course. Why was love always in her thoughts? A few kilometres further, she said, "You're trying to be romantic, remember? And you're not succeeding. Surprise, surprise."

"I haven't warmed up yet. Being romantic with you takes a lot of concentration."

Closer to Dubbo Jack called Bernard on his mobile phone. After a lengthy conversation he disconnected. "Bernard booked us a room at the same motel in case we want to stay here tonight."

"One room?"

"Place was booked solid, and he only got it on a cancellation."

How very convenient. "Do we need to stay? It's not even lunch time."

"I want my ankle x-rayed. Pat said there could be a hairline fracture."

"Can't you wait until we get to Sydney?"

"I'd rather sit in Casualty here for an hour than half a day in the city, thank you very much."

Three tedious hours at the Dubbo Base Hospital resulted in no fracture.

****

Hannah made tea while Jack sprawled on one of the twin beds playing the invalid because he had a pressure bandage on his ankle. Even with her back turned her skin prickled. She knew he was remembering their session in bed, undressing her in his mind. Planning his next move.

Be strong. Resist him. Don't let her mind wander back there, don't allow herself to dwell on the sensations, the emotions he aroused in her. Too dangerous. He was off limits. But here they were again. The two of them. In one small room. Not the same as sharing the shearers' quarters somehow. They'd been in extreme circumstances—survivors. Motel rooms had a certain...connotation. There was a degree of sleaze associated with unmarried couples sharing a motel room. They did it for one reason only. Sex.

With Jack.

But this room had two single beds. She set the cups on their saucers with a clatter. A teaspoon slipped from her clammy, clumsy fingers and landed on the floor.

"That one's yours." Jack. From the bed. Sprawled long-limbed and inviting.

She ripped open a little paper sachet holding a teabag, and pulled the tag right off.

"How come Pat got the idea we'd be happy to share a double bed?" Hannah spun around to face him.

He shrugged with elaborate innocence. "I've no idea. But what could I say?"

She thumped his cup of tea on the bedside table. Liquid slopped into the saucer. His lips had an indescribably sexy curve. She'd kissed them. They'd kissed her, roamed over her body, driven her crazy...

"No chocolate biscuits?"

"No."

A hand snaked out and pulled her unresisting down beside him. "Wish we had a double bed tonight." Those lips landed on hers and were just as intoxicating as every other time.

Hopeless.

Hannah melted against him, her brain shut down. She had to put her arms around him or she'd fall off the narrow bed. He shifted and drew her closer so she could lie beside him. His hands roved over her body doing the things they'd done the previous morning, sending rational thought flying.

Hands tugged her T-shirt free of her jeans, fingers lifted it to tease her breast through the soft cotton bra. She sighed into his mouth, wriggling to allow her hand access to the waistband of his pants. He helped by releasing his hold for a moment and wrenching his shirt off over his head.

"Mmmm." Not sure whose voice was whose, whose hands were whose, whose breath was whose. Cascades of delight coursed from breasts to belly. Heat rose.

Someone knocked on the door. Hannah froze.

"Ignore them." His breath was hot on her cheek. But the knock came again accompanied by a woman's voice.

"Jack? Jack darling, are you there?"

He sat up abruptly. "Good grief. It's Penny."

Chapter Eleven

Hannah leapt off the bed and scurried into the bathroom. Jack opened the door and greeted Penny, but their voices were muffled by the intervening walls and door.

A flushed face stared at her from the mirror. Hair awry, as usual. She tucked in her T-shirt, washed her face, brushed her teeth, took two deep breaths and opened the door. A fallen sock lay in her path, but she pretended it wasn't there and prepared herself to meet the glare of the other woman. No. She was technically the other woman. No. They'd broken up. Whatever.

What was she doing here?

Penny was much prettier in person than the photo Jack had in his wallet. Her arm lay snug and familiar around his waist and she was gazing into his face. A proprietary gaze, of total devotion. Hannah clutched the back of a chair in case her wobbly knees gave out.

"You must be Hannah." The steel-tipped voice didn't go with the baby doll face.

"Yes. I suppose you two have a lot to talk about." She didn't dare glance at Jack. She might spit in his eye.

"Yes, we do. We can go to my room." Penny owned a smile which must have cost her parents a fortune in orthodontist bills. "Give you some privacy. You must be sick of the sight of each other. I know Jack can be difficult sometimes...my grouchy old bear." She hugged him to her. "I can't imagine how you managed." The blue eyes met Hannah's.

"With difficulty. He's such an old bear at times, you're right."

"How long have you been here?" The question barely managed to squeeze out between his clenched teeth. Caught out at last.

"Since yesterday. Marilyn rang me the day after you disappeared. I decided to fly over yesterday with the news film crew to be closer, in case..." A pause ensued just long enough for all the terrible implications of the 'in case' to be imagined. "Marilyn called me this morning to tell me. She's been marvellous. So understanding and thoughtful. I couldn't wait to see you, darling."

She stretched up on her toes and kissed his cheek, clinging to him. Penny and Marilyn would get on like a house on fire. Two doting women. He should be in hog heaven.

"Come on, darling. We'll take your things to my room. Leave Hannah in peace." Hannah received a sickeningly sweet smile.

"No." His firmness startled them both. "We need to talk, Penny." He turned from open-mouthed girlfriend to stunned travel companion-come-lover. "I'll be back. Excuse us, please."

Penny's smile changed to a laser-eyed stare. She released her grip and stalked to the door. Jack flung Hannah a last intense but inscrutable look, then followed her.

Hannah collapsed on to the bed. It was starting. Just as she knew it would. Jack and his women. How could she let him kiss her again? No way would she end up like Penny, chasing him around the country, unable to accept he'd moved on. But he hadn't moved on from Penny. She'd walked out on him. He'd told her himself, and blamed his foul mood on it that first day.

Grouchy old bear? Apt, but not quite how she would have put it. Much too polite. Was he still emotionally involved with the woman? Face to face all of a sudden, did he want her back? He must, or he would have sent her packing on the doorstep.

She stared at her hands and stretched out the fingers. Ringless.

Penny had rings. One in particular on her third finger, left hand. Was it an engagement ring? No, Jack wouldn't have proposed to her. He wouldn't propose to anyone. Not his style even when the woman was carrying his child.

Who would he choose to spend the night with? Blonde Bimbo or Annoying Hannah? Mr. Romance had a big decision to make, and a lot of ground to make up whichever way he went. Annoying Hannah sure wouldn't let him touch her again. In fact, the lock on this room would work perfectly.

Her stomach growled. She needed food. How long would Jack be? Or would he change his mind, be sweet-talked into staying with her? Locking him out would drive him back to the woman sure as eggs. Did she want that? A few days ago she wouldn't have cared what he did, but now... The hollowness in her stomach must be from hunger.

There was a pizza shop across the street. Twenty minutes later she returned with two large Supremes emitting mouth-watering aromas. As she crossed the parking area Penny emerged from a room further down the row. Her face had lost the chirpy confidence of earlier. Lonely and miserable. Hannah knew all about playing the solo blues.

Their paths would intersect in a few paces. She steeled herself for the collision of wills. Where was Jack? His car had gone. Had he fled the scene and left them to fight over him? Coward. The sisters should stick together in the face of men like him.

"Hello." Penny tried a smile. What had he said to her?

"Where's Jack?"

"I don't know. Off on his own somewhere as usual. I shouldn't have come here. I should have known it was over."

Rarely had she seen a more complete change. Confident lioness to whimpering mush in the space of thirty minutes. Oh Jack, Jack, you heartbreaker. There but for the grace of God...

"I've plenty of pizza here. Like some?"

"Oh, Hannah." The sad face brightened for a moment. "You really are very kind."

"We can't have you moping about on your own. He's not worth it, I'm sure."

"I'm beginning to think no man is."

Inside, Penny perched herself on the edge of a chair, holding a slice of pizza between two manicured fingers. "Thanks, Hannah. You're so kind. Jack told me about your recent...umm...medical problems." Oh yes? Up to his old tricks again. "Are the headaches getting better now? You're looking very well."

"Thank you." She hesitated. "I hardly ever get headaches anymore." Except the ones provided by Jack. "And I haven't had a fit for six months at least. I don't hear the voices, either."

What had he been saying?! Alcoholic, vegetarian show-off not good enough now? What a miserable, weaselly way of explaining their connection.

"I suppose you have to keep taking your medication." Penny smiled her complete understanding, encouragement and support.

****

Jack closed the door of Penny's room with a great flood of relief surging through his body. She'd taken it surprisingly well considering the effort she'd made to get here. And she didn't have a clue about his relationship with Hannah, such as it was. The relationship which defied definition as it stood at the moment. He'd have Marilyn to thank for some of the groundwork about Hannah with Penny, plus his own improvisations. He sauntered along the walkway outside the rooms with a pleased smile.

If there was one thing he knew how to do, it was break up and stay on civilised terms. Practice makes perfect. Now, back to Hannah to pick up in the delightful spot they'd left off. Trouble was she'd have cooled to the temperature of Arctic ice by now, judging by the look on her face when he left with Penny. But now he knew the remedy. He knew exactly what she liked.

Romantic! He had to be romantic. Jack paused. They'd passed a bottle shop a couple of blocks down the street. A bottle of wine would loosen her up, then they could go out somewhere for dinner. Or maybe order takeaway and drink the wine in bed. Even better.

Fifteen minutes later he was back with a bottle tucked under his arm. The door to their room was locked. Tap, tap. Tap. Voices. Female voices. Who on earth was in there? Tap, tap, tap, tap. Louder.

Hannah opened the door with a slice of pizza in her hand. "Hello, where did you go? I thought you'd cleared out and left us here when I saw the car was gone."

"I went to get this." He held up the wine. Left us? Who? Not...

"Hope you don't mind, Jack," Penny called from inside the room. "But I met Hannah coming back with pizza, and she invited me in to share."

"You don't mind, do you, Jack?" Hannah smiled that infuriating smile of hers.

"Mind? Why would I mind?" Who would mind having their teary-eyed ex and the girl they wanted to ravish in the same room?

"I didn't know what type of pizza you liked so I got what I like."

"Figures."

She lowered her voice accompanied by the hint of a frown. "I also didn't know if or when you'd be back."

"Of course, I was coming back," he hissed. "I went to get some wine."

"Good thinking! Glass of wine, Penny?" She stepped back into the room.

"Love some. Hannah's a treasure, Jack. You're lucky you were stuck with her."

"Wasn't I?" he growled.

"Have some pizza, grouchy old bear," offered Hannah.

Jack sat on his bed and ate pizza in sullen silence. He could quite cheerfully murder the woman. There were plenty of suitably painful attachments on his pocket knife.

"How are you getting back to Sydney, Penny?" Did she need to sound so concerned?

"I don't know, I thought..." She looked at Jack. He looked back, expressionless. What did she expect? No one asked her to come. Why would he? She'd hurled all sorts of insults at him and accused him of selfishness before she stormed out last week. This was all part of her act. Make him feel sorry for her, do the helpless little woman bit complete with tears. Penny was not a helpless woman. She wanted him hog-tied and compliant. "I'll take the bus," she finished when he offered no solution.

"Why don't you come with us?"

Jack almost choked. Good one, Hannah!

"Would that be all right?" Penny looked from Hannah to Jack with her big, luminous, blue eyes.

"Sure, why not?" Hannah beamed from one to the other. "Then, if I have a relapse there'll be someone to help Jack cope."

Penny stood up. "I'd better go now. Thanks for the pizza. See you in the morning. Goodnight."

"Goodnight, Penny." Jack met her gaze. "I'm

sorry."

"Yes, I know. I shouldn't have come." A feeble smile, downcast eyes.

Hannah closed the door after her and turned to face him.

"What have you got to say for yourself?" He threw his pizza crust into the box with such force it bounced out on to the floor.

"Me?" Hannah picked up the fallen crust with elaborate care. "Exactly what is my 'problem'? Apart from you, that is."

"I told her you'd been ill." Jack got off the bed and went into the bathroom to wash his hands.

"What sort of ill?" Not half as ill as he was going to be in a minute. Women! He'd had it with all of them! "Jack?"

"Mentally ill. You are, aren't you? Most of the time you give a good impression of a looney." He came out of the bathroom to glare at her. "Inviting Penny in to eat pizza! What was that?"

"She looked sad. I felt sorry for her. You're such a miserable, manipulative beast."

"What about me? What about how I felt when I got back and she was here with you?"

"You'd cleared out, the way you always do. Anyway, you can cope. You do it all the time, don't you? From what I can tell, your feelings are never fully engaged, so what you feel is hardly relevant."

"Hannah, you have no idea how I feel. You make these stupid accusations and generalisations..." Disgust halted the flow. "I'm going to bed."

"Me too. And make sure you stay in your own bed."

"You don't need to worry, I can assure you. Forget barge poles, I wouldn't touch you with a flagpole."

"Good."

****

Jack woke with the slamming of car doors and a revving engine. He lay in bed staring at Hannah fast asleep in the other bed. How could he be romantic with a crazy woman like her? Why was he even bothering to prove it to her? He didn't have to. There were plenty more where she came from. Well, not exactly where she came from. But he was fed up with her and her lunacies. Sure she was entertaining in short bursts and sexy as could be...but not enough to outweigh the nuisance value and the irritation.

Why had he ever become involved with her? She had disaster written all over her from the very first encounter. The time had come to call it quits. The interlude was over. They'd drive straight through to Sydney, and he'd be rid of her tonight. He flung the bedclothes off and sprang out of bed.

"Wake up, Hannah." No response, not that he expected one. When he came out of the bathroom she'd rolled over and buried her head under the covers so just a few strands of gorgeous coppery hair strayed over the pillow.

"Get up." He yanked the bedclothes right off her bed.

"Go away, you sadist," she shrieked, and groped for the covers.

"I'll go away to Sydney and leave you here. Come on. If we leave soon we can get there tonight. It's a six-hour drive at least."

She stuck her head under the pillow, groaning. Her foot made a good handle to pull. She kicked hard but he dragged her off the bed and she hit the floor with a thump.

"Ow, you rotten, big bully!" Hannah sat up, wide awake now, rubbing her bottom. "That hurt."

"You'll have to learn to get up in the mornings."

"Why?"

"It's the best part of the day."

"You forget, Mr. Smarty Pants, I'm a night worker." She crawled up on to the bed.

"Not recently, you haven't been."

"Recently, I've hardly had any sleep!"

"Go and have a shower."

Grumbling, she went to the bathroom. Jack stuffed clothes into his bag and bundled her bedding back on to the bed. He looked underneath the bed and dragged out her T-shirt and a sock. She'd be out of the bathroom in a minute because she hadn't taken any underwear in with her. Hopeless.

Hannah came out after her shower, sweet-smelling, naked, wrapped in a far-too-small towel. His fingers itched to snatch it away as she sashayed across to her suitcase and bent over, giving him a show of bare legs below a tantalising glimpse of upper, upper thighs. She turned. The towel slipped as she clutched clean clothing. A flash of rounded breasts.

"Whoops." She grabbed at the towel, opened it wide revealing everything he'd already savoured, then secured it with a firm twist of the wrist.

"Hannah! For heavens sake!" He gritted his teeth against the rush of blood to his groin.

"No time for fooling around, Jack. We have to leave. Penny will be waiting." She slipped past him and darted into the bathroom.

"Thanks to you." He flung his arms wide and cried in despair, "Why, oh, why did I let Bernard talk me into picking you up?"

"As long as I keep taking my medication I shouldn't cause you any trouble." The dimples flirted with him as she peeped coyly around the door.

"You've caused nothing but trouble since I met you." The door closed. "Why would you change now?" Six hours. Just six long hours.

****

Jack drove, insisting his ankle was fine. Hannah

sat in the front. Penny squashed into the back surrounded by camera bags and her own overnight bag. Hannah drove part of the way while Jack dozed in the passenger seat. Penny sat staring out the window, silent. Hannah could only guess as to her thoughts. Not happy ones, she suspected. Jack would not do the same to her. He could romance her all her liked, but he would not wheedle his way any further into her heart than he already had.

They reached Sydney as night fell. Penny insisted they drop her at Strathfield suburban rail station, where she could take a direct train home. Jack carried her bag to the station entrance. He kissed her cheek, turned and strode back to the car with neither a backward glance nor a limp. Out with the old, in with the new. The driver's door slammed and he started the engine without a word. Out with the old, out with the new? End of the romancing? She wouldn't notice.

The house in Balmain was in darkness. Hannah breathed a sigh of relief as the familiar and comforting smell of home reached out to greet her. She switched on the hall light, remembered about the rug and led Jack, lugging her suitcase, through to the living room where he dropped it beside the couch. He stretched and rubbed his back.

She flopped on to the couch with a sigh. Her body still vibrated as if she were driving. Now what would happen? Was this the end? They'd come full circle—the skirmishing had begun here in her living room. Why didn't he just go?

"Mind if I use the bathroom before I leave?"

"Through there." She pointed to the passageway.

Something rubbed against her leg. She looked down through bleary eyes. Freddo wound between her feet. He sported a bandage on his tail, which meant he couldn't hold it up at the usual perky angle, but by the volume of purring issuing forth from his sleek black-and-white body he'd forgiven her. She scratched his head and ran her hand hard down his back, which she knew he liked.

She went into the kitchen and filled the kettle for tea. Maybe she should offer Jack a cup. Thanks to his insistence on driving straight through after lunch, she was hungry, but Steve probably didn't have any food in the house. He hadn't done any washing up for a week, by the state of the kitchen. What a slob.

Footsteps sounded overhead. Steve must be home after all. Unless they had other less savoury company. Perhaps they needed an attack cat rather than hopeless Freddo, who still twined himself around her ankles. Jack, still in the loo, was about as useful as the cat.

Hannah picked up the breadknife and heart pounding, crept into the living room. An apparition in rumpled pyjamas crept towards the kitchen wielding a cricket bat and a ferocious expression. She cried out in fright. He jumped and stubbed his bare toes on one of the armchairs. Freddo rushed past them both and disappeared in a black-and-white streak.

"Hannah! Ow!" Steve dropped the bat and hopped about rubbing his foot with both hands. "Aren't you supposed to be in Gulargambone or somewhere?"

"What are you doing? You scared the life out of me."

"I thought you were a burglar! You could have told me you were coming home in the middle of the night!"

She could have, although it was hardly the middle of the night. She modified her tone.

"Sorry. I didn't think of it. I thought you'd be out. You usually are."

"I'm sick." Steve's voice turned to a croak and he

sagged against the doorframe. "I've been in bed since yesterday. Flu."

Come to think of it, he did look sick—all pale and sorry for himself even without the newly injured toes.

"You look awful. Better go back to bed. Like a cup of tea?"

Using the cricket bat as a crutch, he hobbled back up the stairs, groaning with each step. Hannah went to the kitchen to finish making a pot of tea. She carried two mugs upstairs and sat on Steve's bed. He lay against the pillows, wan and pitiful. Jack was taking ages in the bathroom. Perhaps he'd gone to sleep.

Steve accepted his mug with a weak smile. He took a feeble sip and his eyes flew open.

"What did you put in this!?"

"Lemon and a shot or two of whisky. Maybe three. Did you get my messages?"

Steve took another, deeper drink and smacked his lips. "Yes. What did you do to Freddo?"

She explained, leaving out references to Jack and his surliness, and glossing over the trouble Freddo had caused them, and how it had been his fault anyway, getting under her feet and annoying her when she was in a rush. Doubtful if Steve would be very sympathetic right at the moment. He'd uncovered his foot and was examining his bruised toes.

"Is Freddo all right?"

"The vet hopes there won't be nerve damage. The bones were shoved out of alignment a bit. Might end up with a bent tail. You'll have to pay for it, Han."

"Yes." The toilet flushed downstairs.

"I didn't expect you back for another week."

"I know." How come he didn't ask who else was in the house? Perhaps his ears were blocked from the flu. She yawned. "I'm exhausted. I can't wait to sleep in my own bed. I'll tell you what happened tomorrow."

Steve pursed his lips as he sucked air in between his teeth. His brow wrinkled. "That's just it. Han, you can't sleep in your bed because Matt and Irene are here from Melbourne. They've both got what I've got and they're in your bed. And Jenny's in the spare room." Her bedroom, her music room! All contaminated!

"What?"

"I thought you'd be away. And they didn't know they'd get sick."

"So what am I supposed to do?"

"The couch?" Steve coughed pitifully.

Hannah glared at him, then picked up her tea and left the room. She marched down the stairs and into the kitchen, where Jack was lounging against the bench with a mug in his hand. Freddo wound about his ankles purring like a lawn mower.

He took one look at her face. "What's the problem?"

"Steve's filled the house with sick people and they're in my bed! "

"How many?"

"Two in my bed, one in my music room."

"Where are you going to sleep?" A definite gleam in his eye.

"Steve suggested the couch."

"Looks comfortable." He put his mug down. "Thanks for the bathroom and the tea. I'll be on my way now."

She followed him through the living room.

"Goodnight," he said.

He strode down the hallway. Now or never. Courage.

"Jack?"

He stopped.

"Have you got a spare room?"

"Yes." Although he turned to face her, she couldn't see his expression because of the shadow from the hall light.

"With a proper bed in it?"

"Yes."

Hannah drew a deep breath and walked to within a pace of where he stood. His face was impassive. He knew what she was going to ask, and he wasn't going to make it easy. She'd have to beg.

"Jack? Can I stay with you, please? Just for tonight. Please?"

He stared at her without uttering a word. She waited. Nothing.

"Fine," she snapped. "Forget it. I know you can't wait to be rid of me. Thanks for the lift. Good night."

What a waste of a grovel. Should have known he wouldn't care. Must have been mad to even think he would say yes, let alone offer to help. She marched to the couch and began removing the pillows and tossing them on to the other chairs. Was there enough extra bedding in the house? Her continental quilt would be covered with flu germs. There might be another blanket somewhere in the back of the linen cupboard.

"All right." Long-suffering. "One night."

Hannah froze mid throw. "I'm only coming with you because I have to. Right?"

"Right. Why else would you? Why else would I let you?"

"Right. Take my bag?"

"Yes, boss." Jack picked up her suitcase again. He put it down. "Like to take the bricks out first?"

Chapter Twelve

An unlived-in air pervaded Jack's house in Glebe. A sad little one-floor terrace needing company and a coat of paint. He used it as a stopover between trips. Somewhere to dump gear, change clothes, organise his next assignment.

They ate take away Chinese in tense silence broken only by muttered requests for rice or more soy sauce. Afterwards he showed her the spare room and announced he was going to bed.

Skis leant in one corner, and a bookshelf crammed full of magazines and files took up most of one wall. A computer sat on a small desk. The narrow single bed covered by an orange and blue Mexican-patterned blanket was squashed between it and the wall.

Jack came in with an armful of bedding and dropped it on the bed. "Bathroom's through the back next to the kitchen."

She nodded. "Thanks. Does the roof leak?"

He ignored her. "I'm going to bed."

Hannah spread sheets and blankets, changed into her pyjamas, hopped into the narrow bed. Despite her exhaustion, sleep eluded her. Being near him, being in his house, was too disquieting, too difficult, and altogether too upsetting. She'd go home as soon as she could. Get back to normal. The way she'd been before he crashed into her life.

When she woke next morning, late, the house was empty. Jack must have been out, in and out again because there was new milk in the fridge and fresh bread on the bench. She showered in the poky little bathroom and enjoyed a leisurely breakfast poring over the newspaper which he'd left folded on the table.

Hannah licked jam from her fingers, wiped up the blob she'd dropped with appropriate accuracy on the photo of the previous Prime Minister, licked her finger again to turn the page. The doorbell rang, strident in the quiet house.

A plump, grey-haired lady with a very anxious expression peered past her down the hallway. "Hello. Is Jack at home?"

"No, I'm sorry."

"I am Lucia from next door. I want to ask him a very special favour."

A favour? Right up Jack's alley. "Perhaps I can help? I'm Hannah. Come in and have a cup of tea. I'm sure Jack would love to do whatever it is."

Lucia, clutching her tea cup in both strong, workworn hands, poured out her woe between slurps.

"Forty years anniversary. So romantic. My Luigi's idea. Every photographer is all booked, and I don't want my brother Carlo with his camera although he offered. I want special photographs. What am I to do? Luigi saw Jack's car home again and he said, 'Go and ask Jack, he takes pictures for a living.'"

Here was an opportunity not to be missed. "He sure does. I'm positive he'll be delighted to help."

"But will he be free? All the photographers are booked months ahead." Lucia dabbed at her eyes with a small lacy handkerchief. Hannah patted her arm.

"He'll be free. We came back early because of the terrible floods."

"Thank you, Hannah. You are such a kind girl."

Wasn't she just? "Don't worry about a thing. I'll send Jack over for the details." Chase him over with

195

a broom if necessary.

The front door opened and closed.

"Here he is now." Lucia looked towards the sounds as if they heralded the second coming.

Jack's glance landed first on Hannah. Her smile was far too innocent. What was she up to? Then he saw his innocuous neighbour. "Ciao, Lucia."

"Ciao, Jack."

"I've just been telling Lucia how you would love to help her," said Hannah.

Jack's eyes narrowed. "I thought you might have gone home by now."

"No, still here." Her smile was too innocent. She was up to something. The doorbell rang. "Excuse me."

She leapt to her feet. "I'll go. You listen to Lucia."

She scampered away before he could object. His ears strained to hear who it was but couldn't catch more than the murmur of voices.

Lucia clutched her hands together, eyes filled with tears. "I need a photographer for Saturday night. All the family is coming, and the other photographer has let me down. Hannah said you would be free and I would be so-o-o grateful."

Jack hesitated. This sort of work was the pits, plus he had the other thing to worry about. Finding and photographing a woman. A deadline. He didn't have the time and he certainly didn't have the inclination.

He started to say, "I can give you some names..." when Bevan and Hannah appeared in the doorway. Bevan, in his casual designer clothes and wearing his urbane friendly face. Checking up on him.

"Jack. Glad you're home safe and sound." The smooth expression and good-buddy handshake gave no hint of the steel beneath the surface.

"Like a cup of tea, Bevan?" Hannah turned.

"Jack?"

"Love one, thanks, darling," Bevan said. Darling? He'd only just met her. "What a treasure."

Hannah went into the kitchen, smiling.

"She is," announced Lucia.

Jack stared from one to the other. Had he missed something? "You've known her thirty seconds. Believe me she wears off very quickly." He slumped on to a chair.

"She has a kind heart." Lucia turned to Bevan. "Jack is going to take photographs for my fortieth anniversary."

"Well as a matter of fact..." He folded the newspaper and pushed it aside. Something sticky...jam. Scowling, he pulled out his handkerchief and rubbed at his hand.

"Congratulations! Well done. How very romantic." Bevan, who had two ex-wives and was working on the third.

"It is, isn't it?" Here she was with more tea and cups. She'd made herself extraordinarily at home in his kitchen. "Jack wouldn't understand, though. Romance."

"Don't." He must have looked as angry as he was because she, for once, stopped talking.

"How's the Natural Woman coming along?" asked Bevan into the sudden silence. Maybe he should have let her keep on. Jack pursed his lips.

"Natural woman?" Hannah's eyebrows shot skyward. "Would this be natural as in *au naturale*, as in nude?"

Jack scowled, Lucia giggled. Bevan said, "No, it's for a very prestigious book we're doing incorporating the work of ten of the top Australian photographers. The theme is Natural Woman, or a portrait of a woman. Some of the shots could be nude, of course, but the idea is to capture the essence of a woman's character. How she sees herself

197

rather than how the photographer poses her, combined with the skill of the photographer as an artist."

"Interesting. Who's your model?"

"The photographers are using women who are close to them—wives, daughters, mothers, intimate friends."

"Marilyn?" Hannah wore a sly grin.

"No, I was going to use Penny." Jack caught Bevan's eye.

"He and Penny split up." Hannah told Bevan. "In Dubbo. She's gorgeous. Would have been perfect."

"Be quiet, Hannah," snapped Jack. "I'm sorry, Lucia, but I can't do your wedding. I have to find someone for this thing."

"You don't have anyone?" Bevan's voice rose in dismay.

"There was a girl on the tour but she was too busy."

"Libby?"

"Of course, Libby." Jack paced about the small room.

"You'd better find someone." Here came the steel. "You've got two weeks. I knew you shouldn't have gone on that trip."

Jack clenched his fingers into tight fists. "So do I, now. It was a disaster from the start."

Bevan hadn't finished. "And if you don't come up with the goods, you can forget about the next trip."

"Come on, Bevan." Shouting now. "You know that's not fair. You know I'll give you a fantastic result on the wilderness thing." He flung his arms wide, then let them fall by his sides.

Hannah stood up. "Lucia, I think it's time we left."

"Yes," she agreed. "I am disappointed, Jack."

"I'm sorry." Hannah was glaring at him as

though he'd spat on the Queen. She shouldn't have interfered in his business. In his life.

Bevan suddenly extended a hand. "What about Hannah?"

Hannah? Hadn't she done enough?

"What about me?" She and Lucia stopped. Jack stared at her. Hannah?

"Take photos of Hannah." Bevan beamed with pride.

"No," Jack said in complete unison with her.

The smile collapsed into bewilderment. "Why on earth not? It's obvious. She's a close friend, she's interesting, with loads of personality, plus she's attractive."

"She hates having her picture taken, she can't stand the photographer, and she's leaving right now," said Hannah while Jack said, "She's not a close friend, she's a pain, she argues as a way of life, she's a disaster area."

"Be quiet!" They stopped mid-rant and stared at Bevan. "Hannah. Is there something Jack can offer you to change your mind about this? It's important to his career. It's a very prestigious book you'll be in."

Hannah closed her eyes for a few moments. She took a deep breath. Jack watched her. She'd never agree. Her eyes opened, looked right at him.

"I want nothing from Jack." He knew it. "I was hoping never to have to see him again." Likewise. "But I'll do it and these are my conditions." Oh, Lord! "He does Lucia's photos. He doesn't complain."

Bevan tilted his head, questioning. Jack nodded, with great reluctance. Lucia gave a little cry of delight. She clapped her hands and flung her arms first around Hannah, then Jack. When she had subsided, Hannah added, "And he has to be romantic the whole time. Until the shoot is finished."

Bevan laughed and laughed, stopping just long

enough to kiss Hannah. "Darling, you're priceless. Jack being romantic—we need to get it on video. This is something I would love to see."

"Me too." Hannah's smile became a smirk. "He won't be able to, of course."

"I said I could," said Jack. "But being romantic with her is like trying to be romantic with a tornado."

"You'll just have to do your best then, won't you? That's my other condition. Take it or leave it."

Jack resigned himself to the inevitable. Combined, these two were an overwhelming force. "Who's the judge?"

"I am," said Hannah.

"She is." Bevan slapped Jack on the back. "Good! Now we're all settled, I'm off."

"I'm going too," said Lucia.

"I'll see you out."

Jack went to sit in morose solitude in the living room, ignoring them.

Hannah opened the front door. Lucia paused on the step. "Why don't you come to our party?"

"I'd love to." And Jack would love it, too. "Thank you very much, Lucia."

"Dinner and dancing at the Italian Club in Leichhardt. Formal. Seven thirty for eight, next Saturday. You come. Make Jack bring you."

Hannah cleared away her breakfast things and washed up the extra cups. Jack went out. She wandered about the little house. A lot of books on photography and travel. Not much fiction apart from blockbuster airport novels. His CD collection revealed he preferred jazz, but she knew that because of Miles Davis. Also The Beatles, a variety of rock bands, plus some interesting ethnic music most likely collected while he was away. No classical.

Two large, framed photographs hung in the

living-come-dining room. On closer inspection the beautiful one of the mountain wasn't an Ansel Adams after all. Neither was the pool with leaves floating. Jack's. He was very, very good at what he did.

She sat at the table and stared at them. No wonder he went off on his own for weeks at a time. These weren't the sort of thing you could do in a weekend with crowds of people around. These were works of art requiring time and careful attention to detail.

What a real pain she'd been to him. Disorganised, messy, rude to his relatives, outspoken, silly, ignorant of his stature in his profession, an irrational dislike of said profession— plain tiresome. Hannah rubbed her face with both hands. Hopeless, just as Marilyn had said.

But! She was helping him out now. She could have said a flat-out no. Why didn't she? Answer: because of Lucia. Lucia and her romantic husband. How wonderful to be married so long and still feel the same way about your partner. Jack was incapable of recognising true love when it was staring him in the face!

She rang home. Steve eventually answered, croaking and almost voiceless. The house was still contaminated. She couldn't go home. Her bed would need fumigating, thanks to Steve and his feeble friends. Nothing for it but to tough it out here with Jack.

What would these photos entail? Bevan had said something about photographing the woman the way she wanted to be seen. In another room would work. Hannah chuckled. How about a whole series of pictures of empty rooms with just articles of her clothing to identify her? Or her violin sitting on a chair waiting for her?

Jack came home hours later. Hannah, in shorts,

lounged in his tiny back garden on an ancient deck chair in the sun reading an old *National Geographic* featuring his pictures. The click of his camera brought her upright, bristling with indignation.

"Don't scowl. Remember the agreement?" His eyes were roaming up and down her bare legs.

"I let you take my picture, didn't I?"

"Only because you were asleep."

"I wasn't asleep."

"Stay there." He walked around in front of her for another shot, then lowered the camera. "Why did you agree to this?"

"For Lucia. She was terribly upset. You'll be her number one boy. By the way..."

His eyes resembled ray guns, capable of disintegrating her on the spot. "What else?"

"Lucia invited me because I'm such a nice, kind girl, and you have to take me."

She'd rendered him speechless, for once. Hannah followed him inside, where he sprawled on the couch and began reading the paper, blocking her out with newsprint. What was she supposed to do, stuck here with him? There was no piano, she didn't have her violin. No TV, and he'd lost interest in taking her photo. Maybe they could play cards. Was he expecting her to cook dinner?

"Jack. What about dinner?"

His attention returned to her for a moment. "We're going out."

"Where?"

"It's a surprise."

"Do I need to get dressed up?"

He wrinkled his brow. "If you like."

"Jack!"

His lips stretched into a thin smile. "You always look perfect to me." He turned the page with a noisy rustling and refolding.

"Don't give me that! Where are we going?"

"Out."

"I'll go as I am, then."

"Fine. Might get cold, though."

She went to the spare room and changed the shorts for tight black pants, and the T-shirt for a long-sleeved shirt, slightly crumpled from its week in a suitcase. He probably didn't know what an iron was. He grinned when she reappeared, but didn't say anything.

"When are we going?"

"Whenever you like. Are you hungry?"

"Yes."

"Let's go." The ubiquitous camera was slung round his neck.

Hannah followed him to the Volvo. He held the door for her as she slid into the front seat. She said nothing as he drove over the Harbour Bridge, headed towards the coast and then North Head, on a road which appeared to be temporarily closed to public access, judging by the signs. Was trespassing his idea of a Saturday night out? The surprise could be a night in gaol. Or a night in the old quarantine station, which was supposed to be haunted.

He parked on the rugged headland with a staggeringly beautiful view of the city and the harbour. Lights twinkled in the dusk away to the right and the endless, rolling Pacific Ocean spread to the left and centre. The dying sun behind them sent golden shafts streaking over the ocean, turning the horizon into a hazy purple and gold tapestry of light. The roar of waves pounding against the ancient rocks down below was the only sound.

"It's beautiful." She stared into the distance, a gentle, warm breeze lifting her hair. Click! Ignore it. The view was too breathtaking, far too lovely to spoil with words. Click, click, click. Silence save for the natural—the wind and the ocean.

Jack open the boot of the car, then came various

clunks and rustling noises. A steady hiss made her turn. A small folding table with two chairs and a gas camping lamp, providing a soft glow in the dusk, had materialised from nowhere.

A picnic. She should have guessed. Camping was his thing. Hannah smiled to herself. He'd chosen a spectacular spot. Quite the romantic.

Jack lifted a big wicker basket and an esky from the boot. From them he produced plates, cutlery and two tall champagne flutes, plastic bowls of salad and a container of cold chicken and lobster. He popped the champagne cork with practised ease and poured her a glass without spilling a drop.

She grinned, feigned shock. "Jack. What about my drinking problem? And I'm a vegetarian."

He smiled. "I was mistaken, remember? But I did bring orange juice just in case."

"Champagne will do just fine." She whipped her hand out and took the glass he offered.

"Thought so, by the way you downed it in Bathurst."

Hannah gave a shout of laughter as she remembered the couch incident. "Poor Fran. I'd forgotten."

"Sit down." He held her folding chair for her.

"Jack. I'm amazed and surprised and speechless." She gazed at him through eyes gone moist.

"I've achieved the impossible. Would you prefer chicken or lobster?"

"Both."

"Of course."

They ate without speaking, savouring the food, the view, the balmy spring air, the company. Every so often Hannah's gaze snagged on his, and the soft lamplight made his eyes deep warm pools she could drown in. This Jack was attentive and gentle and mysteriously different.

"I don't run to coffee, I'm afraid. I thought perhaps we could stop somewhere on the way home for dessert." His voice floated towards her on champagne-filled air.

"Lovely." And it was. And he was. "Is camping always like this?" Might not be so bad after all.

"No." Dark eyes bored into hers. So unbearably attractive. She dragged her eyes away. Danger lurked there in his gaze. She knew firsthand.

"Pity. Jack, these photographs. What do I have to do?"

"Not a lot. I've got plenty of you playing already. You need to think about how you'd like to be photographed."

"I have." She told him her idea of the empty rooms and he actually laughed.

"We could do one like that. The last of the group. With the violin and maybe an item of clothing You're always leaving stuff behind. Could be quite good."

"My suit bag?" He laughed again.

She drank more champagne. If he was like this all the time she could quite easily have a relapse and start falling in love with him once more.

"What do you like to do? Apart from music?"

Hannah wrinkled her forehead in concentration.

"Nothing much. Music is me. It's my life." She looked at him, unable to offer anything more, and to her surprise he nodded.

"I know. Like photography is to me."

He extended his hand and closed his fingers over hers. Shafts of electricity ran up her arm. She shouldn't let him touch her. He short circuited her defence mechanisms without even knowing. But her arm remained unmoving, her hand clasped in his.

"Hannah, I..." The roaring of an engine interrupted him. Bright headlights shattered the intimacy.

Jack stood up and walked around the Volvo to

greet the new arrival. An official-sounding voice said something, and they both appeared, starkly illuminated in the headlights. The uniformed man looked tough, with a square face and stocky, rugby player's body.

"What's the problem?" Hannah rose with precarious care. Mustn't fall over. Drunk and disorderly.

"Park's closed. You shouldn't be here. Didn't you see the signs?"

She glanced at Jack's grim face, then at the Ranger. She clasped her hands together the way Lucia did, inserted a quaver into her voice. "But it's so beautiful and romantic! We've just...Jack brought me up here to propose."

The man's face relaxed and he laughed. "What did she say, mate?"

"You came along just at the wrong moment." She giggled. Jack gaped. No help whatsoever.

"Don't let me interrupt. Go on, answer him."

Hannah stepped forward and flung her arms around Jack's neck.

"Yes, please, darling." She kissed him, hard.

"Congratulations." The Ranger slapped Jack on the back. "Like me to take your photo?"

"This," said Hannah, because Jack looked too stunned to say anything, sensible or otherwise, "is one of the best photographers in the world. Jack Rotherford."

Out shot a beefy hand which Jack shook with a bemused expression. "I saw you on the news. Got back safe?"

"Give him the camera, Jack." He did. She wrapped both her arms around him and smiled.

"Give her a hug, mate. She's your fiancée now. Smile. How about a kiss?" Jack stared down at Hannah with the same look on his face as Freddo when he saw the cat box. The look indicating something unpleasant is about to occur. His lips brushed hers and the camera flashed.

"Thanks," said Hannah.

"Delighted." Their new friend handed the camera to Jack. "Wait till I tell them back at base who I nearly busted up here."

"Do us a favour?" Jack interrupted. "Keep it quiet for now? We don't want to spread it around just yet."

"Oh, sure, mate. No problem. Sorry, but you are going to have to leave."

"It's all right, we were going anyway." Jack shook hands again. The Ranger climbed back into his ute and roared away down the track.

Jack began to pack up the picnic with a stiff quietness about him that boded ill.

Hannah drained her champagne. "Boy, we were lucky. Pretty quick thinking, I thought."

"Except now half of Sydney will think I'm getting married."

"Who'd care?"

"I would."

"But you're not getting married. Did you think I was for real?"

He snorted his answer. "But he thinks I am, and all he needs to do is tell a few people with mouths like yours and hey, presto, it's in the papers."

A surge of anger blasted away the cheer. "All you need to do in that case is leave the country."

"I will, believe me. The sooner the better." The boot slammed shut. "Get in the car."

"I'll walk." Idiot! It's miles and pitch black.

"Get in the car and don't be so stupid!"

She flung open the door as he started the engine. The car bounced and slid over the dirt track with Hannah clinging to her seatbelt in grim silence. The ungrateful so and so...

"What do you mean 'a mouth like mine'?"

"You just can't keep quiet."

"If I'd kept quiet we'd be in gaol."

"We would not!"

"Fined, at least."

They reached the tarred road and passed the No Entry signs.

"Can't you read?"

"Married," he spat. "I can't believe you said married."

"I don't know why you're so upset. There's no danger of me marrying you."

"You got that right!"

"You're the very last person I'd even dream of marrying."

"Likewise." And by the look on his face he meant it.

"Did you marry the mother of your son?" The words popped out, uncensored. She tensed, waiting for the inevitable explosion, and he'd be within his rights this time. Too late to take the regrettable question back now.

"No, I did not."

"Why not?"

He pulled to the side of the road and slammed on the brakes. The Volvo skidded to a halt. Hannah clutched the seat belt in alarm. When he cut the engine her hand slid to the release button. Just in case she had to make a hasty exit.

"Right!" he shouted. "I'll tell you, seeing as you're so concerned about my son and my past. Anything to shut you up."

She opened her mouth, but he held his hand up, and she subsided against the seat in silence.

"I met Carol when I was twenty and she was eighteen. We fell in love. She was a student still living with her parents. I was working and hoping for a break into magazines, the international market. It came. I took it and left for Europe. Carol stayed. She was pregnant, but I didn't know until later. When I did find out, she'd already met Martin, and he wanted to marry her and bring the baby up as his."

Hannah absorbed what he told her. It was sad and it sounded plausible and true, and it didn't sound like Marilyn's version. And he was right. She had done her usual trick of judging and making assumptions based on minimal information.

"I'm sorry."

"Now drop it," he growled.

"Can I ask just one thing?" She took his silence as a yes. "Do you regret not being able to call your son yours?"

Jack stared out the windscreen. He shook his head. "I would have been a terrible father. Carol and I would have split up. She wouldn't go with me, you see, wanted to stay here and go to university. Even before she knew she was pregnant. I think deep down she knew I wasn't the home-building family-man type. Martin is. They've been married ever since, with two daughters as well."

****

Hannah couldn't sleep that night. Not a wink. She got up before dawn, careful to make no noise, packed her suitcase, rang a taxi and waited outside on the footpath for it to come and take her home. Flu germs or not, uncomfortable couch or not, deal or not, she couldn't stay in Jack's house a moment longer.

Everyone was asleep when she crept into the Balmain house. Except Freddo. Even he seemed like a friend. Her things were still dumped on the floor where she'd left them. She plonked her suitcase down beside her violin and sat on the nearest armchair, with the cat sitting at her feet staring at her hopefully with his yellow gaze.

"Do you want breakfast?" He blinked. She

dragged herself into the kitchen and opened the last tin of cat food. Steve hadn't done any shopping for days. Which was understandable. Perhaps she should have stayed here and cared for him. Not those people in her bed, though.

At nine she set out to do some supermarket shopping, armed with an extensive list. When she returned in a taxi, laden with grocery bags, Steve was lying on the couch watching football on TV. He helped carry stuff in from the front step, then went back to lie down.

"How are you feeling?" She kicked off her sandals.

"I'm a bit better today."

"And the others?" More than a bit better, please. Especially the delirious one with hallucinations.

"They've gone."

"Why didn't you tell me?" Hands on hips.

"Forgot." The TV volume went up a notch. "You were at your friend's, you were all right."

"Steve!" Was it a guy thing or was it peculiar to Steve, this denseness?

He stared at her, his expression blank. "What?"

"Forget it."

"Some guy called for you. And Bernard." His attention returned to the game.

Her stomach went for the high jump. Jack? He'd be furious. "Who was it?"

"Bernard. I said. Call him." Steve winced as a player with the ball disappeared under a heap of opposition bodies.

"Who else?"

"Huh?"

"Steve? The other call. Who was it?"

"Don't know. Aah, did you see that? The ref's blind." He thumped the couch with his fist. Hannah left him to it.

She unpacked the last of her clothes and stowed

the empty suitcase under her bed. If Jack wanted to take pictures of her, he knew where to find her. Romantic! Pah!

Chapter Thirteen

After lunch Hannah bussed and trained and walked to Bernard's house across the harbour in leafy Artarmon. Marilyn flung the door open and actually gave her a peck on the cheek. Must have assumed Jack and Penny had patched things up and Hannah's fiendish plan was thwarted. Simon and Libby already sat on the white leather sofa.

Marilyn bustled in with a tray full of cups, a coffee pot, cake and biscuits. "Help yourselves. After what we've all been through we needn't stand on ceremony, need we? Nothing like a disaster to bring everyone together."

"It was hardly a disaster, sweetie," said Bernard. "Except for the people living out there."

"It was almost a disaster for Jack. And Hannah."

Hannah smiled warily. This pleasantness was almost more unnerving than the usual nastiness.

"First of all, I'll give you these. For the concerts we've done so far." Bernard handed them each a cheque. "The Arts people want us to complete the remaining concerts early next year. But the good news is we have a concert in two weeks in Mittagong at the Mozart Festival. Last minute cancellation by the other group." He gave them the date. "The Clarinet Quintet with Terry Lindsay from the City Symphony."

Good. Lots of rehearsal, lots of practice. No time to think. Hannah reached for a shortbread biscuit. The doorbell rang. Marilyn fluttered off to answer it. She was all in lemon yellow today, with gravity-defying, high-heeled sandals. A big, disturbingly friendly, under-ripe banana. Her voice rang down the hallway.

"Lean on me, darling. You poor thing. Is the ankle still swollen? You're still limping. It must be terribly painful." She reappeared clutching Jack by the arm.

"Hello, everyone." Tall, self-assured, handsome. Using up all the air in the room.

Shortbread crumbs went down the wrong way as an image of their last pre-Park Ranger moments together galloped through Hannah's head, and a multitude of sensations flooded her body. Warm, romantic evening, fabulous view, ocean waves crashing in the background. Champagne. Hypnotic eyes. Gentle voice. He'd held her hand and been about to say something. Spluttering and coughing, she leapt off the couch, spraying biscuit fragments from her lap as she went.

Safe in the kitchen she grabbed the bench and coughed, eyes streaming, face hot and perspiring. This is what it must be like to choke to death. What Jack wanted to do to her most of the time. She managed to reach for a glass and fill it with tap water, then slurped in desperation, drowning the coughs and washing away the offending biscuit chunks. Life once more unthreatened, her brain began to consider other pressing matters.

How could she not have realised he would be here? Was she totally mad? Why hadn't she prepared herself? She was an idiot. Three deep breaths, wiped her eyes, cleared her throat and strode back to the living room.

"Are you all right?" Marilyn looked unnaturally concerned. Everyone stared.

Hannah nodded. "Yes, thanks. Piece of biscuit went down the wrong way. Just needed a drink of water. What are we talking about?"

She took her place again, taking care to avoid catching Jack's eye. Avoided looking at him at all as he lounged on a chair between Libby and Marilyn. She knew he was staring, his eyes were like fingers, probing and pressing. Bernard continued with rehearsal plans for the Mittagong concert.

When he'd finished, Jack said, "You're all invited to the opening of my exhibition, if you'd like to come." He handed out black and silver invitation cards designed to look like photographs. Hannah took the one he offered, avoiding touching his fingers.

"We can all go together," said Simon.

"How exciting." Libby studied the invitation and looked up, smiling. "Thanks, Jack."

Hannah stuffed the card in her bag without looking at it at all. She had no intention of going to the opening. Her and her big mouth. They might embarrass him and we couldn't have that, could we, Mr. Super Ego? Someone might have been talking to the Ranger and, shock, horror, think they were engaged. Maybe she'd sneak in later when the exhibition had been running for a while.

"Have we finished, Bernard? I'd better go. Thanks for the coffee and cake, Marilyn."

Marilyn glanced up from her cosy monopolisation of the phoney invalid, and smiled. "You're welcome, Hannah." Far too much politeness. Jack simply stared, his expression blank.

Hannah's feet took her towards the station on auto pilot. Jack was angry with her, not speaking. Why did it matter more now than before? Maybe he'd decided he already had enough pictures for his stupid book.

She found her ticket after a thorough search of pockets and handbag, ran it through the turnstile, then put it in her jacket pocket for easy finding at the other end. The next train wasn't due for seven minutes, so she sat on a green bench in the late afternoon sun and stared at her toes.

"Hannah." Jack stood squarely in front of her, blocking out the sun. "Why did you clear off this morning?"

"Isn't it obvious?" She stayed glued to the bench even though her pulse was fidgeting and jumping like a crazed flea.

"Not to me." His voice rose a fraction in volume. "Tell me."

"I didn't want to stay. Can't you understand? You didn't want me there, you made yourself very clear. Me and my big mouth." Hannah craned her head forward and peered down the line. If only he wasn't so handsome. And if only she could forget what those hands had done to her...

"But I didn't say you had to leave!" His arms waved in the air in frustration. The voice rose another notch. "And you just disappeared. What about our agreement?"

"Jack, I went home. I'm sorry if your pride got hurt, but really I don't want to..."

"What?"

She hesitated. "Argue with you any more." Her voice dropped. Her gaze skated across his face to his chest, completely incapable of meeting his eyes. Where was the train?

"I couldn't believe you'd gone." Jack's voice softened. "Why didn't you at least wake me so we could talk about it?" He sat down beside her. Too close. His warm thigh touched hers.

"I can imagine how that would have been received. I was only staying a night or two. Thanks for the bed. There's nothing to talk about."

The train appeared at the bend further down the track. Hannah sprang forward.

"There is!" he cried from behind her.

"Don't shout at me."

The train hissed to a stop. The doors slid open.

"Don't get on the train, Hannah! We need to talk this through."

She half turned, still couldn't meet his eyes. "No, we don't. You've got your life and I've got mine. I won't get in your way any more, Jack. Goodbye."

"But, Hannah…"

She stepped into the carriage and sat down, quivering from head to toe but proud of herself. Good going. She'd maintained her control, stated her points clearly without resorting to shouting or collapsing into his arms in tears, both of which had been quite possible at any given moment. The doors closed, and, as the train eased out of the station, she caught a glimpse of Jack watching with his hands on his hips and a face like thunder. And right behind him on the green bench where she'd left it, lay her handbag.

"Ooohhh." Hannah covered her face in shaky, clammy hands.

Would he pick up her bag? Probably. He'd recognise it. But was he too angry? Surely he wouldn't leave it there on the bench. Maybe he'd hand it in to the station master. She'd have to go back.

Forty minutes later she ran from the train, up the steps, over the line, down the steps on the other side and rushed panting down the deserted platform to the empty green bench.

A laconic station worker informed her, "Jack has your bag."

"Is that all he said?"

"Yeah." He wandered off down the platform in an attempt to look busy.

The next train wasn't due for twenty minutes. The sun had dropped lower, as had the temperature. Her toes were getting cold. She had her ticket but no money, thus a lengthy walk home from the city in the dark when she got off the train. A taxi? But there was no money in the house to pay the driver, and Steve may not have enough cash, either. If he was at home. And her keys were in her bag.

An hour later, as she slogged up and over the steep arch of the Anzac Cove Bridge towards the lights of Balmain, her simmering anger made a corresponding rise to the boil. One sandal strap kept slipping down over her heel. Blisters were inevitable.

Jack must have known she had no money. Jack had his car. He must have assumed she'd come straight back looking for her bag, so why didn't he wait, at least for the next train? He could have driven her home. And when and how was she supposed to retrieve her bag?

Paying her back for this morning. How petty! He was a child. Hannah marched around the corner of her street, full flowering rage having fuelled the last part of her journey and given energy to her flagging legs. The strap on her left sandal broke, and she kicked it off and hurled it into someone's garbage bin along with its partner. She walked the remaining half block in bare feet, and gave the doorbell a vicious twist. If Steve was in bed he could get out, sick or not.

The front light snapped on. Steve's face peered around the door.

"Oh, it's you." He leapt aside as Hannah charged in. She forgot the rug and skidded unceremoniously, flapped her arms like some crazed bird and saved herself by grabbing the door frame of her music room.

"That rotten mat!" she yelled, and continued on down the hallway to the bathroom, where she turned the taps on full blast in the bath, then went upstairs to her room and collapsed on to her bed, footsore, hot, exhausted and close to tears. Steve stood in the doorway, her handbag in his hand.

"Your friend Jack dropped this in." He put it on the end of her bed. "About an hour ago. He's a nice guy."

She clenched her fists and thumped them into the bed. An hour ago she was just starting out on her marathon trek, and Jack was sitting here cosily chatting to Steve, the pair of them laughing about silly Hannah's forgetfulness.

"Jack is not a nice guy."

Steve shrugged. "Whatever you say. Where are your shoes?"

"I threw them away."

"Any particular reason?" His eyebrows crinkled.

"They broke when I had to walk home from the city because I left my bag at the station in Artarmon, and I had no money, and Jack didn't wait for me to get back so I could get it from him, and he's not a nice guy, he's horrible! It's his fault I left it there in the first place."

Hannah sat on the edge of the bed breathing hard. Steve ventured nothing for a few minutes, then eased out of sight. Eventually she went to turn off the taps and pour bath crystals into her steaming tub.

"Are you feeling better?" she called. Poor long-suffering Steve. From her father's side of the family. The less hysterical, less dramatically-inclined branch of the family tree. The sporty ones with straight, controllable, fair hair.

"No." He appeared in the doorway. "I'm still in pyjamas, in case you didn't notice. I think I've had a relapse."

He was still in his pyjamas and he had dark rings under his eyes. His skin had a pasty, unhealthy pallor under the sportsman's tan, and there was the unmistakable, stale odour of illness around him.

"Go to bed, Steve. Why are you up?"

"I'm up because I've had a constant stream of people ringing the doorbell."

"Have you eaten?" He shook his head. "I'll make us dinner after my bath. You should have a shower and change your pyjamas, too. Good thing I'm home now to look after you."

"Mmm." Steve gave her a doubtful look and disappeared.

Hannah lay in the heavily-scented, steaming water and soaked away the anger and disappointment of her encounter with Jack along with the grime of the city. She studied her blisters. One large one on the right heel and two smaller ones where the uppers had rubbed across the tops of her feet. What a disaster of a day, and all Jack's fault. Why couldn't he have just left her alone? Couldn't he make do with the pictures he had? And as for the romance thing. Forget it! Even he would see how hopeless it was.

Hurt male pride. Jack wasn't used to being treated in so abrupt a fashion. It made him furious.

The phone rang later while they lounged in the living room watching TV. Hannah picked up the phone and blocked out the movie with a finger in her other ear. "Hello."

"So you got home safely." The voice was warm and intimate.

"No thanks to you." Gripping the receiver in a suddenly sweaty hand, she darted in to the kitchen.

"What was I supposed to do? I went out of my way to return your bag. I'll leave it where I find it next time." The warmth departed in a flash.

"If you hadn't distracted me I wouldn't have left it there in the first place."

"So it's my fault?" He laughed. "You're ridiculous."

"Well there you go, Jack. That's me, just as

219

you're so fond of reminding me. I'm an idiot. And I've got blisters as well. Thanks for going out of your way and returning my bag," She disconnected.

The phone rang again almost immediately, but she let it ring, staring at it until Steve yelled, "Answer it, Han, what are you doing?!"

She snatched it up. "Don't call me again!"

There was a pause after which an unfamiliar, tentative voice said, "I'm trying to contact Hannah Crawford, the pianist?"

"Whoops. You have. I am Hannah Crawford. I'm sorry, I meant someone else." Her mind still reached for Jack. "Did you want piano lessons?"

"Sorry. No, I want an accompanist." Maybe she shouldn't have hung up on him.

"Yes, fine. What's your name and what is it you wanted accompanied?"

"Oh. I'm sorry! I haven't introduced myself. What must you think? My name's Graeme. Graeme Fletcher," he repeated, as if he needed to confirm the fact to himself.

"And what instrument do you play, Graeme?" She'd been unnecessarily rude to Jack. Why couldn't she think first? Her and her big mouth.

"Flute. I've been asked to give a recital." If Jack called again the line would be busy, and she'd never know. He'd give up. Should she call him and apologise?

"What are your rates?" Graeme asked.

Hannah explained, he agreed. Hannah returned to the couch and the tail end of the movie.

Had she chased Jack away completely? Had he had enough? She'd win her bet he couldn't be romantic, but it was a hollow victory. And what about her side of the agreement? Would he still do Lucia's wedding if he thought Hannah had dipped out on his photos? But she hadn't dipped out. As far as he knew she was thinking about how she wanted

to be photographed. And she simply hadn't decided.
****

The uneasy feeling she'd been too harsh on the phone grew stronger over the following two days. Jack needn't have driven to her house with her bag. The way she'd spoken to him anyone would think she hated and detested the man when she didn't. They'd made love together once and, almost certainly, nearly, twice. She had, anyway, and now she had a sneaking, very uncomfortable and at the same time exhilarating feeling he had, too. He'd murmured such wonderful things to her...but he was an expert. Maybe it was just his way.

And then, of course, there were the roses. Delivered to her door on Monday morning by a man with Flowers R Us on his shirt. Twelve beautiful red roses.

"Who's a lucky girl?" he said, and handed her a card before thrusting the flowers into her hands

No one had ever sent her flowers before. No one had ever given her red roses before. Jack—being romantic again. He hadn't given up. She thrust her nose into the heavily perfumed petals, and a tear or two dropped to sparkle like diamonds on red velvet.

She arranged them with extra care in a tall glass vase and stood them on the dining room table, where they glowed in the light from the window and sent their heady scent through the house. The card read:

I'm sorry
Jack

****

Bussing home from teaching on Wednesday, she pulled out her diary and studied the performing commitments. Would Jack go with them on tour again? He'd most likely be away. Hacking through a jungle or rafting down a wild river.

Jack. Always popping into her thoughts. They'd

spent the whole of last week in each other's pockets, and now his absence was like the gaping hole when a filling fell out or a tooth was removed. Despite having been an annoying nuisance of a tooth.

If she rang him what could she say? "Thank you for the roses," would be courteous. But would she be doing the one thing she swore she wouldn't? Pursue him, a man who didn't love her. Like poor Penny. A man who'd made his situation very clear in regard to having a family. No future for her in his direction at all.

At home the roses glowed from their place on the table, their perfume a constant reminder. My love is like a red, red rose. What good was romance without the love?

****

Jack's silence for the remainder of the week was deafening. Was he waiting for her to call about the photos? Waiting for her to tell him what she wanted? Outside music, her life wasn't very entertaining. Steve made some ridiculous suggestions. Desperate to hear Jack's voice on Friday afternoon she rang, but had to leave a message. "It's Hannah. Thank you for the roses."

Saturday was Lucia's party. She had a personal invitation. Why not go? Good dinner, plenty of wine, a crowd of partying Italians. See Jack. Prove she wasn't pining for him. Discuss the technicalities of her photographs. See how he looked in a dinner suit.

As official photographer, a sight not to be missed in itself, he could take all the pictures he liked of her in her slim-fitting, spaghetti-strapped dress with the plunging neckline. The deep green, silky material shimmered in the light, and she'd chosen her highest, sexiest, stiletto-heeled shoes to show off her legs under the short skirt. He liked looking at her legs. He could look and remember and be frustrated. A small, white opal pendant on a fine, gold chain

222

dropped into her cleavage. Her wild hair she pinned back with a clasp.

The function room on the first floor of the club was packed with people already in full party mode when she arrived. Butterflies tangoed in her stomach. Neapolitan hits from yesteryear vied with the roar of alcohol-fuelled conversations. Lucia must have invited every one she knew, and maybe some she didn't, like Hannah, to help celebrate.

"Cara," she cried, when Hannah's turn came in the welcoming queue. "Luigi, this is Jack's special friend, Hannah."

"Thank you for inviting me."

Luigi shook her hand. "You saved the day for us. Bella, bella. Jack is a very lucky man."

"We wonder why he has no wife," Lucia leaned forward with a confidential expression.

"He travels too much."

"And you?" asked Luigi. "Will you stop this travelling?" A pair of knowing brown eyes studied her.

"I've only known Jack two weeks." He wouldn't stop for her. The opposite was more likely. He'd go further and faster.

"More than enough time to fall in love," he said. "I knew as soon as my eyes fell upon this beautiful girl, there would be no one else in my life." He kissed Lucia's cheek, and she placed a loving palm on his cheek.

"I believe there is someone special for me as well...but I don't think it's Jack." How could her mouth be quivering? Surely she wasn't going to cry in front of these two with their sympathetic brown eyes and their love.

"But you would like it to be." Lucia squeezed her arm.

Hannah moved away before she blubbed on Lucia's shoulder and wet her beautiful cream satin dress. She waylaid a waiter and took a glass of champagne. Not a familiar face in sight. Not even Jack's. Maybe this was a mistake. Her skirt felt far too short all of a sudden. Where was Jack? Slacking off somewhere? Cursing her for forcing him into it.

"Just move across a little to the left, please," came a voice from behind her. His voice. "You too, please, Hannah." In her ear, his breath tickling her neck.

She did as she was told and faced Jack's camera while a stranger cosied up beside her.

Click, flash. "Thank you."

Jack moved closer and edged her away as the group reformed.

"I didn't think you'd come."

"Lucia invited me."

"But I still didn't think you'd come."

"Why not?"

He stared into her eyes for a moment, looked away. Didn't reply. Didn't he want her here? Too bad. Lucia and Luigi did.

"Thank you for the roses, Jack. They're gorgeous."

His serious expression relaxed as their eyes linked again. The camera loomed between them. Click.

"You seemed like a red roses girl."

"Did you get my message?"

"Yes. Have you thought about the photos?"

"Steve suggested I do something more exciting than reading or sleeping, which is what I really do when I'm not playing music."

"What do you do for entertainment? You can't stay home in a coma all the time."

"Go to the movies, sometimes the theatre. Or the opera."

"Opera?" His face sagged, and the look of patronising condescension was replaced by one of apprehension.

"Yes! The Opera House is very romantic. We could have dinner by the harbour, and then see a nice long tragedy. In Italian. Or maybe German."

"I'll come over to your place for a few hours next week and take some shots of you at home, asleep or eating."

"You're supposed to be romantic as well, don't forget." Hannah couldn't prevent a sly little smile. "When's your deadline?"

"The opera?" He groaned. "I hate that sort of singing."

"You may learn to love it. I'll check performances and tell you when."

A grimace, another groan with eyes closed. They flicked open and he glowered at her. "Okay, if I must."

"Wonderful."

"Gotta go. I'm working."

"Sorry." Hannah pulled a suitably contrite face.

His smile was wry, but he shrugged. "You can do your penance and dance with me later."

"Can you dance?" Now that really did just slip out!

He shook his head at her in resignation and walked away to another group of chattering guests. Soon after, dinner was announced. Sliding partition doors were folded back to double the size of the room and reveal beautifully set tables sparkling with glass and silverware. A large arrangement of pink flowers and fernery formed the centrepiece of each table. Where was Jack? Surely he'd be eating with the guests? Lucia wouldn't expect him to eat with the musicians out the back, later.

Hannah chose a seat at random. Impossible to save a place for him. He might not even want to sit with her. He'd have to fend for himself.

"I'm Angelo. Tell me about yourself." The young

man on her left leaned over and managed to peer down her front.

"I'm Hannah." She spread her serviette over her exposed thighs. "I'm a musician."

"I'm a musician, too." Angelo, wine bottle in hand, crooned too close into her ear. "I sing the music of the soul, of *amore*. You understand?" Wine gurgled into her glass.

Oh, yes. She understood perfectly. Jack was up the front, camera at the ready. A priest said Grace. Angelo's attention was claimed by a middle-aged pair on his left. Hannah picked at her bread roll. There was still room for Jack.

A thin, blonde woman pulled out one of the remaining empty chairs. The woman's companion looked across and laughed when Hannah's elbow knocked cutlery on to the floor as she put her half-chewed bread roll back on the plate. She bent to pick up her lost fork and straightened up, red-faced. Jack was watching with an amused smirk from across the table. Fortunately the large floral arrangement obscured most of his view.

"Enjoying yourself?" He had to almost shout to be audible over the band and the blare of talk. "You've found a friend, I see."

Hannah peered through the liliums. Who's the blonde? Did she come with him?

"Hannah, this is Sylvie."

Definitely not romantic, Jack!

Chapter Fourteen

"Hello, Hannah." Sylvie wore a wide, friendly smile as she leaned around the flowers.

"Hello." Hannah dodged a lilium and smiled back. What if she threw her bread roll at Jack? Better still, her knife. Sylvie was lovely.

She drew a deep calming breath. This would call for extreme caution and definite thought before action or speech. Jack poured wine into Sylvie's glass, and she smiled and clinked her glass against his. Hannah couldn't hear a word they were saying, but they looked sickeningly cosy together. Delicious food arrived.

Each time Angelo offered to fill her glass she refused. The last thing she needed was to get drunk with Angelo leering and Jack sitting watching the whole show with his camera and his elegant, blonde companion to hand and thinking heaven only knew what. Maybe he'd include a picture of her and Angelo in his book as an example of how she liked to entertain herself.

Jack announced he wanted a shot of the group at the table. Everyone shuffled chairs about and leaned closer to each other. Angelo draped an arm over Hannah's shoulders.

"Smile," said Jack. "Come on, Hannah, big smile." She smiled. Click. "Thank you." He moved to the next table.

She excused herself to visit the Ladies. When she returned couples were dancing, and the waiters had cleared away the dinner dishes and were serving coffee. Jack and Sylvie had disappeared.

Angelo claimed her before she could sit down.

"Dance with me." He grabbed her hand and tugged her between the tables.

"No, thank you." Hannah stalled at the edge of the dance floor. Angelo lost his grip. An arm scooped around her.

"Having fun?" Jack's voice. Warm-toned. Mildly amused.

"No! What a slimy...ugh."

His grip tightened and he took hold of her hand. The band was still playing something slow and dreamy. She could pretend he was a proper, real romantic hero being comforting and protective. His cheek pressed lightly against her hair.

"You're the most awful flirt."

Hannah pulled her head back.

"I am not! Angelo is repulsive. Are you jealous?"

He laughed softly. "Calm down." His arms tightened their hold.

"Where's Sylvie? Will she mind you dancing with me?"

"I don't think so. She's a sophisticated woman. And..."

"What?" Was he going to say "you're not," by any chance?

"Nothing." They shuffled past a stalled couple.

How would sophisticated Sylvie like another woman crawling over her date? Hannah moved closer, nuzzling her face into his neck, breathing in the warmth. His hand was on the bare skin on her back, sending tingles of electricity through her body. What a sexy man. Would Sylvie mind if she ripped his clothes off in the middle of the dance floor? Lucia might.

"You're not asleep, are you?" His soft voice caressed her ear.

Hannah murmured, "No. Are you?"

"No."

"Thank you for saving me."

"No worries. I've had a lot of practice saving you."

Hannah smiled. "I saved you on the hillside."

"You did. Grumbled a fair bit, but you did."

They shuffled in silence for a few moments. She loved the smell of his body.

"You look good tonight." A whisper of sound. "Beautiful."

Hannah nestled closer. Their bodies fit perfectly together. "Thank you. You look very nice yourself."

"Thank you. Hannah?" The tune came to an end.

"Mmm." Lost in his arms, the spell of his voice gentle in her ear.

"Admit I can be romantic."

She gulped and came awake. This was Jack. This was reality. This was a battleground. One arm was still around her waist, the other now on her shoulder.

"You have to be honest." He was looking down at her, amused. Almost laughing.

She screwed up her face, considering. While her heart thumped and humiliation burned. "You're not doing too badly. How long before you leave?"

"About two weeks."

"Not much time to convince me."

"I won't need more than that. I only need a few more shots. Anyway Bevan's deadline is Friday. You said until this shoot was finished, not until I leave." He smiled down into her eyes with a supremely confident expression. "I'd better do some more work." His fingers slid with tantalising slowness down her arm. "Thank you for the dance."

Nothing more? They walked back to their table. The middle-aged couple remained alone, seated, drinking coffee and ignoring each other. No point staying on.

She picked up her bag. "I think I'll leave."

"How are you getting home? I can't leave yet."

"Taxi."

"Goodnight." He leaned forward. His lips brushed her cheek while she held her breath to avoid saying something extremely toxic. "Wait a minute."

Up came the camera for a close-up of her face, then he stepped back for a full-length shot.

"Great legs." Click, click. "Sexy girl." Down went the camera. "I'll come by tomorrow for some more photos. Mid morning suit?"

Hannah nodded, stunned into silence by his blatant lack of involvement. He gave her a little wave and walked away. How could she be so stupid as to think he enjoyed dancing with her? Too much champagne? Must be. Champagne and slow dancing with Jack's arms around her, and Jack's smell in her nostrils, and the memory of Jack's body imprinted on hers.

Jack who had calmly arrived with another woman and introduced them to each other as if he expected they'd be best of friends. Boy, did he move fast. This must set some sort of record even for him.

****

He arrived on the doorstep at eleven the next morning.

"Coffee, Jack?" Steve stuck his head out of the kitchen.

"Sure, thanks." Jack looked at Hannah. "Have a good time last night?"

Her cheeks warmed as his eyes rested on her face. Was he remembering how she'd moulded herself against his body when they danced? Was he thinking to himself, 'Here's another one throwing herself at me'? His lips wore the hint of a smile.

"Yes." Who was Sylvie? And where did she spring from? Why wasn't he using her as a model if they were such good friends? "What do you want me to do?"

"Just be yourself." He took the cap off his camera lens. "You can manage that, I take it?" His attention reverted to the camera as he peered at her through the viewfinder and made some adjustments. Click.

Click.

"Where do you practise?"

She led him to the front room right by the door where she had her shiny black upright piano, a music stand with some of the quartet music open on it, stacks of music on the floor, and an overflowing desk with more music, a metronome and pencils. Pictures of musicians were stuck to the wall, along with some cartoon drawings and an Escher print of a mind-boggling tower with water running uphill. Her violin was in its case on the divan. A pair of sandals lay where she'd kicked them off in the centre of the room.

He smiled. "This looks like you." Some quick shots secured the moment in history.

"Messy, you mean?" She sat down on the piano stool.

"Yup." Click. A picture of her looking up at him. "Play."

Hannah swivelled around and started doodling on the piano. Her fingers drifted into "Pavane for a Dead Princess" by Ravel, and after a while she realised he had stopped taking photos and was leaning on the door frame, listening. She came to the end and sat embarrassed because the piece was sad and beautiful and expressed all she felt in regard to him. He would have seen it in her face. Photographed it.

Exposing her. The way Raoul had done but mentally rather than physically. Prying into her emotions and her soul. She looked at Jack. His expression almost made her think he cared.

"Who's Sylvie?" she wanted to ask.

He straightened up, opened his mouth but didn't speak. His eyes drove into hers.

"Coffee's ready," shouted Steve.

"Coming?" Jack flicked a smile at Hannah and disappeared.

She followed, but she didn't join them in the living room, she sidled through to the kitchen and fiddled about wiping the benches down. Her hands were shaking.

Steve said, "You know what she really likes to do? Soak in the bath."

"Steve!" Hannah burst through the doorway.

"A bath would be good." Jack looked at her with one eyebrow raised. "Bubbles?"

"Sometimes."

"Very sexy."

Steve chuckled. "Go on, Han. No one would see anything except your head, and maybe a knee or a foot."

"No!"

"You could wear your swimming costume," said Jack, cajoling. "And just pull the straps down under the bubbles."

She folded her arms across her chest.

"Hannah, I've got some good shots of you playing. I've got you dressed up, I've got you on the headland the other night, I've got a couple from the tour, but I want something more intimate. A glimpse of the secret you no one sees."

"Except me if I sneak a look through the keyhole." Steve ducked as Hannah swung a hand at his head.

Jack gazed at her, his expression serious, and Hannah knew she had to take his request with similar seriousness. It was an important project for him and he knew what he was doing. As an artist herself, she had to respect those facts.

"Take me to the opera?" Tell me who Sylvie is.

He nodded.

"Do you want to do this right now?"

More nodding. "Might as well. You could change your mind."

"You got that right." Her swimming costume hadn't been sighted for years. Not a favourite pastime, swimming. Especially in the bath.

Hannah turned the taps on and poured half a bottle of lavender-scented bubble bath into the tub. Those bubbles had to be thick and opaque. Then she went upstairs to search for her costume. Five minutes later she stood at the top of the stairs. "I can't find my swimming costume."

"Why aren't I surprised?" Jack stood up.

Steve laughed. "Borrow mine."

"Very funny. I can't do this without it."

"Do it in your underwear," suggested Steve. Hannah sat on the top step with her hands over her face.

Jack went up the stairs and stopped so his head was level with hers. She looked forlorn and nervous. Maybe frightened. Of him? Surely not. He wanted to hug her. He wanted to hold her as he had when they danced. When she stopped being defensive and tough, and her body admitted how she really felt.

He lowered his voice so Steve wouldn't hear. "You could, you know. It'll be different, Hannah. I'm not like Raoul, you know that."

"Or we could do this another day. After I've bought a costume," she mumbled through her hands. "Or not do it at all."

"We could. If you'd be happier. But we're all set to go, and all you need to do is strip off and get in the tub before I come in."

She lowered her hands from in front of her face. "Will you take me to the opera? Next week?"

If she'd cooperate, he'd take her to the moon. "Yes. And dinner first and supper after. Very romantic."

"And not complain?"

Jack shook his head, hoping he could manage that part. Was she weakening? Her face wore a tiny frown, weighing up the pros and cons. She jumped up with a broad smile. "I'll yell when I'm ready."

"You...con artist!" He went back downstairs to Steve. "Has she always been like this?"

"Pretty much. Like Aunt Tildy. I'm going out. Catch you later. Have fun."

"Oh, it'll be a riot." Jack gritted his teeth, picked up his camera and went to the bathroom like a gladiator. "Are you ready?"

"Yes."

An overpowering lavender scent hit him in the nose first, then he was confronted by the mountain of bubbles billowing out over the sides of the bath and onto the floor. Hannah's disembodied head was just visible in the foam. His foot skated from under him on wet tiles, but he saved himself by grabbing at the door handle.

"Are you in here somewhere?"

"I might have used too much." She grinned through bubbles on her cheeks and hair. His breath caught. Those sparkling eyes and those dimples. She had to be the most beautiful woman he'd ever seen. Suddenly he wanted to prove to her just how romantic he could be, and not because of their silly deal.

"You'll have to get rid of some of it. No one uses that much. You look as if you're drowning in meringue." The lavender scent was giving him a headache.

"What's wrong with meringue? I like it. Take a picture."

"How can you stand the smell?" He edged forward to line her up. She'd piled her hair up in loose bundles. Strands fell about her face and neck, damp and wispy in the moist warm air. Sexy as could be. Concentrate! "Look away to the right. Good. Now smile, not too much. You're supposed to be alone in the bath."

"I am, usually. Want to get in?"

"No. Can we get rid of some of that stuff?"

"It'll dissolve eventually."

"Hannah, can you be a bit cooperative, please?" She was enjoying this. So much for her hatred of being photographed. She was teasing him and loving every minute of it.

She batted at the foam with her hands. Clumps flew into the air and landed on Jack. He retreated to the doorway. Hannah laughed. A couple of rapid shots captured bare arms and dimples and flashing eyes as she played. Foam flew everywhere, the tiled floor became even slicker and more slippery.

He slipped his shoes and socks off and ventured back in. The suds level had dropped now because most of it was on the floor. He moved closer and crouched down to her level. A bare leg emerged in the style of a fifties movie star with its owner pouting, pointing her toe and running her hands along from ankle to knee.

"You don't have to pose." But he grinned and took the photo anyway. "What do you do when you're in the bath? Why do you like taking baths?"

Hannah relaxed back against the end of the tub with an inflatable pillow behind her neck. As they spoke, he clicked. The more shots he took the better, in this brief window of opportunity. Who knew when she'd change her mind?

"I lie here and think. It soothes me if I'm upset."

"Are you upset often?" She didn't look upset now. She looked...too desirable. But he'd been there and it was disastrously complicated. Apart from the fact she wasn't interested in him. And she'd made it very clear she was after all the things he'd spent his adult life avoiding.

"No, but I was recently. When you left me to walk home from the City."

"I didn't know what you were going to do. If there's one thing I have never figured out, it's what you're going to do next."

She smiled and closed her eyes. The bubbles pinged softly as they dissolved around her. Jack studied her. Could this romance idea become serious? Was he actually wanting to be romantic for its own sake? Holding her in his arms as they danced had been a fantastic experience, he'd had to force himself to let her go. What had she done to him?

"Don't move." Click. Click. He moved closer. Click. Close up. Click. Her eyes stayed closed. He studied her face. Then his eyes strayed lower. No bra straps on her shoulders, which were just visible now. Her skin was pink flushed and shiny from the water. He longed to run his fingers over her body again, all the curves and secret places...Jack rested his camera carefully on the clothes hamper.

"Stay right there." He leaned forward and brushed her lips with his own.

Hannah's eyes flew open. She gasped. Her expression changed from surprise to something else, and he leaned forward again, resting one hand as precarious support on the edge of the tub and the other on her cheek. Wet arms wrapped around his neck, and her lips met his in an explosion of passion just like the other time.

He had a split second in which to register her reaction before he felt himself sliding dangerously as his feet lost purchase on the floor. His hand lost its grip on the bath, his legs shot from under him and he toppled into the bubbles. A shaft of pain shot up his arm as his elbow cracked against the side of the bath

A foaming tidal wave of water slopped on to the floor. Hannah still had hold of his neck, struggling to pull herself up, at the same time pulling him down. He managed to get one arm over the side of the bath and haul himself off enough so she could get her head above water. She released her stranglehold and came up spluttering and coughing while he rearranged himself at the other end. His right elbow was numb.

"Are you all right?" She nodded and ran her hands over her face and hair. Bubbles swirled between them. The tap stuck into his back.

"Are you?" Was that the twitch of a smile starting on her face? She'd pulled him in deliberately?

"Yes. Why did you do that?" So furious he could barely speak. "Now I'll smell like a...a..." Jack heaved himself up and stepped out, waterlogged and heavy.

"Lavender bush?" she suggested, beginning to laugh out loud.

He grabbed a towel from the rail and scrubbed his hair and face. "At least my camera's safe from you." His jeans clung damp and uncomfortable to his legs. "I'll have a bruise on my arm to match the others I got from you and the tree trunk."

"Me? You started it. You kissed me. I can't help it if you're accident prone."

"You pulled me in."

"Why did you kiss me?" Why indeed?

"It seemed like a romantic thing to do."

Hannah gave a gurgle of laughter. "You'd better warn me in future when you're going to be romantic, so's I don't get a fright."

"You're impossible." He stripped off his soaked T-shirt.

"You'd better take off your jeans, too." Her eyes were almost on stalks. Too late. Any romantic intent he'd had was drowned. "Don't mind me."

"Steve got anything I can borrow?"

"Ask him."

"He's gone out."

"Have a look in his room. He won't mind. He likes you, for some peculiar reason. But then, Stevie always was a little odd."

"I'm not going to go poking about in Steve's room. You go."

"I'm not getting out with you standing there."

"Why on earth not? You're not naked."

Hannah said nothing.

"Are you?" There'd been such turmoil when he'd fallen in, details hadn't registered.

She still said nothing, and a slow smile spread across Jack's face as he reached for his camera. He squelched over to the edge of the bath and peered down at her.

"Water level's dropped a lot, bubbles are dissolving *molto vivace*. Mmm." He raised the camera and pretended to frame a shot. "Very nice, I must say. I could probably sell these to Penthouse. Maybe if I wait a little longer we'll have more flesh and less foam."

"Get out of here," she shrieked. The bath sponge flew at him followed by a bar of soap. Jack backed out with a derisive laugh, grabbed the towel and his T-shirt as he went, and pulled the door shut.

As soon as the door closed, Hannah pulled the plug and stood up. The bath mat was soaked, and although the worst of the flood had drained away, the floor was wet and dangerously slippery. Bubbles still clung to her body. The lavender scent was overpowering, headache-inducing. She stepped into the shower cubicle to rinse it off. Lavender-scented Jack. What a hoot.

She grabbed her robe from the hook on the wall and opened the door cautiously. "Jack?"

"Hurry up and get me some clothes," he yelled.

"Do you want a shower?"

"No, just get me some clothes." He appeared with the towel wrapped around his waist.

"Where are your clothes?" She stifled the erupting laugh. "You do stink pretty. Just like my grandma."

"In a plastic bag. Shut up and get a move on."

Hannah went into Steve's room and opened the drawer housing T-shirts. She pulled one out at random. It had 'I was cursed at Salem' on the back, given to Steve by his mother after a trip to the U.S.

Jack dragged it over his head. "I was cursed in Balmain."

"Do you want to wear Steve's underpants?"

"As long as they're clean."

"Of course, they're clean." She threw a pair to him. "Track pants or shorts?"

"Either. I don't care. I just want to leave in decency. Although." He frowned. His jaw moved as though he were grinding his teeth. "I really need a few more shots, and I don't think I could face coming back here again."

"More? You've taken plenty."

"I haven't quite got what I want yet. Maybe...what's your favourite room?"

"My music room." She sniffed ostentatiously and smiled.

The frown upgraded to a scowl. "Do you go out walking or exercising? Is there a place you really like?"

"No. Told you I wasn't very interesting."

"What about your bedroom?" Impatient now.

"You're not coming into my bedroom with a camera."

His expression told her she'd gone too far. Again.

"Go away so I can dress. Then I'm leaving. I'll

make do with what I've got," he said, tight-lipped.

"I'm sorry, Jack." And she was. Suddenly and completely.

"You can't help being unhelpful. Or maybe you can. I don't know. I've had enough. I'll tell Bevan it's his fault when he complains."

Chapter Fifteen

Jack rang on Tuesday morning, brisk and businesslike.

"I've got some good prints," he said without preamble, as her heart leapt and bounded in her chest. "But I need another one."

The thought of facing him again after...she couldn't. What could she say to him? Too humiliating. "I don't think I can," The words crawled from her mouth.

There was silence broken only by his long slow exhalation. "Suit yourself, Hannah, but you did agree to this, and I did do Lucia's party." He paused. "And Bevan wondered why I didn't want to use you in the first place. I should never have agreed."

"Neither should I." Her voice shook.

His didn't, he was furious. "Just what is your game?"

Silence. "I...I don't have one...I'm sorry. Goodbye." Hannah extended her hand slowly and disconnected. She continued her practice for Graeme's flute recital but had to keep stopping because the notes blurred together and tears dropped on to the keyboard, making her fingers wet.

Why couldn't her relationship with Jack be straightforward? He was complicated, and he made her complicated where she was, in reality, quite simple. She wanted to know what her game was, too. She had the awful suspicion she'd fallen in love with him, but was in denial because it was such a humiliating and potentially soul destroying thing to have happened. Like getting the Black Death. And she'd tried so hard not to.

It was absolutely impossible to tell him. It would be the worst sort of torture for her, and too gloatingly mundane for him even if he could stand the sight of her. He'd yawn, look down his nose, and sneak a glance at his watch. But she needed to apologise for her stupidities and show him she wasn't a careless, thoughtless idiot all the time. She wanted his respect, at least.

The camera! She could replace the camera Jack had dropped. It had been her fault, sort of—well—almost certainly completely her fault.

Hannah rushed to the living room and grabbed her bag from the table. She'd scrawled the details down somewhere, in secret, so he wouldn't know she felt guilty about it. In her diary. The almost illegible numbers and brand name meant nothing to her.

The phone book listed plenty of camera stores, and she learned the camera was not an obscure model, but one she could obtain at a reasonable price at any time. After lunch Hannah went shopping.

She wrote a note to accompany her gift, saying she hoped this would be an adequate replacement for the camera which had been broken, as she felt she was partially to blame. That phrasing was good because it shared out the responsibility and didn't refer to the circumstances. Her apologies came next, in a general way, for everything, and she finished by saying he was free to use whichever photos he chose for the book as she trusted his judgement. She signed it simply, 'Hannah' and slipped it into the wrapping paper, pleased with the comprehensive coverage and the feeling of sins at long last expiated. The next move was his.

Not desperate at all. Composed and adult.

All the same she went about her practising and rehearsing with a lump of lead in the pit of her stomach. There was no word from Jack, romantic or otherwise, but she didn't really expect any. On Thursday at six she went upstairs to sit on her bed and wonder about going to his opening. Wouldn't she just be torturing herself? But she couldn't stay away.

Go. Be aloof and sophisticated.

She opened her wardrobe. What does one wear to an exhibition opening? Freddo wound around her ankles. He, as usual, was no help at all. She pulled out a black, floaty skirt with a scalloped hem line and dragged it on over black tights. Low-heeled pumps completed the lower half, but what about the upper? A ruby red, crushed velvet, sleeveless top. Not too dressy, but dressy enough. Drape a Chinese silk shawl over her shoulders. No, she'd wear her black jacket. Very sombre, but perfect for her mood.

Her hair could do its own thing. She didn't need to impress anyone, and the only man for her had seen her at her worst and would be unlikely to care how she looked now. A Hannah couldn't compete with the Pennys and Sylvies of the world as far as appearance goes.

****

Jack paced about the gallery. He wasn't so much nervous as apprehensive, couldn't stand still. The display of his work didn't worry him, nor the prospect of critical judgement. He didn't much care what the critics thought. His pictures were good and he was pleased with the care and attention Anne-Marie had taken to ensure they were framed and captioned exactly as he wished.

She'd even taken the late addition in her stride and laughed when she saw it. "It's perfect, Jack. I've never seen you look so happy. There aren't many photos of you in existence. We'll hang it right here by the door."

He looked at it now, transported to the moment when the camera had clicked, capturing the time and place for eternity. But today! He'd had a tremendous surprise late this afternoon. A card had arrived yesterday in the mail, for a parcel awaiting collection at the local post office. He and Anne-Marie had been so busy setting up the exhibition, he'd only remembered to collect his package on the way home to change for the opening.

No idea who sent it. He didn't recognise the writing, wasn't expecting anything from anyone, hadn't ordered any equipment. It wasn't his birthday, and October was too early for Christmas.

Hannah's name leapt out at him as his eyes flew to the bottom of the short note. He read it through. And read it again, slowly, sitting at the dining room table. Stared at the still-wrapped parcel. She'd replaced the camera. How did she know what to get? How could she afford it? It would have cost thousands of dollars, and she hated anything and everything to do with photography. He tore the paper off and read the details on the box.

Typical Hannah. He smiled and sighed as he held the student version of the broken camera. He'd been given one just like it for his twelfth birthday. Just a few letters different in the model number between student and top flight professional, an easy mistake to make, especially by Hannah, the expert. But she'd tried.

The note again. It sounded like a farewell, a cutting of bonds, a tying off of loose ends. The last streamers breaking as the ship left the wharf. She'd made a decision in regard to him, and this was the last unresolved issue. His hand had hovered over the phone to call her back. But he hadn't. And she hadn't. After what he'd said, it was no wonder.

Would she come tonight? He cared what she thought. He cared about her. How had it happened? Hannah, with more strings attached than a harp, making him feel the extreme and unusual sensation of guilt...and the even more disturbing thought that perhaps he'd fallen in love with a woman who didn't want him. He wasn't used to having to ask a woman how she felt about him, it was usually blindingly obvious, but Hannah—she had him floundering. She didn't take his romantic overtures seriously, still treated the whole thing as a joke when, for him, it had become anything but.

Then she looked into his eyes, and he thought he saw the glimmerings of passion. Deep, heartfelt passion. When she danced in his arms and snuggled close. Was she pretending? The rapport they'd shared on the headland before the ranger had turned up. Had he imagined it?

"Jack, this is so exciting, I'm so proud of you." Marilyn burst through the doors with Bernard in tow. She swept across the empty room in a swirl of gold and black silk, her heels tip-tupping on the parquet floor, arms spread wide. Bernard extended his hand and slapped him on the back.

Guests poured in. At six forty-five the State Government Minister for the Arts declared the exhibition open.

Now he could leave. It wasn't so simple, of course, people kept talking to him and asking him about the places he'd been and what he thought about particular events and asking for technical photographic details, most of which would have been interesting under different circumstances. Now it was tiresome and annoying. He wanted to be alone. He wanted to think about Hannah and this new and unfamiliar feeling he had. Hannah! Of all the women in the world...he must be crazy...she'd infected him.

She hadn't come. She didn't care.

He caught a glimpse of Sylvie over by the door. Then he saw the unmistakable profile of Simon lifting a snack to his mouth. Hannah would have come with him, if she was coming at all.

Heart pounding, Jack edged around a chattering group, nodding and smiling as they praised his work. Two women blocked his view of Simon. Someone congratulated him again, and he had to pause and be polite for a moment or two. But Simon was easy to see in a crowd.

"Hello, Simon, Libby." They were alone. No Hannah. Where was she? Why hadn't she come? He wasn't prepared for the flood of disappointment threatening to close his throat.

"Jack! This is fantastic." Libby stood on tiptoe to kiss him.

"Goes for me too, without the kiss," said Simon.

"Thank heavens. Tongues would wag." Jack forced a laugh. "Thanks for coming."

"Here take these." Jack spun around.

There, behind him, Hannah, clutching three precariously balanced glasses of champagne.

Libby said, "We haven't seen this wall yet, Simon." They moved away with their drinks.

He gazed down at her. She wouldn't look him in the face, studied the champagne in her glass instead.

"Hannah," he began softly, but perhaps she didn't hear in the roar of voices because she said, "Marvellous exhibition," and stared around the crowded room.

She sounded as if she had an ice-cube down her back—and dressed for a funeral as well. "I got the camera today, Hannah. Thank you. You didn't need to."

She nodded. Her lips trembled on a smile. "I think I did. Was it right?"

He nodded, swallowed a rush of emotion, wanted to kiss her. "It's perfect."

"Good."

"Hannah, I..." She looked so cool and unnaturally aloof, he hesitated.

"Jack. Hannah, hello," cried a voice. They both

turned.

"Hello, Sylvie." Nice woman, rotten timing.

Hannah managed a smile and, "Hello," through clenched teeth. Did he enjoy having all his exes in the room at the same time? First Dubbo, now here. But he had no feelings, certainly no concern for how she felt.

Sylvie pulled forward a silver-haired, bespectacled man who'd been hovering behind her. "My husband, Ralph. Jack and Hannah."

Who was this woman? With a husband whom she introduced to Jack after going out with him to a party?

Ralph pumped Jack's hand with enthusiastic vigour. "Delighted to meet you. I've admired your work for years, and I couldn't believe it when Sylvie said you'd invited us tonight."

Jack smiled. "I'm glad you could come."

Sylvie turned to Hannah. "Ralph was green with envy when I said I'd met Jack Rotherford at Lucia and Luigi's party. Sat next to him, no less." She laughed. "He couldn't go. Had the flu."

Hannah summoned a proper smile this time, fuelled by overwhelming relief. "My housemate had the flu recently, too,"

"Men are such terrible invalids, aren't they?"

"Now hang on," protested Ralph. "Help me, Jack."

"I live alone," said Jack, "So I have to doctor myself. Hannah doesn't do First Aid."

Her eyes flew to his face. He was smiling. A tender smile. Her own lips curved. "No. And you were a terrible invalid. He fell in a rabbit hole and hurt his ankle," she told Sylvie and Ralph.

When they moved on, she turned to Jack. "Why did you make me think she was your date?"

"I enjoy seeing you suffer." But his eyes said something else. Hannah looked away. He put a gentle finger to her chin and forced her to look at him. "Have dinner with me?"

She nodded. When he was gentle and sweet, she was lost. Why couldn't he be like this all the time? How could she tell if it was an act or the real thing?

"I'll tell Anne-Marie I'm leaving."

"Hello there, you two." Bevan, with outstretched hand and wide smile. "Our Jack's a genius, isn't he?"

"I haven't had a chance to see yet," said Hannah.

"Come with me, darling." Bevan tucked her free arm through his and led her away from Jack, who was immediately cornered by someone else. They stopped in front of a spectacular photo of a waterfall in a rainforest.

"How are you two getting on with the shoot?"

"It's horrible," blurted Hannah. "I don't know why I agreed to do it."

"Have you seen any of the results?" She shook her head. "I think you'll be pleased. They're wonderful. Jack's captured the real you."

"You don't know the real me, and neither does he. I don't know the real me. I thought I did but not anymore."

"Jack has that effect on people. Particularly women."

"That's not what I meant." It stung, being lumped in with all his other conquests even though it was true. "He's infuriating, smug, selfish and obnoxious."

Bevan laughed. "But is he being romantic?"

"In patches. I think a sustained effort is beyond him."

"We'll have to keep him up to the mark. It was all part of the deal." He nodded his head and firmed his mouth. A mischievous gleam lit his eye. "Have dinner with me tonight. Let's make him jealous."

"He's already invited me."

Bevan looked over her shoulder and raised his

voice "Ssh, here he comes," Jack appeared beside her. "I'll fight you for Hannah's company at dinner tonight."

"Grow up, Bevan. Hannah can decide."

"You should fight for her hand," chided Bevan.

"Jack invited me first so I'd better go with him, thank you."

"Off you go with my blessing. And Jack, the powers that be have okayed the wilderness project. All systems go, as soon as you sign the contract."

Jack grinned and grasped Bevan's hand with both his. "Excellent! That's the best news I've had since...I can't remember."

Hannah smiled dutiful support, but her heart thudded to her feet like a stone. His trip. Leaving. She'd forgotten. What a selective memory she had. Still, if he left she'd be able to keep her debilitating passion secret.

"When are you going, exactly?" Her peremptory question interrupted their conversation..

Jack turned to her with a blank face. "What?"

"When are you leaving?"

"Monday week. But I'm always ready at the drop of a hat." The men laughed. Bevan must know all about his well-trodden avenues of escape. From women like her who thought they were in love with him. Jokes for the boys. "Why don't you come to dinner with us, Bevan?"

"I'd hate to spoil a romantic evening." He winked at Hannah.

"You won't." In her peripheral vision Jack's face hardened.

"No, I'd be *de trop*," Bevan said. "Excuse me." He pecked Hannah's cheek, shook Jack's hand and left them.

"Are you sure you want to have dinner?" Jack's cool gaze met hers, his voice tight.

"Don't you?"

249

"Just answer the question, can't you?"

"Yes. I'm hungry," snapped Hannah.

"Come and meet Anne-Marie. Then we'll go." To her relief, this was a much more relaxed tone.

Anne-Marie kissed Jack's cheek. "I'm surprised you stuck around this long. Is this the girl?" She smiled at Hannah.

"Which girl?" Hannah cast a suspicious glance at Jack who managed to look innocent.

"Didn't you see on the way in?" asked Anne-Marie. "The photo of our hero?"

"No, I've hardly seen anything, it's so crowded. I'll come back another day."

"I'll show you on the way out," said Jack.

They pushed their way towards the door. Jack stopped in front of a photo. His name was across the top in large letters and his biography down the side. Hannah looked, and burst out laughing. Part relief, mostly pride.

"I told you it would be a winner. Not a thumb or a blurry outline to be seen."

"Only because I set it up for you, and all you had to do was press the button."

"Which one's the horse?" asked Simon, looming over her shoulder.

"You look very happy there, Jack," said Libby.

They walked out of the Gallery together. Libby and Simon turned left, Jack indicated right.

"Where would you like to go?"

"Wherever you like. I eat anything." Hannah's stomach churned like a washing machine. She shouldn't drink champagne without eating. But maybe it was nerves. The anticipation of being alone with Jack in her newfound knowledge of love. Who'd have thought it? How can you fall in love with someone who irritates you most of the time?

"There's a Greek place near where I live."

"Fine." She walked beside him to the familiar

blue Volvo. He looked different in a jacket and tie, shaved, hair brushed. Hard to imagine him as the intrepid photographer, camping out and living rough. Now he was urbane and sophisticated, aloof and distant as he strode beside her. Well known and respected. An identity. She treated him abominably. Most of the time. Why would he bother with her?

"I've never seen you wearing a tie before. Apart from the bow tie on Saturday."

"I own one and this is it. Anne-Marie made me wear it. She threatened me."

"Wow, she didn't look so tough."

"Believe me, she is." He reached up and undid the tie and top button of his shirt then stuffed the tie in his pocket. "Much better."

Apart from the public persona, of which she was learning more and more, Hannah didn't know a great deal about this man she loved. As they drove she began to list the points, trying to fix him in her mind, colour in the outline. Assembling facts.

She knew he liked mints, bananas, her sandwiches, drank coffee with milk and sugar, and tea with just milk. He wasn't wild about cats. He didn't care about having the latest fashions, or a brand new car. He liked his neighbours. He had a son. He could be annoying, grouchy and had a temper, but underneath was kind and thoughtful. He could be selfish. He liked Miles Davis and Jimi Hendrix and was open to learning more about classical music. Except opera. He was a good driver. He didn't snore and was better than a hot water bottle in bed. His touch electrified her, his kisses were mind-blowing, and he had the best body she'd ever laid her hands on. Hannah giggled and flushed in the darkness.

"What are you laughing at?"

"I was thinking of how little I know about you."

"And that's funny? I don't know much about you

251

either, you know." He paused. "And yet we've slept together." He chuckled.

She stared out the window as they approached Sydney University. Jack turned down Glebe Point Road and parked outside a restaurant tucked away in a side street. Before she had unstrapped herself he leapt out and ran around to open her door with a flourish. Inside, a smiling waiter ushered them to a table and took orders for drinks.

"Where are you going on your travels?" Half way round the world no doubt—into the wilds of Patagonia, up the Amazon, over the Himalayas, under the polar ice cap, camera at the ready.

"Tasmania."

"Tasmania?" Hannah laughed in astonishment. Only a few hours' flight away. Her Aunty Lorna lived in Tasmania. "I thought you were going somewhere exotic."

"Ever been to the Tasmanian wilderness?"

"No."

His face lit up. "It's marvellous, Hannah. I'd love you to see it."

"Does it involve camping?"

"Yes."

"Forget it."

"When did you go camping last?"

"Apart from sleeping in your car? When I was ten."

"And one experience put you off camping for life? Crazy." He shook his head.

"It was the worst experience of my life." She had a quick think and amended it to "The second. The first came later."

He grinned. She frowned. "You know what I mean."

He nodded. "The dirty pictures man."

"Yes. I went camping with some family friends. The father was one of those gung-ho boy scout types.

Put me off scouts for life, as well. Sang songs round the campfire with him plunking on an out-of-tune guitar; hiked for miles through insect- and snake-invested bush, carrying tons of gear, with him insisting we sing Ten Green Bottles, except it was about a thousand wretched, green bottles; ate blackened sausages he charcoaled over a fire, which he couldn't light for ages. Got up at dawn after no sleep because we put up tents on a rock field, minus two poles because he'd forgotten them, and to top it off, survived a thunderstorm in the middle of the second night with a flash flood running through the tent and soaking my sleeping bag. Then we had to hike in the rain back to the car, which had a flat battery because the idiot had left the radio on for two days. Great fun was had by all."

By the time she'd reached this point Jack was laughing so hard she had to stop talking and join in. The waiter hovered, listening and grinning, with his notepad to take their orders.

"And that's it?" asked Jack when he'd gone. "That's what put you off camping?"

"Isn't it enough? I vowed I'd never sleep in a tent again. Not that I slept at all."

"Don't you think it's time to give it another go?"

"No."

"But you've changed your mind about having your photo taken." Jack held her eyes with his. "Why?"

"I didn't have much choice, did I? You popping up everywhere with your camera." She dropped her gaze, then looked up again. His eyes hadn't left her face. "And I still don't like it. I put up with it."

"Mmm."

"And you're not a sleaze like Raoul." Just a heartbreaker.

"Thank you. You promised to let me take photos of you."

"You have. Lots."

"Just a couple more."

Hannah hesitated. "I thought you'd finished. What sort of photos?"

"You looked extremely sexy in the bath..." Jack studied her through half closed eyes.

"You don't want..."

"Of course not. How could you even think such a thing?" His grin made her smile despite the sudden chilled shock.

"What a horrible joke."

"Sorry. But it's all just so silly."

"What?"

"Your aversions."

"Silly to you maybe. I'll admit my camping thing may be out of date, but no one can take away the memory of the scumbag with his camera."

"What happened?"

Hannah bit her lip, took a sip of wine. "It's not something I'm proud of. I was young and stupid and reckless. I acted before I thought. Something I haven't fixed yet."

Jack put his hand over hers on the tablecloth. "We've all been young and stupid." Was that how he justified his relationship with his son? Or maybe how he dealt with it. "It's part of your unique charm," he added.

How could she tell if he was doing being romantic, or serious?

"A girl from school had posed for him and said he paid good money. He wanted teenagers in school uniform so I went along one day after school. Didn't tell my parents, of course. Anyway he wanted school uniforms all right, but he also wanted no knickers and eventually no uniforms. They got us pretty drunk. He had a mate there too, his assistant."

"Did you tell your parents?" His hand was still on hers.

She nodded. "They hit the roof. He ended up in court, et cetera, but it was in the papers for a while. Not my picture or name, they were suppressed, but it was nasty and grubby and..."

"It's no wonder you don't care for photographers," finished Jack.

Hannah tilted her head as she studied him.. "You're all right. I wouldn't have agreed to the bath otherwise."

He smiled and squeezed her hand. "Thanks. Although I didn't agree to the bath I got. Steve's clothes are in the car."

She sniffed with ostentatious deliberation, and he laughed. He looked down at their interlocked hands.

"Hannah...I'm sorry for what I said on the phone."

"I'm sorry, too. I mean, sorry I hung up on you."

His tone softened. "I don't blame you." Her whole body tingled with warmth.

Food arrived, and conversation ceased.

On the way to Balmain after dinner, Jack said, "So? Am I capable of being romantic or not?"

Why on earth was this so important to him? Why was he persisting with it, when it was pointless and meaningless?

"I'll give you a very qualified yes—yes-ish. Not much action this last week."

"I've been busy getting the exhibition ready."

"Well that's just it, isn't it? A truly romantic man, a man wooing a woman he really cared about, wouldn't let his work get in the way. He'd find little ways of letting her know she was special and always in his thoughts."

"Makes it difficult."

"You were the one so anxious to prove it. I was quite happy to leave it alone." So he didn't care, and it was all pretence. "You don't have to try any more,

255

Jack, time's up tomorrow. Pity it was such a strain. I knew it would be."

"You think you've won, don't you?"

"Do I? Won what? I didn't realise we were having a contest." Won? Lost, if only he knew. But she wouldn't tell him.

Jack double parked outside her house. He grabbed the bag containing Steve's clothes, tucked her arm in his and walked her to the door, where she reluctantly untangled herself to rummage for her key.

"Thank you for dinner. I enjoyed it."

"So did I." His arms slid around her. Hannah's heart thumped in anticipation as he bent his head and kissed her. A nice, friendly, chaste kiss. She waited for more, the passion he'd shown before, but he drew back, gazed into her eyes with a very searching look, and let her go.

"Goodnight." He gave her the bag.

"Goodnight."

He twisted the key and opened the door for her. She had no choice but to step inside. Jack walked to the gate and turned, smiling the smile which always caused her a nuclear meltdown. Hannah gripped the door to prevent herself running down the steps and throwing herself on him, begging him to come inside and share her bed. No. Ravaging him in the street. He walked to his car. And left.

Chapter Sixteen

Hannah went inside and closed the door. Steve had fallen asleep on the couch in front of the TV, with Freddo on his lap. He stretched and yawned. "What's the time?"

"Five past eleven." She slumped down next to him. Was this what she had to look forward to? The pair of them nodding off in front of the TV every night. Better than living by herself, nodding off in front of the TV alone.

"Steve, do you think you'll ever get married?"

His head whipped towards her. "Yeah, sure. Why not? Why? Have you been proposed to?"

Hannah snickered at the shock in his voice. "I went out with Simon and Libby." She paused. Her lip trembled. "And came home with Jack."

"The photographer. I thought you didn't like him, he's horrible, you said."

"I do like him."

"Isn't that good?" He raised his eyebrows. Confused. As usual.

"Not in this case."

"Why not? You make things too complicated, Han. Just like Aunty Tildy."

Hannah stared at him, anger rising from the desolation like red-hot, molten lava. "Why does everyone tell me I'm just like my mother?" she yelled. "I'm not like her. I'm me. I'm different!"

"Calm down." Steve stroked Freddo on his lap. "You've just proved my point."

"Sorry." The anger subsided. Maybe they were all right about her. Maybe there was no use denying

257

it. How could you fight your genetic inheritance?

He continued, "But of course you're different. Tildy's far more dramatic than you'll ever be. You've got the blood of the stoic Crawfords in your veins, remember. Uncle Brad's a pretty strong influence on you all. He'd have to be, to keep Tildy under control and happy."

"How can you stand living with me, Stevie?" The sides of her mouth turned down mournfully.

"We stoic Crawford side of the family enjoy the excitement. I'm going to bed."

His blond, stubbled, comfortingly familiar figure went up the stairs. So like her father in many ways. Calm and reliable. Was Jack calm and reliable? She felt safe when she was with him. She trusted him. She irritated him.

Too much had happened lately. Like Dickens— "the best of times and the worst of times."

The best. She had found the love of her life. Was he her perfect other half after all? Jack? Grouchy, cynical, jet setting, playboy Jack? But none of those things were true of him, except maybe the grouchy bit. If he was perfect for her she wouldn't be facing:

The worst. Jack didn't love her. He lusted after her but he didn't love her, and no one could make someone else love them if they didn't. Hearts don't love to order.

Hannah couldn't think any more.

She went to bed to lie tossing and turning all night, her head filled with the memory of Jack's arms around her, and his kisses and his voice, whispering...How much she loved him. And the other uncomfortable thought—they'd known each other a very, very short time. "Love at first sight," Libby had said, joking. She, and certainly Jack, knew that wasn't the case. But it did happen to people, and they mustn't worry about not knowing each other.

Perhaps he was her perfect other half. She just

hadn't recognised his shape because she'd been looking for something else, and he didn't seem to fit at all. But was she his?

And it was all academic and irrelevant and hopeless because he couldn't wait to leave for his big adventure—not to get away from her, because he didn't care one way or the other about her, but because it was his dream come true. How could she possibly compete with his dream?

****

Tildy called to announce she would be visiting the following Thursday and staying for a few days.

"I'm auditioning for a movie." Her excitement burst through the phone. "With Geoffrey Rush in the lead."

"How wonderful, Mum." Tildy would take her mind off Jack. Tildy eclipsed everything.

But Jack called the same day. For one wild moment she imagined he might have changed his mind. He'd stay—for her. Then the whole catastrophe reignited. "About the opera, Hannah," he said. "I signed the contract this morning, and it's got some pretty tight scheduling...Bevan's company owns me for the next year."

And that was the end of that. Don't burst into tears. He couldn't stay even if he wanted to. Bevan's company would sue him within an inch of his life for breach of contract.

"Forget about it, Jack. This whole romance thing...to be honest I was finding it a strain. Romance without the emotion, without any...love...doesn't work, does it? I don't know why I even wanted you to do it."

"I'm sorry I wasted your time." His voice was as stiff as hers.

"Enjoy your trip."

He broke the connection. Her arm stretched out all by itself and replaced the phone with great precision. She walked out the back door and sat in the sun on the grass but couldn't see much because there were too many tears. Freddo rubbed against her legs and she didn't even push him away. She leaned forward, closed her eyes and rested her wet cheek on her bent knees, arms hanging weakly down beside her.

Now Jack wouldn't call her. Maybe ever again. She should be pleased to have broken off their odd relationship, and not the other way around. She should be strong and independent, not sitting out here crying and being comforted by the cat. Hannah wiped her face with both hands and stood up with newfound resolve. Get on with her life. Jack wasn't the man to fulfill her plans for a family, never had been. She'd known from the start, mustn't dwell on it.

****

Her mother arrived on Thursday after lunch. Hannah walked into the open-armed embrace.

"It's so good to see you, Mum."

"Darling Hannah. I've missed you." She held Hannah away. "Now tell me where I go, which cupboard you're hiding me away in."

Her megawatt smile flashed, and the thick mane of wavy, chestnut hair rippled about her face as she ran a bejewelled hand around the nape of her neck to lift it free of her collar. Three silver bangles jingled when she lowered her arm. Hannah picked up the bags and led her through to the living room and up the stairs.

"I've put you in my room. I'll sleep in the music room."

"I'm sorry to be a nuisance." But Tildy had already swung the smaller of the bags onto the bed and begun taking out a blouse. "I just need to hang a few things and freshen up. Why don't you put on the kettle? I'll be down in a minute."

Hannah withdrew to the kitchen, where she did as she was told and made a pot of tea. Ten minutes later Tildy swept in on a wave of L'Air du Temps perfume and a change of clothing.

"Your father sends his love, of course."

"How's Maddie?" She led her mother out into the back garden to sit on the two rickety cane chairs on the little patio area. Freddo, of course, appeared to investigate the newcomer inquisitively.

"Positively radiant, and Colin hasn't stopped grinning since he heard the word 'baby.'" Tildy inspected the chair before lowering herself onto the seat. "Are you all right with their news, darling? We all realise it must be hard for you."

Hannah nodded. Tildy bent down to stroke Freddo. "What a lovely cat. He must be Stevie's?"

"Yes. Except for his tail which I paid for. It cost about ten times more than he's worth. It got stuck in a door."

"And what about you? Tell me about you." Her mother fixed Hannah with her clear, blue-eyed gaze.

"I'm fine." She desperately composed her features into casual nonchalance, clutched her mug of tea and took a sip.

Her mother burst out laughing. "You really are a hopeless actress."

So she hadn't inherited everything from Mum. Her father was transparent when it came to heartfelt emotions. She'd got the worst of both of them—excitable emotions and an inability to conceal them.

"Who is he?" There was no evading the question.

"He's a photographer. Jack Rotherford."

"The Jack Rotherford."

"Yes."

"Will I meet him?"

"No."

"Why not?"

261

"Because I've finished with him." Hannah's face crumpled as the realisation hit. Maybe it really was true. Tildy was by her side in an instant, comforting arms around her.

"What happened?"

"He doesn't love me. He's going away on his lifelong dream project on Monday. For a year at least. We had a fight, so we're not even friends now. All we ever do is argue."

Her mother was silent, hugging her until Hannah pulled herself together. Tildy sat back in her chair, but kept hold of Hannah's hands in both of hers.

"Darling, Brad and I were apart a lot in the early days. Anything can be overcome."

"Jack made it clear he wouldn't change his life for a woman. Even if he did love me, which he doesn't, it wouldn't work. He's just like Adrian. His work takes precedence over everything. He has a son who's grown up thinking his stepfather is his real father, and Jack doesn't even seem to mind," she wailed.

"You mustn't make judgements on other people's decisions. You can't possibly know all the circumstances. The girl may have wanted to stay for all sorts of reasons. Maybe they were very young."

She nodded. "They were. It's just...it seems so callous to abandon a child...when I..."

"Does he know?"

"No, telling him wouldn't make any difference. All I want is to find a man to love who loves me, and have lots of babies. Is that too much to ask? Why can't I find someone? You did. Maddie did."

"You will." Tildy smiled and touched Hannah's cheek with soft, caring fingers. "You were always such a sensitive little thing. You're like me—bit of a tendency to the dramatic. It can create big problems."

Hannah smiled. "Someone else said the same thing."

"Who?"

She straightened, lifted her chin with dignity and looked down her nose at her mother. "The Mayor of Bathurst's wife."

"Oh, my." Tildy pressed a hand against her chest.

Hannah laughed. "I must tell you what happened, Mum..."

Here was one person she knew without a doubt would love the story of the couch. Then she told her Harvey Beddowes' tale about old Kev's teeth and the horse. Tildy laughed so much, Freddo fled to the rhododendron.

****

Her mother stayed for the Mozart Festival in Mittagong the following weekend, travelling with Hannah and Simon in his car to meet the others at a prearranged café for lunch.

"Tildy Crawford!" shrieked Marilyn, causing heads to turn.

Tildy metamorphosed into the polished star and extended her hand to shake Marilyn's. Gold bracelets jangled.

"You must meet my nephew Jack Rotherford."

"I'd love to, but I'm only staying until tomorrow."

"He should be here any minute," said Marilyn. Hannah froze. Jack? Here? Can't be so busy getting organised after all.

"How marvellous." Tildy squeezed Hannah's hand hard under the table. Five minutes later Jack strolled in and pulled up a chair between Simon and Marilyn. The Jack of old, distant and disagreeable, and by the expression on his face, wishing he were somewhere else.

"Darling this is Hannah's mother, Tildy

Crawford," Marilyn waved an arm and endangered her glass of water. "The actress."

"How do you do, Tildy?" Jack extended his hand across the table. He smiled at Simon and Libby, then his eyes flicked to Hannah. "Hello."

"Hello." She snatched up her glass and drank. Water slopped over her chin.

"Still can't drink properly?" he murmured. His eyes caught on hers. Did he remember? Kissing...

"Tell me about your trip, Jack," said Tildy.

"The Tasmanian wilderness," he began eagerly, while Hannah's mind swirled with memories, her lips relived the sensation—his mouth on hers—the first time they'd kissed and meant it. She'd spoiled it. Who was the romantic one in this farce? It was beginning to look more and more like Jack. All she did was mess things up.

The Clarinet Quintet was the first item on the afternoon programme. Jack took photographs from afar, didn't intrude. Hannah didn't mind his camera now. He was hearing her play, and she wanted him to be impressed, see she wasn't a total fool.

At interval, Tildy and Marilyn were easy to spot. They stood out like a couple of exotic parrots in a room full of pigeons. Jack was with them. He looked like a hawk. Cool and distant. Observing. He appeared, mentally, as if he'd already left for Tasmania.

"Darlings, you were wonderful!" Tildy clapped as Hannah approached with Simon.

"The quartet's playing better and better," Marilyn informed her.

"Hannah has a secret admirer," Tildy announced into a break in the conversation. "I wonder if he's here." Simon and Marilyn raised their eyebrows simultaneously. Hannah gasped. Tildy continued, "He sent the most gorgeous bunch of roses. Red roses," she emphasised, and nodded at Marilyn, accompanying the look with a knowing wink.

What? Where did that come from? One of her soapie scripts? Was this to make Jack jealous?

"I haven't met him but he sounds very..." She paused. "Passionate."

Hannah couldn't look anywhere near Jack. Now he wasn't aloof and distant. His eyes were boring into her, she could feel them. He radiated electricity. The type they ran through cattle prods and electrodes for torturing people.

"You won't. It's a pity but Mum is leaving first thing tomorrow," Hannah explained. Sooner if it could be arranged. Now would be good.

Jack excused himself and walked away. She stared after him, aghast. Tildy nodded imperceptibly at her and inclined her head in the direction of Jack's fast disappearing figure. Chase him? She expected her daughter to chase after him like some shameless groupie?

"My goodness, Jack's fascinating. And so handsome." was Tildy's next remark to Marilyn. She thrust her arm through Hannah's and squeezed, comforting, as Hannah's shocked brain groped for a life raft of sanity in this roiling sea of despair and lunacy.

****

On the way back later in the evening, Simon said in a bewildered voice, "What was all that about? I thought we set you up with Jack the other night at the opening. Libby was convinced of it."

"Whaaat!" screeched Hannah, causing Simon to swerve violently. Tildy gave a cry of delight from the back seat and clapped her hands. "And as for you, Mum! Roses? Jack sent me red roses."

"Oh, really? You didn't tell me. No wonder my tactic backfired a little. Got quite a reaction, though."

"All of you should keep out of my love life, such

265

as it is. I don't need any help messing it up, thank you. I can do that quite well myself."

But Tildy addressed the subject again after dinner, when Steve had gone out. She sat opposite Hannah in the living room, chatting about the forthcoming baby, and what names might be chosen.

"Marilyn hasn't the slightest clue Jack's in love with you. She doesn't know as much about him as she thinks."

From baby names to Jack in one easy leap? Hannah nearly spilt her coffee. "He is not, I repeat not, in love with me. You saw him today, he barely spoke to me."

"Why not?"

"Because he can't stand me."

"Don't be so silly, Hannah," snapped her mother. "The man loves you, he's just too dense to see it. Or too proud to admit it."

"Well, he hasn't got much time left. He's leaving for the wilderness on Monday."

"Tell him you love him. Don't be such a spineless wimp. Don't let him get away."

"I will not chase after him like every other woman does, Mum . It's too humiliating. He knows where I live."

"In which case I can do no more. On your own head be it."

"Thank heavens."

****

Tildy left the house early in the morning. Hannah waved as the taxi disappeared round the corner. Now her support was gone, and tomorrow Jack would be gone. They would, between them, leave a hollow shell of a Hannah, for despite all Tildy's optimism and confident utterances, she knew Jack wouldn't be declaring undying love for her. He wouldn't be grovelling on her doorstep asking forgiveness. He was too proud, and had too many to choose from, to bother with an annoying red-haired woman with a tongue disconnected from her brain. And more prosaically, he'd signed a contract which would take him away, regardless. For a year.

Hannah took Tildy's sheets to the laundry. A parcel sat on the washing machine. A gift-wrapped, rectangular parcel with her name on it in Jack's writing—shaped like a large book.

Steve! Hopeless! Must have put it there for some obscure reason and forgotten. Why didn't Jack mention it?

Hannah took the parcel to the living room and sat at the table. She stared at it before undoing the wrapping paper. An album of photographs. She studied the beautiful black leather cover with gold edging, and ran her hands over the smooth surface. Her fingers shook as she turned to the first page.

In Kurrajong, with the sun shining through her hair like gold. The group arriving at the concert hall in Bathurst, with Hannah and Simon exchanging glances behind Marilyn's back. He hadn't missed it after all. An image pierced her mind—Jack laughing at her discomfort. His smile. The warmth in his eyes. She turned the page.

Her performing. Astonishing, expressive pictures displaying her love of the music, her total absorption. She turned the page again. Many photos she didn't know he'd taken. Sitting in Louise's garden with Simon; groping about under the table; standing under the tree in the rain feeling sick; laughing at something somewhere, her face alight with pleasure; walking along the deserted road towards the flooded bridge. A dozen more. Their whole trip encapsulated and presented to her, with love and tenderness shining from every page. He'd made her look beautiful, just as he said he could.

The photos he'd taken after they returned. Lounging in his deckchair in shorts; standing on

North Head with the glorious molten sunset; in the bath, acting like Marilyn Monroe; playing with the bubbles; lying back with her eyes closed just before he'd kissed her...And last of all the photo she'd taken of him with the horse, laughing and happy.

Tears streamed down her face. Of all the romantic things he could possibly have done...He needn't have bothered with roses and dinners. If they'd still been on speaking terms, she'd go camping with him wherever he chose. Up a mountain, in a desert, on a glacier. How could he leave this treasure with a dope like Steve? Why didn't he give it to her himself?

But wasn't it just like him to have the last word? His parting shot. To prove a point.

Hannah went upstairs to get dressed, taking the album with her hugged tight across her chest. Later, the phone rang. Steve had gone out for a run. She roused herself from her torpor of misery and summoned the energy to lift the receiver.

"Hello, Hannah." The phone slipped in her nerveless fingers, then she clutched it so hard her hand ached.

"Jack. I thought..."

"What did you think?"

"You wouldn't speak to me again."

"Why not?"

"You walked away."

He didn't answer for a moment. "Did you get the album?"

"This morning. Steve put it on the washing machine and..."

"Hannah. Did you like it?" He sounded anxious. Was he worried he'd failed at the last, with his final throw? But she was past pretending.

"It's wonderful." Her voice caught. "It's the most romantic thing I've ever seen."

"So you admit I could do it."

Silence.

"Hannah?"

"I don't want to play this game any more, Jack." Softly.

"What game?"

"This stupid one. You proving you can be romantic to...I don't want to do it any more." Her voice shook. He didn't understand. "It was a stupid idea."

"Why?" Soft and intense in her ear. "You were the one who said I couldn't be romantic. I just proved I can, and you won't admit it."

The doorbell rang, strident and jarring in the quiet of the house.

"Someone's at the door."

"Hannah, why don't you want to play any more? Why won't you admit it?"

"Because it's not a game to me," she whispered. "And I do admit it. You can be romantic. But you said..." Ring, ring.

"What did I say?"

"You'd only do it if the woman made you feel that way."

"Yes."

Ring.

"But Jack, you were doing this just to prove something, not..."

Ring, ring, ring.

"I'll have to answer it." Tears of frustration pushed at her eyelids.

"Okay, I'll hang up."

"No, don't. Please don't, Jack."

"Why?"

Ring.

"Because I love you," she blurted, and flung the phone down. Drat this persistent nuisance at the door. Jack would hang up while she was dealing with them, and she would never have the courage to call him back or to say it again. He'd be gone.

Ring, ring, ring.

She ran down the hall and wrenched the door open.

"Say that again." Jack, standing on the doorstep with his mobile phone in his hand. He slipped it into his pocket, and smiled that smile, and her heart had a nuclear meltdown.

"I..." Her knees turned to jelly. She clutched the door for support.

"Yes? You?"

"Love you," she said. He stepped forward and wrapped his arms around her.

"I love you, too," he said just before he kissed her, and it wasn't the nice, friendly, chaste kiss like last time they'd stood on this spot together.

Hannah managed to murmur, "Come inside," and untangle herself enough to close the door behind them. They shuffled down the hallway, lips and bodies interlocked, bouncing off the walls, giggling and loving.

"Where's the booby trap rug?" He asked between kisses.

"Mum said either she'd nail it to the floor or throw it out so Steve put it in his bedroom."

Jack held her away and glared at her. "By the way, who is sending you red roses?"

"Mum made it up." She grinned. Good work, Mum. "To make you jealous. Did it work? She thought it backfired. I was furious with her."

He laughed, then his dark eyes turned serious. "Hannah, did you really like the photos?"

"Yes. They're wonderful."

"I told you I could make you look good."

"Yes, you did. You're better than Raoul. Although I never did see the shots he took."

"Hannah?" Jack took her hands and led her to the couch. "Do you think maybe I'm your perfect other half?"

"Do you think you are?" she challenged. "Isn't it romantic claptrap?"

His voice came softer and gentler than she'd ever heard it. "I can't bear the thought of you being with someone else, and I don't want to be with anyone else."

"Well, you must be. It wouldn't work otherwise, would it?"

He shook his head. "Do you feel the same?" A little boy, unsure and anxious.

She smiled her answer at him. The worried look relaxed into a smile mirroring hers. What a changed man he was. Amazing.

Then she remembered. "But you're leaving tomorrow. You're going away on your trip to do your book." Her voice rose to a wail. "What are we going to do? We've just found each other."

"I'm not." Jack reached for her, pulled her close. "I'm not going. How could I go and leave half myself here? That's why I went to Mittagong. To see you one last time, and when I did I realised I had to find out how you felt about me. I didn't know, you see," he whispered into her hair.

"Neither did I, until I saw the photos, then I thought maybe you did."

She clung to him as he kissed her again. What had he said? Surely she'd misheard?

"Did you say not go? But you can't not go. It's your dream. You've wanted to do this for ever. You signed your soul over to Bevan, you said."

"I know. And you said once if I found the right woman, I'd do anything to keep her. You were right. I can't go if all the time I'm away I'm wishing I was with you."

Hannah sat up straight and pushed him away. "No, Jack. You can't stop what you're so good at and what you love. I won't let you. You'd end up hating me for it." He stared deep into her eyes. She held his gaze. "You mustn't."

He bit his lip, brow wrinkled. "What will we do?"

"You have to go."

"I can't."

"You did it before."

He rose to his feet and stared down at her, frowning. "It was different. I explained. I was young and ambitious. I didn't realise..." When he next spoke his voice had softened. "Hannah, you asked me if I regretted not knowing my son?" She nodded. "I didn't at the time, not really. But as I get older, I realise what I've been missing, and then seeing you with little Veronica...I want a family too, but with you, only with you."

She stood and wrapped her arms around him. He squeezed her tight.

"I lost my baby, Jack. Before," she whispered. "I had a miscarriage. I fell. I was three months pregnant." Tears trickled down her cheeks. "I wanted a baby so much."

"But you can have more? Can't you?"

She nodded, drew a deep breath. Soft fingers wiped her face.

"What happened to the father?"

"I divorced him." Hannah studied his face as the surprise registered. "He wasn't there when I had the accident, he was away with work. He was always away with work. He didn't even come home when he heard what had happened, just rang me in hospital and made all the right noises, but he said it wasn't worth his while to fly home because it wouldn't serve any purpose as I was all right, and he had an important meeting. He was in L.A. at the time."

Jack stared into her eyes. "I won't do that to you, Hannah," His voice rasped with emotion. "Believe me. We've both lost a child, let's not lose each other."

"I don't want another man like Adrian in my life."

She rested her head against his shoulder, and he held her, stroking her hair.

"I'm older and wiser and I love you more than I love anything."

"Even your camera?" She squinted up at him.

"Even my camera. Got any more secrets?"

She giggled and shook her head. "You've just discovered my biggest one. I love you."

He held her face between his palms and kissed her with great tenderness. "I love you, Hannah Crawford."

"But we can't be together. Now we want to, we can't. It would ruin your career to break your contract, and I can't afford to go with you."

He sat down on the couch and pulled her onto his lap. "How about this? I'll come home after Tassie, before I do the next session in South America. You join me whenever you have time. It'll only be for our first year. After that, no more travelling unless we both go, and if you're pregnant nobody goes anywhere."

"Do they have five-star tents? Are there hotels in the wilderness?"

Jack smiled and placed his palm against her cheek.

"We'd better get married at some stage." He leaned forward to kiss her again.

"Married?" What would Marilyn say? Very un-Jack.

"Yes. Will you?"

"Yes." Hannah folded her arms around his neck.

But Marilyn as mother-in-law?

About the Author...

Elisabeth Rose lives in Australia's capital, Canberra. Her early years were spent reading, riding horses and generally enjoying an idyllic childhood on an apple orchard. She completed a performance degree on clarinet, travelled Europe with her musician husband and returned to Canberra to raise two children. Twenty years ago she began practising Tai Chi and now teaches classes in that as well as teaching and playing clarinet. Reading has been a lifelong love, writing romance a more recent delight. She has two books released with Avalon.

Thank you for purchasing
this Wild Rose Press publication.
For other wonderful stories of romance,
please visit our on-line bookstore at
www.thewildrosepress.com.

For questions or more information,
contact us at info@thewildrosepress.com.

The Wild Rose Press
www.TheWildRosePress.com